The Girl with the Violin

Glenda Poulter

Also by Glenda Poulter

Single Stories

Never Too Late

The Girl with the Violin

Glenda Poulter

Affinity
Rainbow Publications

2026

The Girl with the Violin

Affinity E-Book Press NZ LTD.
Canterbury, New Zealand

Edition First

ISBN: 978-1-991357-40-3 (paperback)

Editor: A Koenig
Proof Editor: Lisa M
Cover Design: Lisa M
Production Design: Affinity Publication Services

ACKNOWLEDGMENTS

I would like to thank and acknowledge my beta readers, Sarah Shaw and Suzi Vilkman. They helped me make Evie and Freddy's story better with their insights and suggestions.

I'd also like to thank the acquisitions team at Affinity Rainbow Publications for choosing to publish this book. Thank you to Lisa M, Affinity's beta reader; my line editor, Angela Koenig; proof editor, Lisa M.; and book cover artist, Lisa M. Without each of you and your diligent work, *The Girl With the Violin* would not be the book it is today.

Last, but certainly not least, I'd like to acknowledge my daughter, Kathryn "Kaycee" Hawn, who patiently answers all of my text message questions about grammar and punctuation, thus making my writing sound better than it actually is.

DEDICATION

This book is dedicated to our elder lesbians and the life some were forced to live apart from the one they loved the most.

As always, it is also dedicated to my partner, Lisa Beemon. We know how blessed we are to be able to spend our lives together into old age.

TABLE OF CONTENTS

Chapter One	1
Chapter Two	6
Chapter Three	18
Chapter Four	25
Chapter Five	36
Chapter Six	49
Chapter Seven	57
Chapter Eight	60
Chapter Nine	69
Chapter Ten	82
Chapter Eleven	90
Chapter Twelve	99
Chapter Thirteen	102
Chapter Fourteen	111
Chapter Fifteen	117
Chapter Sixteen	125
Chapter Seventeen	131
Chapter Eighteen	135
Chapter Nineteen	140
Chapter Twenty	149
Chapter Twenty-one	163
Chapter Twenty-two	166
Chapter Twenty-three	177
Chapter Twenty-four	181
Chapter Twenty-five	185
Chapter Twenty-six	188
Chapter Twenty-seven	194
Chapter Twenty-eight	196
Chapter Twenty-nine	203
Chapter Thirty	207
Chapter Thirty-one	216

Chapter Thirty-two	223
Chapter Thirty-three	226
Chapter Thirty-four	235
Chapter Thirty-five	245
Chapter Thirty-six	255
Chapter Thirty-seven	269
Chapter Thirty-eight	277
Chapter Thirty-nine	281
Epilogue	289
About the Author	294
Other Affinity Books	295

CHAPTER ONE

Present day

Grace peeked into her 94-year-old great-grandmother's bedroom. "You awake, Grams?"

Evie pushed herself up in bed and smiled. "For you, my dear? Always. What is that you have in your hand?"

Grace leaned over and kissed the leathery cheek Evie tilted up, and then perched on the side of the bed. "You know, Taylor and I are going through that big box of photos Grandma and Mom found in y'all's attic?"

Evie laughed. "Find any pictures of my pet dinosaur?"

"You're not that old, Grams." Grace laughed too. "No dinosaurs, but a lot of people we can't identify. You feel up to going through some of them with me?"

"Hand me my glasses and let me see what you've got."

Two heads, one gray and the other dark auburn, bent over a stack of black-and-white photos. For an hour, Evie identified the faces in the old pictures, sometimes with a story about the situation or event depicted. But when she picked up the last photograph, she fell silent. Grace watched as she traced an outline around the person in the picture and chewed her bottom lip.

"Grams? Are you okay? Who is that?"

Evie shook her head and took her glasses off. Grace handed her a tissue from the box on the bedside table. Evie dabbed tears from the corners of her eyes. She studied the picture again before turning it over and looking at the back. She pointed to the date printed there in faded ink.

"June seventeenth, nineteen thirty-seven," she read. "Freddy's birthday."

"June seventeenth? That's your birthday too."

Evie nodded. "Yes, it is. Freddy and I were born in the same hospital. Her mom, Miz Addie, and my mother shared a room. They became best friends 'til the day they died. I 'spect they're hoofing it up in heaven. Freddy and I shared everything, almost like twin sisters probably would. In fact, when we were little, strangers often thought we were twins."

"Freddy is kind of a strange name for a girl, isn't it?" Grace took the photo from Evie's hand and studied it. "I wish I could see her face better. That hat looks a bit big for her."

Evie laughed. "That was her mother's new cloche, and Freddy had to try it on. Her daddy had just gotten his hands on that camera and made her pose for this picture. Miz Addie was a big woman, and you can see how small Freddy is. That hat came down to her nose."

"What's with the violin?"

"Ah. She could make that violin sing. Her whole family was musical and sometimes would play in three or four churches on one Sunday. And not all of them were Baptist, which just bugged my daddy half to death. As far as he was concerned, anyone not white and Baptist didn't have a chance of going to heaven. The Prilouxs belonged to our church, but that didn't stop them from taking their music to a Methodist or Calvinist church."

"You still haven't told me why she's named Freddy," Grace said.

"Freddy is short for Frieda. Frieda Grace Priloux."

"Grace?"

Evie nodded. "She was named after her gran'ma, and I named your grandmother after her. Your grandma named your mom Grace after herself, and Cecelia named you Grace after herself. But in my head, you're all named after Freddy. That's just how special she is. Was."

"Did she have any kids?"

Evie shook her head. "No. She died young and unmarried."

"Oh. I'm sorry, Grams. It must have been hard for you since y'all were so close."

"It was." Evie's voice cracked. "I still miss her."

"What are you two up to?"

Grace turned and smiled at her mother as she came into Evie's room. Cecelia went to the other side of the bed and kissed Evie's cheek. "Gracie, what did you do to make Grams cry?"

Evie laughed and patted Cecelia's hand. "Memories made me cry, my dear, not this child. She brought me some photos to look at and, oh my, the memories they brought back. But I'm getting tired, and I think I need to take a break."

Grace nodded. "Sure, Grams. Thanks for telling me about the pictures. I'd love to hear more about Freddy sometime."

"Of course. I love that you're interested in this old woman's life."

"Would you mind if I recorded our conversations?" Grace asked. "That will make it easier to save them."

"On one condition," Evie said.

Grace took her great-grandmother's hand. "What's the condition?"

"You bring your sweet Taylor with you next time."

Grace laughed as she kissed the old woman's hand. "I'll do that. I know she'll enjoy seeing you again."

†

Later that evening, Grace and Taylor cuddled on the sofa as Grace recounted her afternoon with her great-grandmother.

"She said I can record our conversations but only on the condition that you come with me to see her next time," Grace said as she circled Taylor's palm with her thumb.

"I'm glad she doesn't have a problem with our relationship." Taylor kissed the side of Grace's head. "I really like her. I bet she was a force to be reckoned with when she was younger."

"From the stories Grandma and Mom have told, I think you're probably right." Grace took a deep breath. "But I think Gramps abused her, at least emotionally and verbally. She's opened up so much since he died. Grandma told me Grams always deferred to Gramps. She said he was constantly demeaning her. And not just Grams, but Grandma and Aunt Betts too."

"How do you think your great-grandmother and grandfather got together? It sounds like they were polar opposites."

Grace shrugged. "I don't know. I guess that's one thing I'll have to ask her about."

Taylor turned on the sofa until she and Grace were face-to-face. She leaned over and kissed Grace lightly on the lips. "I think we've talked long enough," she said. "There are other things I'd rather be doing."

Her fingers were busy as she spoke, unbuttoning Grace's blouse and tracing the outline of her bra over her breasts. Grace took a sharp breath when Taylor reached into her bra and tweaked a nipple.

"Yeah," she managed to say before Taylor covered her lips again.

CHAPTER TWO

A few days later, Grace and Taylor tapped on Evie's door.

"Come in, come in," Evie called from her chair by the window. "Forgive me for not getting up. Standing seems to be a bit harder every day."

"That's okay, Grams," Grace said. She bent and gave her great-grandmother the obligatory peck on the cheek.

Evie held her hands out to Taylor, who took them in both of hers. "It's good to see you again, my girl," Evie said. "This one's been trying to keep you all to herself. Give me a kiss, right here." She tapped her cheek.

Taylor laughed and did as she was told. "It's good to see you again too, Evie. Thank you for inviting me."

"Is this the day y'all have chosen to interrogate me?" Evie said as she sat back in her chair. She motioned to the stack of photographs and the small recorder Grace had set on the table while Evie and Taylor chatted.

"I don't think I'd call it an interrogation, Grams," Grace said with a grin. "I'd like to go through these photos we looked at the other day and some more we brought, and let you tell us the story behind them. I'll record them with this," she picked up the recorder, "and then we'll download what you tell us to the computer."

Evie held her hand out. "Let me see that contraption."

Grace handed her the recorder and watched as she looked at it, turning it over in her hands.

"Where's the tape?" Evie asked.

Grace and Taylor laughed.

"No tape, Evie," Taylor said. "It's digital. It records your voice on a tiny chip and then, when we plug it into the computer, a program transposes what you said to text."

"You're speaking Greek to me, dear," Evie said with a shake of her head. "I'll take your word for it."

Grace flipped through the photos and chose one. The old black-and-white photo was of a group of young people lounging on and against a large sedan. She turned it over and read the writing on the back.

"'The crew at the lake. Dean, me, Freddy, Carson, Louise, Tucker, August 4, 1937.'" She handed the photo to Evie. "What was the occasion here, Grams? Looks like y'all were having a lot of fun."

Evie laughed as she studied the photo. "Tucker's girlfriend, Hazel, took this photo with Tucker's new camera. She refused to be in any of the pictures, so she became our official photographer. It was a Saturday, if I remember correctly, out at Lake Worth. It was one of the first times Dean came out with me and my friends. Look how much taller he was than the rest of us."

"How tall was he?" Taylor asked.

"I remember thinking he was a giant when I was a little kid. To me, his legs were like tree trunks," Grace said.

"Six feet, four inches." Evie laughed. "Our friends used to call us Mutt and Jeff."

"Who?" "Why?" Evie and Taylor asked at the same time.

"Oh, my. I forget how young you girls are. Mutt and Jeff were cartoon characters. Mutt was very tall, and Jeff was very short."

"You'd think it was the other way around," Taylor said. "I'd think that Mutt would be the short one. I'm going to have to Google them."

"Google?" Evie frowned. "Oh, you're going to do something on the computer, right?"

Taylor laughed. "Yes, ma'am. Google is a search engine on the internet that helps us learn new things, both necessary and just for fun."

"Who does the car belong to?" Grace asked. "Do you remember what kind of car it was? It's really cool looking."

"It was Tucker's car. His daddy bought it for him a couple of years earlier. All I know is it's some kind of Ford. Tuck was the only one in our group who had a car until Dean came along, but his was too small for us all to fit in."

"Wasn't this during the Depression, Grams? What did Tucker's father do that he could afford to buy him a car?" Grace sifted through the photos in front of her and picked out a few more with the car in them. "He liked having his car in the photos, didn't he?"

"Oh, yes. He was really proud of that car. I thought he'd wash the shine off it as much as he gave it a bath." Evie paused for a moment. "These pictures bring back a lot of memories."

"Good or bad?" Taylor asked.

"Both. And some in between. Back to your question about the Depression. Yes, all of these pictures were taken during the Depression, but our family was lucky and didn't suffer as much as some families did. Tuck's dad was a gangster. He kept a lot of the speakeasies in Fort Worth and Dallas stocked with liquor he smuggled in from Mexico. Everyone knew what he was doing, but for the most part, they looked the other way. Tuck's dad was a good man though. He made sure a lot of his neighbors were taken care of as much as he did his own family. I know he paid for Carson and Louise's wedding, and another friend's dad's funeral. He came to church about once a month and put a hefty sum in the collection plate."

"Wow. What did your father think of a gangster giving ill-gotten gains to the church?" Grace asked. "From what you've said in the past, I wouldn't think he would look too kindly on it."

"At first, he didn't. But as things got worse and worse, he accepted the money as a gift. That helped a lot of people who were members of the church. I know it paid the mortgage on the church and the parsonage more than a few times." Evie shook her head. "It was a bad time for a lot of people, but we were so young, and most of us were in families that didn't suffer like so many others did. We didn't know how bad it was until we were grown, marrying, and having our own kids."

"That reminds me," Grace said. "How did you and Gramps meet? Y'all seem to be from such different worlds that it seems strange your paths crossed."

"At Earl and Mamie Harrison's wedding. Earl and Dean were firemen on the same truck and were good friends. Dean was Earl's witness. I wasn't actually invited, but I was there with Freddy and her family. They provided the music at the wedding reception."

"You crashed a wedding and met your future husband? That sounds like the plot in a movie," Taylor said with a grin.

"It wasn't that romantic," Evie said. A small frown flitted across her face before she smiled at the girls. "Except that I have y'all, my family, I wish I'd never met him."

"Oh, Grams." Grace took her great-grandmother's hands. "Was being married to him that bad?"

Evie shook her head, but Grace saw something in Evie's eyes that confirmed her suspicion.

"Why did you marry him?" she asked.

"That's a long story, my dear, and I'm tired. Can we do this another day?"

"Sure," Gracie said. "I have an idea. Why don't I leave you my recorder? That way, you can tell the story when you feel like it, and we won't be interrupting with a lot of questions."

"That sounds like a good idea," Taylor said. She picked up the recorder from the table and showed Evie how to use it. "You push this button to record and this one to stop. It's as simple as that."

"How much will this thing hold?" Evie asked. "I talk a lot."

Taylor laughed. "So that's where Gracie gets it. Don't worry, Evie. This recorder will hold almost twenty-four hours of your storytelling. It's fully charged, so you shouldn't have any problems."

Grace helped Evie to her bed and left the recorder within easy reach on the bedside table. Evie's eyes closed, and she was asleep before the girls could dim the light and take their leave.

†

Evie woke a few hours later. She lay in her bed, and the memories that seeing the old photographs had brought played in her mind. She smiled to herself as she thought of Freddy with her violin, standing alone with a hat two sizes too big on her head.

"Oh, Freddy. If you only knew how much I miss you," she whispered.

She reached for the intercom to summon Cecelia to help her. Her hand skimmed the recorder as she pushed the button. She picked up the recorder and scrutinized it. The contraption looked nothing like any recorder she had ever seen. She pressed the record button, and the little green light came on. She immediately pushed the stop button since she wasn't quite ready to tell her story.

"Whatcha got there, Grams?" Cecelia asked as she came into the room and turned the light on.

"The girls left me this recorder so I can tell them my stories without them interrupting me every few seconds. Can you help me to the bathroom, please? I'm about to pee my pants."

Cecelia helped her up and placed her walker in front of her.

"What are the girls going to do with all this information they're getting from you?" Cecelia asked through the closed bathroom door.

"I don't know," Evie said. "I guess they're writing it down somewhere. Maybe Taylor's using it for that paper she has to write for school. Come help me get off this pot."

After Evie was up and had washed her hands, Cecelia assisted her back to bed. "Are you sure you want to go back to bed? It's still kind of early."

"I know, but I'm tired, and that chair isn't as comfortable as I thought it would be. I'll just put a bunch of pillows behind me, and I'll be okay."

"Okay. Supper's chicken pot pie, if that's okay with you. It's leftovers." Cecelia made sure Evie could reach her glasses and her water glass as well as the recorder.

"Sounds good," Evie said. Once Cecelia had left the room, she picked up the recorder again and examined it. "I guess you and I are going to become friends. Let's get started."

†

1937

"Here, Pipsqueak. Carry this for me." Freddy's father handed Evie a small drum. "Just follow Freddy. She'll show you where to put it."

Evie grinned at Richard Priloux's nickname for her. Though her family shortened her name from Evelyn to Evie, they never used fun nicknames. The Prilouxs were as different from the Hardens as white was from black. And Evie liked the Prilouxs' way a lot more than she did her family's. She turned and skipped after Freddy until she caught up with her.

She and Freddy joined Freddy's mother and brother on the small stage at one end of the long white tent. Evie set the drum down and looked around her. People were scurrying around, putting tablecloths on the round tables scattered through the tent, while others arranged fresh flowers on each table. The scent of the flowers joined the aromas emanating from the buffet table full of food for the wedding guests.

"I've never seen anything like this," she said. "People who get married in Daddy's church just serve refreshments in the fellowship hall."

"We do receptions like this a lot. Well, we used to. Now we do one every once in a while," Freddy said. She took her violin from its leather case and tightened the strings. She ran the bow over them and adjusted the strings again. "I like doing them. We usually get a chance to eat some of the food while toasts are made and everyone talks nice about the bride and groom."

"Yes, but we earn our money once the dancing starts," Gary, Freddy's oldest brother, said.

"Dancing?" Evie's eyebrows went up.

"You are so sheltered," he said with a laugh as he headed back to the truck for more equipment.

An hour later, Evie sat wide-eyed as the tent filled with laughing, chattering wedding guests. The guests roared a welcome as the bride and groom finally arrived at their reception. They went to the table prepared for them before turning, waving, and bowing to the crowd. Freddy's family played a fast rendition of the "Wedding March" as everyone laughed and cheered. The music wound down as an older man joined the young couple. He put both his hands in the air and waved them around until everyone sat down and became quiet.

"Thank you all for coming to celebrate with Earl and Mamie as they start their lives together," he said. Another roar went up along with his hands as he waved them to silence again. "There are some people who have some things they'd like to share with y'all and these kids. I'm first."

Everyone laughed as he turned to the couple. Evie listened as the man, who turned out to be the bride's father, told them how special and blessed they were. She missed what came next as Freddy pulled her elbow to get her attention.

"We have to eat now, or we won't have a chance," Freddy whispered. "Come on."

Evie followed Freddy to the buffet tables and accepted a plate from one of the servers. Her mouth fell open as she walked along the tables. She had a choice of fried or roasted chicken, beef ribs, or sliced pork, along with potatoes prepared in more ways than she knew was possible, and all kinds of other vegetables, and bread. She knew she couldn't choose on her own, so she followed Freddy's lead and chose a couple of pieces of fried chicken, some mashed potatoes, green beans, and a cornbread roll. At the table that was set aside for them, she found her place already set with a glass of tea and a bowl of banana pudding. This was a lot more than the refreshments she was used to seeing at a wedding reception.

The family finished eating just as the bride and groom concluded their own toasts to the gathering. As everyone cheered, the Prilouxs took their places behind the small dance floor and played quietly while the guests formed a line at the buffet tables. Evie sat in a chair behind Freddy, watching in awe at a piece of life she had no idea existed until now.

Gary's right. I am sheltered, Evie thought. She wanted to get up and wander around the tent, but she knew that would be rude. She leaned over so far that she almost fell out of her chair several times. Mrs. Priloux smiled at her as she tried to regain her balance. The older woman crooked a finger at her, and Evie joined her on the piano bench.

"Why don't you walk around a bit?" Mrs. Priloux whispered. "Just stay along the walls, and no one will notice."

"Oh, thank you." Evie grinned and kissed her friend's mother's cheek. "I promise not to garner any attention to myself."

Mrs. Priloux smiled and turned back to her music.

Evie skirted the edges of the crowd, staying close to the walls of the tent. The people attending the reception paid her no mind, laughing and drinking what Freddy had told her was champagne. As she got close to the table where the bride and groom and their attendants sat, she noticed one of the men who had toasted the couple was watching her. She stopped and ducked her head. While she was trying to decide whether to go back the way she came or sneak past the table, the man startled her by lifting her chin and looking at her face. She hadn't heard or seen him approach. She was taken aback by how tall he was.

"You're a pretty little thing," the man said. "I don't recognize you. Who are you here with?"

"The band," she whispered.

"It's a good thing I can read lips since I couldn't hear what you said." He grinned at her. "What instrument do you play?"

His grin was infectious, and she smiled back. "I don't. The violinist is my best friend, and I came along to help set up and take down."

"What's your name?"

Before she could answer, Mrs. Priloux joined them and took her elbow. "I need you to come turn the pages for me on this next set." She looked up at the man. "Please excuse us, sir. I hope she didn't intrude too much on the party."

"Not at all." The man bowed slightly from his waist. "It was nice to meet you, m'lady. Maybe you'll save a dance for me?"

"Umm, I don't dance," Evie stammered. "But thank you."

She almost tripped as she turned to follow Mrs. Priloux back to the bandstand. The man caught her by the waist and steadied her.

"Thank you." His hands were still on her waist. "I can stand alone now. Thank you."

"I'll let you go only after you tell me your name," he said, that grin on his face again.

"Evelyn Harden. Please let go. I need to help Mrs. Priloux."

"My name is Dean Creech. I hope to meet you again."

Dean let go and stood back. Evie could feel his eyes on her back all the way to the bandstand. She slid next to Mrs. Priloux on the piano bench and took a deep breath.

"Are you okay?" Mrs. Priloux whispered. "Was that man bothering you?"

Evie shook her head. "No. He was nice. He just caught me off guard. I don't think I've ever seen anyone so tall."

Freddy perched on the edge of the bench and wrapped her arms around Evie. "I saw that man flirting with you."

"He wasn't flirting." Evie felt her face flush. "Flirting? I've never been flirted with before."

"Except by me," Freddy whispered in her ear. "Don't forget how much I love you."

Evie's face turned a deeper red as she remembered the night before when Freddy showed her how much she loved her. She still couldn't believe her body could have those sensations.

"Dance time." Mr. Priloux bent over the small group at the piano. "Father and bride first, then mother and groom, then bride and groom, best man and bride, and maid of honor and groom. Are we ready? Everyone's music in the right order? Okay. Let's hit it."

Evie watched as the small band took their places once again.

"Watch me and turn the pages when I nod, okay?" Mrs. Priloux said. "I'm glad you're here to help me tonight. It'll make this a lot easier."

Evie smiled and nodded. She was glad to be there rather than at home listening to her father read his sermon to the family. Hearing it once was bad enough, but twice was awful.

The rest of the evening was uneventful. She watched as Dean danced first with the bride, then the bride's mother, and then almost every other woman and girl in attendance. He glanced at her once and held his hand out. She shook her head and turned her attention back to turning Mrs. Priloux's pages on time.

CHAPTER THREE

Present day

"Hey, Grams," Grace said as she came in. "How are you doing? Do you need anything?"

"There's my favorite great-granddaughter." Evie beamed at Grace and then looked behind her toward the door. "Where's your pretty girl? I like it when Taylor comes with you."

"First of all, I'm your only great-granddaughter. Second, Taylor had some research to do for her dissertation, so I dropped her off at the library. And third, Taylor likes you too."

"What's she writing her report on?"

Grace laughed. "It's a bit more than a report, Grams. Taylor's dissertation will be more like a small book than a report. And she's doing it about people like you who live to a ripe old age and are willing to share their stories about their past."

"Is she using me in her report?"

Grace shrugged. "She might. If she does, she won't use your name unless you give her permission to."

"She can use my name all she wants. I'll be dead soon enough not to care."

"Don't say that. You're going to live forever." Grace looked away so Evie wouldn't see the tears in her eyes.

Evie held her hands out, and Grace took them. She marveled at how much larger her hands were than her great-grandmother's. The skin on Evie's hands was leathery yet almost translucent. The blue veins ran like the back roads on the Texas road map. Grace brought Evie's hands to her mouth and kissed each of them.

"I love you, Grams. Thank you for telling us your stories."

"I love you too, my darling. You come from a line of strong women, and I think you're the strongest of us all."

"I don't know about that," Grace said with a laugh.

"Tell me what you thought about how I met Gramps."

"Why didn't you dance with him?"

Evie threw her head back and laughed. "Is that the only part that you caught?"

"No. I was just wondering."

"Honey child, we were staunch Southern Baptists. If Daddy had known that the Prilouxs were playing at a wedding where there was alcohol and dancing, I can guarantee I wouldn't have been there. I had no idea how to dance."

"You learned though. I've found pictures of y'all dancing. And Momma told me you taught her to dance."

"I learned after my daddy was gone to whatever version of heaven or hell was waiting for him. My momma even learned to dance after he died. He held her back in so many ways, and I swore I wouldn't have a marriage like theirs. And then I married a man cut from the same exact cloth Daddy was."

"How did Gramps hold you back?"

"Humph." Evie looked out the window for a moment. "How did he not hold me back? He pretty much made me give up all my friends and kept my family at arm's length—his arms. The only time I left the house without him was to go grocery shopping and to the beauty shop, and he went with me to those places plenty of times. Even church. He dictated which groups I participated in, and then, after the girls came, he dictated what they did outside the house. They weren't allowed any of the activities at school and only a few at church—Girls' Auxiliary, the choir, and a Lottie Moon mission group. We weren't allowed to laugh out loud, and the girls weren't allowed to play anywhere but in their bedroom. No toys. No books. No crayons. Nothing. Now look what you've gone and done. Got me all riled up and sweating. Get me a drink of water."

"What's going on in here?" Cecelia hurried through the door. "I could hear you all the way in the living room."

Grace hurried over with a glass of water and handed it to Evie before falling on her knees beside her chair. "I'm sorry, Grams. I'm so sorry. I didn't mean to upset you."

Evie put her hand on Grace's head. "Not your fault, my dear. Not your fault. Sometimes I don't realize how angry I still am at those two men until something reminds me. I look at you girls, and I'm so glad y'all escaped all that shit."

Grace's mouth fell open, and she looked up at the older woman. She was sure the look on Cecelia's face mirrored her own.

"Grams! Should I find a bar of soap?" Cecelia asked. "I don't think I've ever heard you say a curse word."

"You should've heard me when Freddy and her brothers and I would hold cursing contests. I held my own, but Gary always won."

"Cursing contests?" Grace's voice cracked as she tried to keep from laughing.

†

"Cursing contests?" The look on Taylor's face was priceless. "Oh, my. I wish I'd been there. Your grandmother cracks me up."

"Great-grandmother. She's quick to correct anyone who gets that wrong," Grace said, shaking her head. "I had no idea that Gramps ruled with such an iron hand. Grams said she wasn't allowed to be around her friends unless he was with her. He controlled every aspect of her life, and Grandma's and Aunt Betts'. It just breaks my heart."

Taylor pulled Grace into a tight embrace and rocked her until Grace's sobs let up.

"I'm sorry. I don't know where that came from."

"Your heart," Taylor said. She leaned back so she could look Grace in the face. "You are grieving what your grandmother—great-grandmother—missed out on. Just be glad your moms aren't like that."

Grace smiled at the thought of the two women who raised her to be the best she could be. "I am blessed, aren't I? Mom and Mudda are the best mothers a girl could have. Instead of holding me back, they pushed me forward and still do. They are so proud of you; they almost pop whenever they talk about you."

Taylor turned a pale pink. "Thank you. I think they're pretty special too. But I'm not doing anything all that special."

Grace laughed. "No. Nothing special. Just working on getting a doctorate in social anthropology. Heck, I didn't even know there was such a thing until I met you."

"I googled Frieda Priloux. Guess what I found out."

"Well, going by what Grams has told me, I figure you found her obit. Grams told me she died when a plane she was ferrying during World War II crashed."

"That's not at all what I found out. In fact, Frieda's still alive and lives in Weatherford with her niece. Or rather her great-niece."

Grace's mouth fell open. "You're kidding."

"Nope." Taylor pulled her tablet out and turned it on. "Look for yourself."

She handed it to Grace, who read the notes Taylor had meticulously typed. "Wow. Just wow."

"I took the liberty of calling Pepper, her niece. She's really nice and is a good woman. Frieda has some dementia and has to have twenty-four-hour care. Pepper works from home so she can be there for her. She has dedicated her life to her great-aunt."

"Wow. Just wow."

"You already said that," Taylor said with a laugh. "Anyway, Pepper invited us to come out to visit so you can decide whether you should tell Evie that Freddy's still alive."

"But why does Grams think she was dead? That just doesn't make sense."

"Let's ask her again when we see her next. Right now, I'd like to change the subject, if you don't mind."

"To what?" Grace looked up as Taylor took the tablet from her and pulled her to her feet.

"It's a conversation best held in the bedroom with no clothes on."

†

1943

"Dead? What do you mean, dead?" Evie put one hand to her throat and the other over her mouth. "Freddy? Dead? What happened?"

She couldn't stop the tears from overflowing, even though she knew her crying angered Dean and upset their daughter, Eleanor. But this time, Dean gathered her in a hug before guiding her to a chair. He kneeled down in front of her.

"The bomber she was ferrying from San Angelo to somewhere on the East Coast crashed. She didn't have a chance. I'm so sorry."

"Oh my God. I have to call Mr. and Mrs. Priloux." Evie tried to stand, but Dean held her in place.

"I talked to Richard Priloux just a little bit ago. They just want to be left alone."

"Will they let me know when the funeral is?"

"Oh, honey. There won't be a funeral. Freddy's body was burned to ashes. There's nothing to bury."

Evie covered her mouth and bolted for the bathroom. She landed on her knees in front of the toilet just in time. After she lost the contents of her stomach, she turned and put her head on her arms on the side of the tub. She was so drained she didn't have any tears left. She didn't know how long she had been there when she woke up. She tried to stand, but her legs were asleep.

"Dean? Dean, please come help me up."

Silence and the sound of Eleanor playing in her crib answered her plea. She knew he wasn't home, but tried again, just in case she was wrong.

"Dean? Please come help me."

She reached over and put the toilet seat down before pushing herself up far enough to sit on it. She put her hand on the bulge of her belly that was just beginning to show. Knowing Freddy would never see this child shook her to the core. She finally pushed herself to her feet, washed her face, and brushed her teeth. She staggered to the bedroom, where she found a note from Dean propped on the dresser.

"Gone to the firehouse. Big fire south of town. Be back late."

And that was it. That was the last Evie and Dean ever spoke of Freddy's death. The Prilouxs left Fort Worth shortly after, and Evie never heard from them again. But she kept them close to her heart and wrote them a note every year on Christmas and on the birthday she and Freddy shared. She didn't know where to mail them, so she kept them all in her keepsake box, where they lay unread for nearly seven decades.

CHAPTER FOUR

Present day

"Did you come across the box of notes Grams told us about?" Grace asked as she and Taylor surveyed the contents of the attic.

"I don't remember seeing it, but I was mainly looking for more photographs. Hopefully it's not buried too deep."

The two girls began moving the boxes, checking the contents of each before moving on to the next one. Two hours later, there were only two boxes left.

"I'll take this one," Grace said as she kneeled in front of the box on the right.

Taylor opened the other one.

"No need to go any further. Look what I found," she said. She lifted an ornate box. The box was gilded, and the word "Keepsakes" was emblazoned across its lid. "I somehow expected it to be a bit more sedate."

Grace held her hands out, and Taylor placed the box in them. Grace leaned against the wall and slid down until she sat cross-legged on the floor. Taylor sat down next to her.

"I feel like we're intruding on something intimate," Grace said. She ran her hands over the lid.

"We could take it to Evie and let her open it. I just wonder if that's a good idea. She's still obviously so deep in grief, thinking Frieda is dead."

Grace nodded. Tears slid down her face and dropped onto the box. Taylor put an arm around her shoulders, and Grace turned into her embrace.

"Why would Gramps do something like that?" she asked. "It's so cruel. I can't imagine how much pain it would cause if you disappeared from my life and I thought you were dead."

"That's not going to happen, sweets. I promise. I love you, and no one is going to separate us."

Grace nodded as Taylor held her, and Grace cried herself out.

†

"You must be Taylor Bradford," the girl said as she opened the door to the unique Queen Anne-style house.

"Yes, I am. And this is Grace Jenkins. Are you Pepper?"

Pepper nodded and stepped aside so Taylor and Grace could enter the house.

"Your home is beautiful," Grace said. The artist in her wished she had a tablet and her pencils with her. "Is it all original?"

Taylor nudged her with her elbow. "We're here to talk about Frieda, not the house."

"Oh, that's okay," Pepper said. "Come on into the sitting room. I've put some refreshments out. Hope y'all like sweet tea and pecan tarts. And yes, the house is all original except for the kitchen and bathrooms. Aunt Freddy took immaculate care of it until she couldn't anymore, and my partner and I have ever since."

Grace and Taylor exchanged glances, Taylor with a raised eyebrow.

"Did I say something wrong?" Pepper asked as she sat down and poured them each a glass of tea.

"Well, I, for one, have two questions regarding what you said," Taylor replied. "But one is rather personal."

Pepper laughed. "Yes, my 'partner' is same sex. Her name is Sonya, and we've been together almost twenty years. What's the second question? And then it's my turn for a personal question."

"Personal question first," Taylor said. She took Grace's hand and smiled at her. "Yes, we're a couple. Been together almost four years, but we haven't made it legal."

"Yet," Grace said under her breath. Taylor raised an eyebrow at her, but Grace didn't say anything else.

"My other question is, how long has Frieda owned this property?" Taylor asked.

"Please call her Freddy. I have to think twice when you say Frieda." Pepper stood up and went to a small desk. She came back with an old accordion folder. "I had a feeling you'd want to know some details, so I dug these out."

She set the papers she took from the folder on the table and spread them out. She picked one up and handed it to Taylor. Grace leaned closer to see what it was.

"'Deed of Property,'" she read. "Wow. She paid this off back in '70? When did she originally buy it?"

Grace took the deed and held it where she could read it. "Purchased, December fourth, 1950. Paid in full, December fifth, 1970. Wow. She paid it off in almost exactly twenty years. That's almost unheard of these days."

"You wouldn't believe the offers that have been made for this property over the years. When Aunt Freddy realized she was losing her memory, she drafted papers forbidding the house sell until after her death. I'm praying that the house will stay in the family."

"It must be hard taking care of someone with dementia," Grace said. "I help my grandma and mother take care of Grams, but she is fully lucid. It's just old age in general that has slowed her down."

"Your great-grandmother is Evie, right?"

Grace nodded. "Yes. She's a pretty special spitfire that we all love. What do you know about her? Did Freddy talk about her before she got sick?"

Pepper laughed. "Only all the time," she said. A shadow crossed her face. "She has a big photo album full of pictures of her, but they stop in 1939. The only reason she ever gave us was that Evie got married, and her husband wouldn't let anyone take her picture. Then Aunt Freddy joined the WASPs during World War Two. Even the occasional notes she received from Evie stopped, and she never knew why. Her parents moved to Waco to be close to her oldest brother's family after he died, and they too, lost touch with Evie's family."

"I think we have a lot of blanks that need to be filled in," Taylor said.

Over the course of the next couple of hours, the trio asked and answered questions about their elderly family members.

There were many times that heads shook in disbelief and frustration.

"I can't believe how horrible Gramps was to Grams and Freddy." Grace dried tears from her face for the umpteenth time. "How can someone be so jealous?"

"I think it's more of a control issue than jealousy. He kept her from her own family too, remember?" Taylor rubbed Grace's back. "I'm sorry, sweetie. I hate that you're becoming so disillusioned about your grandpa."

A bell rang from a room deep in the house. Pepper stood up. "Excuse me a minute. Sounds like Aunt Freddy's awake from her morning nap. I need to go check on her and fix her lunch. Y'all are welcome to stay if you'd like."

"Will it upset her for you to have visitors?" Taylor asked. "I know most dementia patients do best when they stick to a strict routine."

"I often have clients come by," Pepper said. "Having visitors doesn't throw her off. Thanks for asking though."

Taylor and Grace looked through the rest of the stack of papers as Pepper went to take care of her aunt. Most of the papers were tax receipts for the property, but there were also a few letters addressed to Freddy from different members of her family. Grace was curious about what was in them, but she and Taylor decided it would cross a line to read them. After a few minutes, Pepper motioned for them to come to the kitchen.

The kitchen was an anachronism compared to the rest of the house. It was modern and bright, with white cabinets and stainless-steel appliances. The only things that fit the age of the house were the chrome-and-red Formica kitchen table and matching chairs with red-vinyl seats. An elderly woman sat at the table with an oversized bib tied around her neck. She was slurping from a cup of tea while Pepper prepared a sandwich for her.

"Would y'all like something to eat?" she asked. "I'm making Aunty and me a grilled cheese sandwich. I can make four as well as I can make two."

"That sounds good. Thank you," Grace said. She mouthed, *Is it okay if we talk to Freddy?*

Pepper nodded and turned back to the stove. Grace and Taylor sat on opposite sides of the table, on either side of Freddy.

"Hi, Freddy. How are you today?" Taylor said. "My name is Taylor, and this is Grace. We're friends of your niece, Pepper. I hope you don't mind us having lunch with you."

Freddy looked up and grinned. "My great-great-niece," she said. "I like having company."

She turned to Grace, but before Grace could say anything, the old woman burst into tears and jumped out of her chair. She threw her arms around Grace and started trying to jump up and down. Grace stood up as quickly as she could to keep them both from falling to the floor. Pepper rushed over and pulled her aunt away from Grace.

"Aunt Freddy, what's going on?" she asked. Taylor handed her a napkin, and she dried the tears from Freddy's face.

"Evie! Evie has finally come to see me. Oh, Evie."

Freddy held her arms open for Grace. Grace hesitated before stepping into her embrace. After a moment, she loosened Freddy's arms from around her and guided her to her chair. She kneeled in front of her and held both of her hands.

"I'm not Evie, Freddy. I'm her great-granddaughter, Grace."

"Grace? But that's my name. I think." Freddy scrunched her face. "Sometimes, I forget what my full name is. Freddy Grace Priloux, I think."

"That's right, Aunt Freddy." Pepper was back at the stove rescuing the sandwiches, which were starting to scorch.

"Freddy, Evie named her first daughter Eleanor Grace, who named her first daughter Cecelia Grace. And she named me Grace Marie. We're all named after you. That's how much she loves you," Grace said.

Pepper set the sandwiches on the table. "Eat, Aunt Freddy. Then we can talk some more about this, okay?"

Without another word, Freddy leaned over and began to eat. Grace watched as she devoured the sandwich in just a few bites. Freddy looked up and grinned.

"I'm done eating. Now we can talk."

"Aunt Freddy, first, I want you to answer a few questions," Pepper said. "What day is it?"

"Wednesday."

"That's right. Now, do you play any musical instruments?"

"Yes, silly. The violin. I played in orchestras all over the world. Did you forget?"

Pepper laughed. "No, sweetie, I didn't forget. I just wanted to see if you're lucid enough to talk."

Freddy's face fell. "I am perfectly lucid. Please, can we talk?"

Pepper patted her hand. "Yes. But if you get upset or start to get confused, we stop, okay?"

"I'll tell you what, Freddy," Taylor said. "I'll record everything we say today and leave the recording with Pepper. That way, you can listen as often as you want—to help you remember. Is that okay with you?"

"I think that's a marvelous idea. Now, Grace, tell me about your great-grandmother, Evie. Is she still alive?" Freddy asked, her eyes bright and alert.

Grace nodded. "Yes, ma'am. Alive and as well as she can be at near ninety-five years old."

"Is she confused?"

"No, ma'am. She is probably the least confused person I know."

Freddy threw her head back in laughter. "That's my Evie. She was always the one with the most level head of everyone in the group of dodo birds we ran around with." She leveled a steady gaze at Grace. "What about that asshole husband of hers? Is he still alive, or has he left this earth for his domain in hell?"

"Aunt Freddy! That's a rude thing to say about Grace's grandfather," Pepper said.

"Great-grandfather," Freddy said. "And I don't care because that's what he was. If she doesn't already know that, then I 'spect she'll find it out eventually."

Grace took Freddy's hand. "Yes, I do know what a horrible person my gramps was. I didn't know until just recently though. Grams has been telling me about her life with him and how controlling he was. He passed away about nine years ago. He had a stroke two years earlier and had been bedridden. Grams took care of him without complaint, but her personality did a one-eighty-degree turn almost as soon as he was in the ground."

"I loved her." Freddy's eyes filled with tears. "I wanted her to run away with me, but she wouldn't. She was so afraid of her father. He told her she had to marry Dean, so she did. But I know she didn't love him. She should have run away with me."

Grace sucked in a breath at Freddy's words. *Grams was—is—a lesbian?* She looked at Taylor and then Pepper. Both shrugged their shoulders, their faces showing as much confusion as she felt.

"Did Grams love you that way too?" she asked.

Freddy's face broke into a wide grin as she nodded. "She did. She loved me, and we wanted to be together forever, like Pepper and Sonny are now."

"Sonya, Aunt Freddy. Her name is Sonya."

"She looks like a Sonny," Freddy said. "And Karen—I mean Carter—with, uhm, what is his name?"

Taylor looked up from her notes, a strange look on her face. "Carter Priloux? It didn't even dawn on me that he could be kin to y'all. He was in some of my undergrad classes at UTA."

Pepper nodded. "Yep. Carter is my brother—was my sister, until ten or so years ago. He was born Karen but never acted like one. Aunt Freddy, Carter's boyfriend is James."

Freddy looked up from picking at the crumbs on her plate. "Hmmm? Did you know the grass is growing? And God's going to blow holes in the sky later today."

"She's gone," Pepper said. "I'm sorry. But I'll tell you, this was the longest she's been lucid in months."

"Is there anything we can do to help?" Taylor asked as Freddy wandered to the back door, where she tried the knob. It was locked, probably to keep her from wandering away. She moved on to the cabinets, which were also latched.

Pepper shook her head. "No. I'll get her involved in putting a jigsaw puzzle together. That will keep her occupied for a few hours. I think it's best if y'all go ahead and leave though. Thanks for coming. Can you see your way out?"

Grace hugged her. "Thank you for having us. Call us if there's anything we can do."

"Or if Freddy says anything else you think we should know," Taylor added.

"Thanks. No, Aunt Freddy. You can't play with that." Grace watched as Pepper carefully took the dish soap from Freddy's hands and put it on an upper shelf.

†

The drive back to Fort Worth was quiet. Grace was lost in thought about the things Freddy had revealed about her and Evie. She jumped when Taylor touched her arm.

"You gonna sit out here?" Taylor asked. "Or come inside? I'm hungry. Do you want something too?"

Grace looked around. They were parked in their driveway. "Wow. I was thinking about Freddy so much I didn't even know we were home."

Taylor nodded. "I know. I had to be careful not to get distracted. Come on. Let's go in."

Once inside, Taylor poured them each a glass of tea. "You want some soup or something? That grilled cheese sandwich just made me hungrier."

"That sounds good." Grace sat at the kitchen table and put her chin on her propped-up hands. "Pepper is a brave soul. I'm not sure I'd have it in me to take care of someone with dementia. Grams has it all together and taking care of her isn't all that easy."

"You're stronger than you think." The spoon clicked against the side of the pan as Taylor stirred the soup. "A person does what she has to do. I think I'm more impressed that Pepper is a twice-removed niece and is taking care of her."

Taylor set a steaming bowl of soup in front of Grace. “Want some bread or crackers?”

Grace slid off the chair and wrapped her arms around Taylor. “Thank you for taking such good care of me and loving my family as much as you do.”

Taylor rubbed her back a moment before speaking. “I love you more than I can express. And the fact your family has accepted me without question—well, that’s a lot more than I ever expected.”

Grace stepped back and looked at her when she heard tears in her voice. She used her thumbs to dry the tears sliding down her partner’s face. “Why are you crying?”

Taylor placed a hand on each of Grace’s cheeks and kissed her lightly on the lips. “Eat your soup before it gets cold.”

CHAPTER FIVE

"Freddy's alive?" Grace's mother and grandmother looked at her like she was crazy.

She nodded. "Yes. Alive and living in Weatherford. She has dementia though. Taylor and I were lucky enough to visit with her when she was lucid. It was sad to watch such an obviously intelligent woman regress after we talked for a while."

The older women looked at each other, their faces mirroring the incredulous looks.

"Why in the world would Daddy have told her Freddy died?" Eleanor asked.

"And how did he keep the truth from her?" Cecelia said.

"Wait, you haven't heard the kicker," Grace said. She pulled an old newspaper from her bag. "Pepper gave me this. It's an article about a local violinist who made good and traveled all over the world to be a guest performer with other orchestras. Her name, according to the paper, is F. G. Artemis.

Turns out F. G. Artemis is Freddy. Artemis was her mother's given name, but she went by Addie."

Eleanor took the paper and looked at the photograph of Freddy playing her violin with the Dallas Symphony Orchestra. "No, here's the kicker. Mike and I were at this performance. She was so good that she actually moved him to tears. I wish I had known who she was. That was over forty years ago."

"You had no way of knowing, Grandma," Grace said. She sat on the ottoman next to Eleanor and leaned her head against the older woman. "And even if you did, what could you have done?"

Eleanor shrugged as she accepted a tissue from Cecelia. "I just feel like I let her down."

"Do you think we ought to tell her?" Grace asked. "I mean, if we do, she's going to want to see Freddy, and Freddy may not be lucid enough to know who she is."

"I think she would know," Taylor said from the doorway. She shrugged off her jacket and hung it on the coat rack.

Grace smiled at Taylor and stood to hug her. Taylor leaned over and kissed Eleanor and Cecelia on their cheeks. Eleanor took one of her hands and kissed it.

"You look good, Missy. I know that means you're doing most of the cooking 'cause this one can burn boiled water," Eleanor said with a grin.

Grace turned pink as Taylor laughed.

"You're right, as usual, Miz Eleanor. Did she tell you she burned boiling water AGAIN?"

"You didn't," Eleanor and Cecelia said in unison.

"I put the water on to boil to make mac and cheese. An idea for that Grapevine mural commission came to me, so I went to my studio to start making some notes. I got sidetracked, and, well—"

"The pan boiled dry, and it scorched. The house still smells like it's burning down," Taylor finished for her.

The older ladies laughed at Grace's expense. Her pink turned red as Eleanor bent and gathered her into a hug. "Darling girl, stay out of the kitchen, please?"

"Back to what y'all were talking about when I got here," Taylor said as she pulled a chair close to the sofa. "I think you need to let Evie know about Freddy. It's only fair to her. We can explain about Freddy's dementia and make sure she understands Freddy may not know who she is. Let Evie decide whether to go see her or not."

"Are y'all out there talking about me?" Evie's voice drifted in over the intercom. "My ears are burning something terrible. Someone come help me out of bed."

Grace pushed the button on the intercom and said, "Coming, Grams." After she released the button, she stage whispered, "Do y'all think she heard us?"

Cecilia shook her head. "The intercom's one way unless the button's pushed. Go help her and see if she'd like to come out here with us."

Twenty minutes later, Taylor and Grace made sure Evie was comfortable in her rocker.

"You need the stool, Grams?" Grace asked.

"No. I'm good for now." She looked at her daughter and granddaughter. "Now I know y'all were talking about me while I was sleeping. I want to know what y'all were discussing."

"We talk about you all the time, Mom," Eleanor said with a grin. "You're the only thing interesting in our lives."

Evie shook her head. "Don't give me that," she said. "Taylor, I think you're the only sane, truthful one in this gaggle of hens. What were y'all talking about?"

"Gaggle of hens?" Grace said. "I am not old enough to be in a gaggle of hens."

"Don't change the subject, child." Evie's face was turning red, and Grace knew she was getting angry.

"Grams, calm down. Your blood pressure's about to go off the charts." She looked at the others. Cecelia gave her a barely perceptible nod, and Eleanor followed suit. Grace scooted the ottoman over so that she sat directly in front of Evie.

"Grams, Taylor did some research, and we found some interesting things out about Freddy. That's what you heard us talking about."

"What did you find out?" Evie asked. Eleanor set a box of tissues on the table at Evie's elbow. "Why do you think I'm going to need tissues?"

Taylor sat on the ottoman with Grace and took Evie's hands. "It's kind of unsettling, so I want you to be prepared, okay?"

"Freddy's been dead since '43. How can anything y'all found out be unsettling?"

Taylor and Grace exchanged looks. Taylor picked up the yellowed newspaper that Eleanor had set on the coffee table. She handed it to Evie, who held it close to her face.

"My glasses are in the other room. What does this say?" She lowered the paper to her lap but then picked it up again and studied the accompanying photograph. Her mouth fell open, and her eyes filled with tears. "That's Freddy. When was this picture taken?"

"In 1970, Grams. She performed using the name F. G. Artemis—"

"That's the name she told me was going to be her stage name," Evie said, one hand over her mouth. "She was alive in 1970? Where was this picture taken?"

"Dallas," Eleanor said. "Mike and I went to that performance, but we didn't know who she was, or I would have told you."

"1970? Dallas? Why didn't she try to get in touch with me?"

"I don't know, Grams," Grace said as she put a tissue in the old woman's hand. "Maybe she did, and Gramps intercepted the call. I don't understand why he disliked her so much."

Evie shook her head as she dried the tears that continued to gather in her eyes. "He had what he felt were legitimate reasons at the time." She took a deep breath. "Is this the only unsettling thing y'all discovered? I'm sure if there's one thing, there's more."

Cecelia walked over and sat on the arm of Evie's chair. She leaned her head on Evie's head. "Grams, Freddy is still alive. She lives in Weatherford with a niece."

"What?" Evie tried to stand, but Cecelia caught her by the shoulders and eased her back into her seat. "She's alive? Oh, my God. Oh, my God. You have to take me to her."

"There's some things you need to know about Freddy before we can do that," Taylor said. "Grace and I went out there yesterday and met her niece, Pepper. Pepper is Freddy's caretaker—"

"All old people need caretakers," Evie said with a grunt. "That's not news."

"Mom, Freddy has dementia." Eleanor grimaced as she spoke.

"Dementia? Such as Alzheimer's?" Evie's voice cracked under the weight of the words.

"It's not Alzheimer's, according to Pepper," Taylor said. "She never specified exactly what kind it is."

"Did y'all see Freddy? Other than the dementia, is she okay?"

"We did see her, Grams." Grace took Evie's hands once again. "She thought I was you. I guess I'll believe you now when you say I look like you did when you were young."

Evie's laugh was fragile. "Tell me more. I want to hear all about her. Please."

"We were blessed to be there when she was lucid," Taylor said. "She told us you two were particularly close and that her heart broke when you quit writing to her. I don't think she knew that Dean told you she was dead."

"She told us she wanted you to run away with her," Grace added.

Evie nodded, a nostalgic smile playing at the corners of her mouth. "Yes, that she did. Dean had gone to Daddy and told him he wanted to marry me, but I said no. Daddy told me in no uncertain terms that I was going to marry him. When I told Freddy, she wanted us to jump in her old jalopy of a car and get as far from Fort Worth as we could. I wish I'd gone with her." She looked at the women listening to her. "But if I had, I wouldn't have you all here with me now."

"Grams, can I ask you a personal question about you and Freddy?" Grace asked. "You don't have to answer if you don't want to."

"I guess it depends on the question and the answer."

Grace swallowed hard and glanced at Taylor. Taylor gave her an encouraging nudge.

"Freddy said she loved you and you loved her, and it was more than a friendship type of love."

Evie nodded her head. "Yes. We loved each other like your mom loves Marie, and you love Taylor. But back then, it was not only considered immoral, it was illegal."

Grace caught sight of the look on her mother's face and almost started laughing. Instead, she patted her mother's knee and said, "We were as surprised as you are, Mom."

"Do you think that's why Dad told you Freddy died?" Eleanor asked. "Did he know how much—and how y'all loved each other?"

Evie put her face in both hands. She took a deep breath before looking up again. "Yes, to both questions. He told Daddy, which is why Daddy was so adamant that I marry Dean. Dean caught me and Freddy kissing one day. We were out gathering the eggs, and we thought we were safe from anyone seeing us in the hen house, but we didn't know Dean had come to see me. Momma told him where we were. All hell broke loose. I was married to Dean within a month, and Freddy was banned from being around me. We'd sneak out to meet each other though, right up until she left for the army. After that, I never saw her again."

She put her face back in her hands and sobbed. Grace's face was also wet with tears, as were Taylor's, Cecilia's, and Eleanor's.

†

1939

"Evie?" Mrs. Harden called up the stairs. "Come down here and help me. Someone needs to go collect the eggs. I didn't get to it this morning, what with the mission ladies calling like they did."

"Coming, Mom." Evie and Freddy bounded down the back staircase into the kitchen. "Freddy and I'll go get the eggs."

"Thank you. And be careful not to break any. Mrs. Riggs wants a dozen tomorrow morning."

"Yes, ma'am." Evie took the egg basket from its hook on the back porch and skipped down the steps, Freddy at her heels. Freddy pinched her hip, and Evie squealed. Her skip turned into a run.

"Don't break any of my eggs," Mrs. Harden called from the kitchen door.

Once inside the hen house, Evie scooped eggs out of a couple of nests before Freddy caught her by the shoulders and spun her around. Before she could say anything, Freddy covered Evie's lips with her own. Evie set the basket on top of the nest boxes and snaked one hand around Freddy's neck as the other one lifted Freddy's skirt and cupped her hip cheek. Freddy groaned and deepened the kiss. Evie broke it off so she could catch her breath.

"Ummm, I love it when you kiss me," she said.

Freddy unbuttoned the top couple of buttons on Evie's dress and kissed her neck and breastbone. Evie moaned as one of Freddy's hands cupped her breast. A moment later, they were kissing again.

"What the—?"

The girls jumped and turned toward the henhouse door to find Dean standing there, the sun behind his back, throwing him into silhouette. Freddy stood in front of Evie and shielded her while Evie rebuttoned her dress.

"What in the world were you doing to her?" Dean demanded, approaching Freddy with clenched fists.

"Leave her alone." Evie stepped between them. "What are you doing here?"

Dean grabbed Evie by the elbow and dragged her out of the hen house.

"Let me go." Evie struggled to get away as Freddy tried to catch up with them.

"I will not," he said. "Not until your father hears about what I just caught you two doing. My God."

Evie looked over her shoulder at Freddy, whose complexion had gone from rosy to gray. "Go home, Freddy," she said. "Go home."

I love you, Freddy mouthed. Even as she was being dragged up the porch steps, Evie managed a smile before the screen door slammed between them.

"What is going on?" Mrs. Harden stood at the kitchen sink, drying her hands on her apron. "What is all this ruckus? Dean, let her go."

"No offense, Mrs. Harden, but if I do, she'll run away, and she has to face the consequences of her sins."

"Sins? What in the world are you talking about?"

"Momma! Help me!" Evie shouted as Dean dragged her through the house and into Mr. Harden's study, Mrs. Harden on their heels.

Mr. Harden stood up as Dean shoved Evie into a chair. She tried to stand up, but he forced her back down. Mrs. Harden tried to gather Evie in her arms, but Dean prevented that as well.

"Mrs. Harden, this has to be between me, Evie, and your husband right now," Dean said. "I'm sure Mr. Harden will fill you in later. Please leave."

"No, Momma! Stay. Please," Evie begged. She looked at her father for help, but all she saw was him agreeing with Dean.

"I don't know what this is about, but if Dean thinks it's important enough to see me about, then you need to go back to the kitchen." Mrs. Harden hesitated a moment. "Now, Edith. And close the door behind you."

Once the door clicked closed, Mr. Harden came around the desk and took Dean's hand from Evie's shoulder. "She's not going anywhere now, son. Sit down and catch your breath so you can tell me what this is all about."

Evie tried to stand up when Dean let go of her, but her father held her in her seat with more force than Dean had.

"I came to visit Evie, and when I got here, Mrs. Harden told me she was gathering the eggs. I didn't know Freddy was with her until I opened the hen house door and caught them—"

"Stop!" Evie screamed. "Stop. Please."

"Caught them doing what, Dean?" Mr. Harden squeezed Evie's shoulder until she winced in pain.

"Sir, I hate to say what I saw. It was depraved behavior in every sense of the word. Your daughter's dress was unbuttoned, and Freddy's skirt was pulled above her waist, and they had their hands all over each other while they kissed. I was—am—mortified."

Before Evie could move, her father slapped her hard across the face, twice.

"How dare you commit such a crime on the sacred grounds of this parsonage and church?" he roared. "How dare you commit such immoral acts at all?"

"Daddy, stop." Evie lowered her face into her hands. "Please stop. How can it be a sin when we love each other?"

Evie's father jerked her head up by her hair. He got as close to her face as was possible.

"Love? Is that what you call it? It is sin. The Bible teaches that love is sanctified only between a man and a woman, and man shall not lie with man nor woman with woman."

He let go of her hair and pushed her out of the chair.

"Get thee out of my sight, child. Go to your room and do not come out until either your mother or I come to get you. Now, go!"

He swung a foot at her, but Evie moved fast and was able to avoid his kick. She ran up the stairs and to her room, where she slammed the door as hard as she could. She sat on the end of her bed and once again put her face in her hands, but she had no more tears. Just as she was about to lie down, she heard a familiar scratch at her window. When she pulled the curtain back, Freddy's worried face peered through the window. Evie raised the window but only about an inch.

"Go away, Freddy," she whispered. "If they find you here, they're likely to kill you."

Freddy shook her head. "I'm not leaving here without you. I have my car down the block. Come on, while there's still time."

Before Evie could respond, a heavy knock sounded at her door. She slammed the window and pulled the curtains closed just as her father entered the room, Dean directly behind him.

"Dean has asked me for your hand in marriage, and I have accepted his offer."

"What?" Evie went pale. "I don't want to marry Dean. I don't want to marry anyone."

"That's too bad. Your mother will come up in a bit to discuss your wedding day. And you are never to see Frieda Priloux again. Understood? I am going over to her house now to discuss this with her parents. I only hope it's not too late to save her soul."

"Daddy! No! Please. Don't do this."

But Mr. Harden and Dean were already gone. Evie turned back to the window and was relieved to find it empty, even as she rued her decision not to run away with Freddy. *What happens now? I can't go through with a marriage to that man. I not only don't love him, I hate him.* Evie lay down on her bed and hugged a pillow to her chest. It wasn't long before Mrs. Harden knocked on the door.

"Oh, child. What have you done?" Mrs. Harden asked. "Sit up here and look at me."

Evie sat up, but she kept her face down. Mrs. Harden used a finger to raise Evie's chin so that they were looking at each other eye to eye.

"Is what Dean says true? Were you kissing and fondling Freddy?"

A tear rolled down Evie's face as she nodded. "Momma, I love her."

Mrs. Harden shook her head. "No, dear, you don't. It is not possible for two women to love each other in the carnal way. As friends, yes. As sisters, yes. In a carnal way, no. The Bible says love is between a man and a woman. You are fortunate that Dean loves you and is willing to marry you after what he saw."

"I don't love him, and I don't want to marry him."

"Love sometimes comes after the wedding, as I'm sure it will for you," Mrs. Harden said. "Now, you and I need to talk about the way a man loves a woman and about how babies are made."

"I've seen horses and cows breed, and colts and calves born. I know all that, and I don't like or want it one bit."

Evie's head snapped back when her mother slapped her. "You speak with disrespect toward me, your father, and future husband. Fine. You know everything you think you should know. Here's something you don't know. Your wedding day is two weeks from Saturday. We only have a few days to make you a dress and get things planned. In the meantime, you aren't to leave this room or have any contact with Frieda Priloux. Period."

Before Evie could respond, Mrs. Harden was gone, and the bedroom door firmly shut.

"Two weeks? Two weeks? Noooooo—"

CHAPTER SIX

Present day

"Are you sure you want to do this?" Cecelia asked as she settled Evie into the front seat of Taylor's SUV. "You know there's a chance she won't have any idea who you are."

"I'll know who she is," Evie said, her lips set in a way everyone present recognized. There was no turning her back now.

Grace and Cecelia gave each other a look as they buckled their seat belts.

"Y'all ready?" Taylor asked, looking over her shoulder and giving Grace a smile.

"As ready as I guess we can be," Cecelia said. She squeezed Grace's hand, but the look on her face revealed how worried she was.

Although the drive was only about half an hour long, it seemed interminable since Evie kept telling Taylor to slow down.

"I'm going the speed limit," Taylor said. "If I slow down anymore, the other drivers will run us off the road."

"The speed limit is too high." Evie had a white-knuckle hold on the "oh-shit" handle and the armrest.

They all breathed a sigh of relief when Taylor pulled into the Queen Anne house's driveway. There was silence in the car while everyone caught their breath. Grace leaned forward and put a hand on Evie's shoulder.

"You okay, Grams?"

Evie nodded. She was looking at the house. "One day, when we were about twelve or thirteen, Freddy drew a picture of a house and told me she was going to buy it for me when we grew up. I swear this is the house she drew. It's beautiful."

"Wait 'til you see inside," Grace said. "It's almost all original and is exquisite. Are you ready?"

"Yes. I want to see her." Evie opened the door, swiveled in her seat, and waited for someone to help her out.

Pepper met them on the porch. She hugged Taylor and Grace and shook hands with Cecelia before turning to Evie. "Miz Evie, I can't tell you how glad I am to finally meet you. As long as I can remember, Aunt Freddy has spoken of you. Even since she got sick, you're her main topic of conversation. Y'all come on in. I've got sweet tea and pecan sandies in the sitting room."

She took Evie by the elbow and guided her inside. Evie stopped just inside the door.

"Oh, my." One hand covered her mouth as she reached out and ran the other along the frame of a picture hanging on the wall. "Oh, my. I drew this for her just before…"

Grace hadn't noticed the picture when they were there the first time. In it, two girls leaned on opposite sides of a tree, their hands clasped behind it. Even though the girls had their backs to the viewer, it was obvious who they were. In the background was a house and garden grown over with colorful flowers. The quality of the picture was amateurish but showed a lot of potential for the artist to improve.

"I didn't know you painted," Grace said as she slipped an arm around her great-grandmother's waist. "This is beautiful."

"It was our dream," Evie said. "This is the last picture I ever drew. Dean didn't approve of it. He said it was a waste of good paper and valuable time. He threw out all my pencils and paints the first day we were married."

"Oh, Grams." Grace embraced the older woman. "I didn't know Gramps was so horrible to you. I'm so sorry you had to live like that."

"Come on, you two," Cecelia said. "Let's go sit down and have some tea."

"Pepper, was that painting there when we were out here?" Grace asked under her breath. "I don't remember seeing it."

"It was hanging in Aunt Freddy's room. She decided a few days ago that it needed to be out here. I don't question small things like that, so I helped her rehang it. I had no idea of its importance."

"It's almost like she knew we were coming," Taylor said. "Do you know if she's clairvoyant or was before she got sick?"

Pepper shrugged. "I don't know, but I don't think so. No one ever said anything about it to me."

"I think some people with dementia become clairvoyant. That's one thing I want to research for my dissertation."

"That's about the hundredth thing you want to research," Grace said, nudging her partner in the ribs. "I think you're going to have to eventually nail it down."

The three young women laughed and went to join the others.

"Tell me about you and Freddy when you were younger," Pepper said as she sat on the sofa beside Evie. "I feel as though I already know you as much as Freddy talks about you, but I'd love to hear your side of some of the stories."

Evie laughed. "The two tellings will likely sound quite a bit different if Freddy has stayed true to herself. She has a way of embellishing things to make them seem more interesting. She is a natural storyteller."

Pepper laughed. "That's true. The problem these days is that she tends to tell the same story over and over, word for word. I nod and say 'uh-huh' a lot."

"Where is she?" Evie asked. "She is here, right?"

"Oh, yes, ma'am. She was wound up this morning like she knew something was up. I didn't tell her anything in case the plans changed. It's hard to explain to her when things don't go as expected. Anyway, I finally talked her into lying down about an hour ago. I 'spect she'll be up in a little while."

"What's it like, taking care of her?" Evie looked around the sitting room. "Do you have to keep her out of places? There's a lot of breakables in here."

"She can be a challenge sometimes," Pepper admitted. "At times, she tries my patience more than a little. Fortunately, Sonya, my partner, has a lot more patience than I do and steps in when she sees me starting to go a bit crazy."

"When do we get to meet Sonya?" Taylor asked.

"I had hoped today, but she had a last-minute call. She's a freelance court reporter, and one of the regulars decided to have her baby a couple of months early, so Sonya had to go fill in for her. Maybe we can set a time we can meet for dinner."

"That was going to be my question," Cecelia said. "How do you and Sonya get a break?"

"There's an organization out here that rescues caretakers," Pepper said. "Once a month, a nurse or social worker comes and stays with Freddy for a day and sometimes overnight. I don't know what we'd do without them. They are, quite literally, lifesavers."

"Pepper! Where are you? I wet myself." Anxiety crackled in Freddy's panicked voice.

"Excuse me." Pepper jumped up and ran out of the sitting room. "I'm coming, Aunt Freddy. Just stay right there."

Evie's face turned gray at the sound of Freddy's voice. Grace joined her on the sofa and put her arm around her shoulders.

"Are you okay, Grams? We don't have to stay if you don't want to."

Evie shook her head. "I want to see her. Even if she doesn't know who I am, I want to see her."

The four women sat in silence, listening to the muffled voices of Freddy and Pepper down the hall. After a few minutes, Pepper led Freddy into the kitchen. She caught Grace's eye and tilted her head, silently inviting them to join her and Freddy.

"Aunt Freddy, do you remember Grace and Taylor? They came to visit you the other day."

Freddy looked up from the sandwich Pepper had set in front of her. Her face lit up when she saw Grace. She held her hand out, and Grace went and squatted beside her. Freddy put a hand on each cheek and gave her a light peck on the lips.

"My Evie has come back to see me," she said, pulling Grace into an embrace. "You came back."

"Freddy, I'm Grace." Grace gently removed Freddy's arms from around her. "Evie is my great-grandmother. She came with me today. Do you want to meet her?"

"Pepper is my great-great-niece." Freddy returned to her sandwich.

Evie sat in the chair next to Freddy's. She sat in silence while Freddy ate. After a few minutes, Freddy turned to her.

"You're old," she said.

"So are you," Evie answered.

"Who are you?" Freddy had a confused look on her face. She looked from Evie to Grace and back again. Grace sat down on the other side of Freddy and took one of her hands.

"Freddy, this is Evie. Your old friend."

Freddy shook her head. "No. You're Evie." She pointed at Evie. "She's too old."

Cecelia put her hand over her mouth and turned away. Taylor was grinning and patting her on the shoulder. Pepper turned and looked out the kitchen window. Even Evie was trying not to laugh.

"Thanks, you guys. Leave me stranded." Grace tried not to roll her eyes.

"You're old too," Evie said, putting a hand on Freddy's arm. "We're both old."

"But Evie is young." Freddy stood up and held her hand out to Grace. "Come see my jigsaw puzzle. Remember how we used to put one together all the time? Momma and Daddy kept them at our house 'cause your daddy thought they were a waste of time."

There are those words again—"waste of time," Grace thought. *Why were things that were enjoyable a waste of time?* Grace took Freddy's hand and let her lead her into a dark paneled room with a large table in the center, a jigsaw puzzle about half finished on it. The picture was of a large red barn with sunflowers prominent in the foreground. Grace heard a sharp intake of breath from Evie.

"What's wrong, Grams?" Cecelia asked.

"That's the same puzzle we were putting together when Daddy forced me to marry Dean."

"It's the only one she'll work on," Pepper said. "And it's out of print. When I found that out, I took a picture of it completed. I found a company online that makes jigsaw puzzles out of photographs. I've had a dozen made." She pointed at a shelf. It held stacks of puzzle boxes. "When one wears out, I replace it with one of those."

"Have you tried to give her a different one?" Taylor asked.

"Yes. Until you've seen an elderly woman throw a temper tantrum worse than any two-year-old could, you haven't been to hell yet."

"You sit there." Freddy pointed to a chair on the other side of the table. Grace obediently sat down and waited for Freddy's next move. Freddy handed her a puzzle piece. "That was the piece you couldn't figure out where it went the last time we worked on this. Can you figure it out now?"

Evie went to stand beside Grace. Pepper moved a chair over for her to sit down. Evie smiled her thanks as she lowered herself into the chair. She held her hand out for the puzzle piece. But before Grace could give it to her, Freddy grabbed it back.

"No. Not her. You. You find where it goes." She shoved the piece back at Grace and looked at Evie. "Go away, old lady."

"I will not," Evie said. "You need to learn to share. Maybe I can help her figure out where it goes. You mind your manners."

Freddy's mouth fell open, and everyone but Evie held their breath. Evie took the puzzle piece back and studied it.

"You sounded just like my momma," Freddy said. She grinned. "You must be a friend of my momma's. Did you know her? Miz Addie? She knew everyone in town."

"Yes, she did," Evie said. "Why don't you and I talk about your momma and let these young'uns go visit? We can work on the puzzle together if that's okay with you."

Freddy nodded and looked over her shoulder at Pepper, Taylor, and Cecelia. Grace stood and joined them. Freddy made a sweeping motion toward them.

"You children go entertain yourselves. This old lady and I have things to talk about."

Chapter Seven

That evening, while Taylor was in the kitchen starting dinner, Grace pulled out the velvet box she had secreted in one of her drawers. She opened it and admired the diamond ring inside. She put it back, but then thought about something Evie had said on their way home.

Evie had said that she wasted time. "I had an opportunity to spend my life with the one person who loved me, and I wasted it."

When I look back on my life, I don't want to feel I've wasted any part of it, Grace thought.

She pocketed the box and went to the kitchen. She leaned on the door frame and watched as Taylor stirred something that smelled fantastic.

"That smells awesome," Grace said.

Taylor looked over her shoulder and grinned. "I'd say thanks, but it's spaghetti sauce from a jar I've heated up. Pasta is about ready. Are you hungry?"

Grace nodded and joined Taylor at the stove. She reached over and turned off both burners.

"Hey! What are you doing? It's not ready yet."

Grace went to one knee and took Taylor's hand.

"It may not be ready, but I'm ready for us to make the commitment to be a family forever. I don't want to waste any more time. I love you. Will you marry me?"

Taylor covered her mouth with her hand and kneeled in front of Grace, nodding. "I'll marry you if you'll marry me."

Grace grinned and opened the small box. "It's not much, but when I saw it, I knew it was the right ring for you. I took your school ring with me when I had it sized. I hope it fits."

She took the ring from its box and slid it on Taylor's left ring finger. She started to pull Taylor into a kiss, but Taylor put her hands on her shoulders to stop her. "Hold that thought," she said as she jumped to her feet. "Don't go anywhere."

Grace watched as Taylor trotted out of the kitchen. She began to stand, but Taylor was already back and kneeling in front of her. She took Grace's hands in hers.

"You beat me to the punch but not by much. I was going to ask you the same thing after dinner." Taylor showed Grace an identical velvet box. She opened it to reveal the most beautiful diamond and ruby ring Grace had ever seen. Taylor took the ring and slipped it onto Grace's hand. "I love you so much more than I ever thought it possible to love someone. Thank you for inviting me into your life and your family's life. Now you can kiss me."

Grace and Taylor fell into each other's arms and then to the floor. A few minutes later, they had wiggled out of their jeans and T-shirts and were celebrating their newly engaged status. Before they got too involved, Grace's phone rang. The girls looked at each other and cracked up laughing.

"There was a time I would have told you to ignore it, but I know we can't do that." Taylor pulled Grace's jeans over so Grace could get her phone.

"It's Mom." Grace slid her finger across the screen. "Hey, Mom. What's up?"

Her eyes grew wide and filled with tears. "Grandma or Grams, Mom? Which hospital? Baylor Southwest. We'll be there as quick as we can. I love you."

†

Two weeks later, Grace pushed Evie's wheelchair as close as possible to the edge of the grave. Evie kissed the white rose before throwing it on top of the casket. She patted Grace's hand and looked up at her.

"A person should never have to bury her own daughter, even if that daughter is an old woman."

"I'm so sorry, Grams. Do you want some privacy? I can come back to get you in a few minutes."

Evie shook her head. "No. I've said what I need to say. Eleanor knows how much I love her. I've already told her to kiss and hug Mike and Betts for me. Let's go home and chow down on some of the food the church ladies brought."

CHAPTER EIGHT

"Uh, honey." The tone in Taylor's voice caused Grace to look up from the book she was reading. "I think you should see this."

Grace put her book down and joined Taylor at the kitchen table. "What are you looking at?"

"I've been looking through all these canceled checks from your great-grandparents' stuff. Until 1950, the checks were typical ones—utilities, car payments, groceries. But then these start showing up every month beginning in March. I'm up to 1960, and they're still showing up."

Grace took the check Taylor held out to her. The check was written to Genevieve Olster for two-hundred dollars. The memo line said, "With my love."

"Who the hell is Genevieve Olster, and why is he paying her every month?" Grace asked.

Taylor took the check back and put it on a stack of checks. "I don't know, but I know I've got more research to do. I'm going to get my laptop and see what I can find out."

Grace nodded absently as she picked up the stack of checks and flipped through them. Gramps had written "love" on every one of them in one form or another. Taylor sat back down and cleared a spot for her computer. Grace scooted over beside her and watched as she typed "Genevieve Olster" into an unfamiliar search engine.

"That's not Google. What is it?"

"It's a much more thorough search engine that I pay a small fortune to the school to use. I get a lot more hits on it, and they are more accurate. Here we go—Genevieve Olster. Birthdate, April 1, 1921. Death date, September 19, 2010. Eighty-nine years old. Never married, but has one son, Lawrence Dean Olster. Dean? Hmmm, that makes this a bit more interesting. Lawrence's birthdate, March 30, 1950—"

"Oh, my God." Grace leaned back in her chair so fast she almost fell over. She jumped to her feet and stomped around the kitchen. "Damn his cheating hide. I wonder if Grams knows about this. Oh, my God."

"Sit down, Grace. There are a lot of coincidences, but so far, no proof. Let's stick with the concept of innocent until proven guilty."

"Hmmmpf. Guilty, guilty, guilty." Grace sat on the edge of the chair.

"There is no father listed for Lawrence, which is unusual for that time period."

"Is he still alive?" Grace was back on her feet.

"Yup. He still lives in the same house where he was raised. Townsend Drive in South Fort Worth. Oh, wow. Get this. He's married to a man, Philip Barker. I bet your Gramps is spinning in his grave."

"Oh, my God. How many gay people did his genes produce?" Grace laughed. "And he was the most homophobic person who ever walked the earth. I can't wait to tell Mom."

"I wonder if that's a good idea." Taylor pushed back from the table. "To find out she has an illegitimate uncle could hit her hard right now. Eleanor's only been gone a couple of weeks. And I sure don't know if I'd tell Evie."

Grace nodded. "Yeah. Now is probably not a good time to spring something like this on them. Hell, I wonder if there is a good time."

Taylor reached out and took one of Grace's hands. "There is something we need to spring on them soon, especially if we want to get married this summer. We still haven't told them we're engaged."

"Yeah. Our timing wasn't the best, was it?" Grace felt tears sting her eyes. "It's still hard to believe Grandma's gone. Grams is so old I thought all of the Creech-born women would live forever."

"Your Aunt Betts didn't, so your hypothesis was already wrong." Taylor handed her a paper towel to dry her tears.

Grace grimaced. "That's true. Grandma was seventy-seven, but Aunt Betts was only sixty-ish when she died. Grandma and Grams say she died of a broken heart after her husband died in that car wreck."

"Do you believe people can die of a broken heart?" Taylor asked with a worried look on her face.

Grace moved over to sit on her lap and wrapped her arms around Taylor's neck. "I know I would. I can't imagine my life without you."

Taylor put a hand on each of Grace's cheeks and pulled her face down into a deep kiss. Just as Grace unbuttoned the top buttons of Taylor's shirt, her phone rang. The girls looked at each other for a moment. Grace grimaced as Taylor handed her the phone.

"Better see who it is," Taylor said.

†

"There they are." Taylor pointed as a black Denali pickup truck pulled into the steakhouse parking lot. She and Grace waved as they watched Pepper back the truck into a parking spot.

"That's some piece of transportation you have there," Grace said with a grin when Pepper and Sonya joined them on the sidewalk.

"It's my baby," Pepper said. "I'd like y'all to meet Sonya, my beautiful wife and main breadwinner."

Sonya laughed as she shook hands with Taylor and Grace. "It's nice to finally put faces with names. It seems all Pepper or Aunt Freddy can talk about is you and your family. Evie sounds like a national treasure."

"She is," Grace said. "How is Freddy doing?"

"Let's get a table before we start talking," Taylor said. "I don't know about y'all, but I'm starving."

A few minutes later, the four women settled into a booth and opened their menus. Their waiter turned out to be one of the young men who sometimes assisted Grace when she was painting large murals, so there was a lot of laughter and teasing while they made their selections. Finally, it was just the four of them again.

"Now, how's Freddy doing?" Grace asked again.

"Amazingly well. I took her to her physician the day before yesterday, and she was amazed at how lucid she seems to be. I told her about all that has happened over the last couple of months, and she explained that the type of dementia Aunt Freddy has could be psychological instead of physiological. It can be slowed or even stopped when positive things happen. But the opposite can be true if those positives turn negative or stop altogether."

"How lucid is she?" Taylor asked. Grace grinned when she saw her fiancé was taking notes on her phone in her lap.

"Watch it, ladies," Grace said. "The consummate researcher is taking notes about what you say."

Taylor's face turned pink, and she put the phone on the table. "Caught," she said. "I'm doing research for my doctoral dissertation in social anthropology, and I find Evie's and Freddy's story just what I need to make it less statistical and more real."

"Wow. I didn't even know there was such a thing as social anthropology. I'd like to hear more about that," Sonya said.

Grace playfully put her hand over Taylor's mouth. "Oh, please, don't get her started. We'll be here for ten hours if you do."

Taylor pulled Grace's hand away from her face. "She's right. Maybe we can get together another time, and I can explain it to you. But, seriously, how lucid is Freddy? She seemed pretty much 'there' last time we visited, except for still not understanding that Evie is Evie."

"That's normal with dementia patients. The last time Freddy and Evie saw each other, they were in their early twenties. In her mind, Evie is still young. She doesn't understand that the time that went on for her also went on for Evie. Evie handled it well by not insisting she was Evie but letting Freddy believe she was just some other old woman." Pepper took a sip of her tea. "But she did something yesterday that makes me think she's coming back more."

"What was that?" Taylor asked, but before Pepper could answer, the waiter served their food, halting their conversation until after-dinner coffee arrived.

"Back to your question from before dinner," Pepper said. "Freddy asked me to buy strings for her violin. Now, she hasn't even had that violin out in about six or seven years. Sonya brought the strings home, and she and Freddy restrung the violin. Sonya also brought bow resin and a few other things that she thought Freddy would need. I didn't know what to expect, so when she put the violin away without playing it, I wasn't too surprised."

"But then this morning—" Sonya shook her head, and Pepper took up where she left off.

"We didn't need our alarm clock this morning. We woke up to the sound of Freddy playing her violin. I didn't know whether I was dreaming or if I'd died and gone to heaven. She hasn't lost any of her talent."

"Wow. Just wow." Grace felt tears sting her eyes. "I'm speechless—"

"And that's a rarity," Taylor said.

The four women all laughed.

Once they settled their bills, the women lingered on the sidewalk, talking for a few more minutes.

"Are y'all headed back to Weatherford tonight?" Grace asked.

Pepper and Sonya shared a smile. "No," Sonya said. "We have reservations at the Hilton downtown. We're splurging because we missed celebrating our anniversary a few months ago."

"Hey," Pepper said. She grabbed Grace's hand and held it up. "I don't remember seeing this the last time y'all were out to the house."

Taylor held her hand up so they could see her ring. "We're officially engaged," she said.

Pepper grabbed the two of them and hugged them. "That's awesome. When's the wedding?"

Grace took a deep breath. "We don't know yet. The day we became engaged was the day Grandma had her stroke. Things were so crazy, and then the funeral. We haven't told the family yet."

"Oh, my goodness," Sonya said. "Y'all've been through the mill lately, haven't you?"

"It's been crazy. I'm not sure even how to tell Mom, Mudda, and Grams we're engaged."

"Mudda? What kind of name is that?" Pepper asked.

Grace laughed. "That's what I call my other mother, Marie. It started as a joke when I was about six years old and then became a habit. She calls me 'Dauda,' and I call her 'Mudda.'"

"I didn't realize your mother was a—" Pepper looked around and lowered her voice. "A lesbian. She does not ping my gaydar at all."

"We get that a lot," Grace said. She checked her watch. "I have enjoyed this so much, but I need to get over there so Mom and Mudda can get a break from taking care of Evie for the evening. This has been great. I hope we can do it again soon."

The four women took their leave and went to their respective vehicles. Grace and Taylor were silent on the drive to Grams' house. As they drove into the driveway, Grace said, "I hate that Pepper had to whisper about Mom and Mudda."

Taylor reached over and squeezed Grace's hand. "I know. I hate it too, but that's the way it is. Are you going to tell your mothers what we found out about Dean?"

Grace shrugged. “I don’t know. I don’t want to cause any more pain than everyone’s already in. I believe I will tell Evie that Freddy is playing her violin again.”

†

“Her violin?” Evie’s hands were on her chest. “Oh, my. I loved listening to her play. She used to make up songs that she called her ‘Evie’s Opus.’ I have no musical training, but the music always made me cry. The last time she played it for me was the last time I saw her.”

†

1942

“I’m so glad you came,” Freddy said as she pulled Evie into her bedroom. “And you brought the baby. Hello, Eleanor. How are you today?”

The chubby, pink-cheeked baby grinned a toothless grin and held her arms out. Freddy took her and spun around the room with her.

“You get to clean up after her if she urps,” Evie said with a laugh. “She ate right before we came over here.”

“Where does Dean think you are?”

Evie shrugged. “He got called to assist a station out west with a big brush fire. He doesn’t know I’m not at home. If he calls, I’ll just tell him I took the baby for a walk.”

Freddy gave the baby back to Evie before gathering both of them into a hug. “I wrote some more on Evie’s Opus. You want to hear it?”

Evie nodded as she perched on the edge of Freddy's bed and set Eleanor in the middle of it. She took some of Freddy's pillows and propped the baby up with them. Freddy picked her violin up from the desk and placed it under her chin. With a quick smile at Evie, she began to play. The bow drew the most beautiful notes from the instrument, and the music flooded Evie's soul. Tears welled up in her eyes, and she covered her face.

When the music stopped, Evie stood up and gathered Freddy in her arms. They kissed while the baby gurgled on the bed.

The next day, Freddy left to join the WASPs.

CHAPTER NINE

Present day

"This is a story about two women, best friends as children, ripped apart as young women, reunited as they approach their ninety-fifth year."

"What are you doing?" Grace asked. Taylor clicked off the recorder and turned with a smile.

"I'm telling your grams' story," she said. "I think this is a great humanitarian story that a lot of people will be interested in."

Grace held her hand up. "Wait a minute. What do you mean 'a lot of people?'"

"The public. One person I keep running into at the library does human interest stories for both the newspaper and one of the television stations. I think this is a story that she can run with. Who knows what else we might learn if more people know about it."

"Uh-uh." Grace shook her head. "I don't think it's a good idea, and I don't think Grams would go for it. You did plan on asking her first, didn't you?"

Taylor frowned. "Of course. I'm not that callous. Excuse me. I have work to do. And, no, it has nothing to do with your family."

She stood up and stormed past Grace into the study. The door closed with a quiet click, a sure sign Taylor was unhappy.

"What the hell?"

Grace knocked on the door and tried the knob, only to find it locked.

"Taylor! What did I say?"

"Go away, Grace." Taylor's voice sounded as though she was crying. "Just go away."

"Not until I know what's wrong."

"Then you'll just stand there 'cause I'm not coming out for a while."

"Fine." Grace went to the kitchen and retrieved a bag of chips and a couple of Dr. Peppers. She returned to the study door and sat down on the floor, her back against the door. "I'll be here when you come out."

She opened the chips and the soda pop, but before she could imbibe, the door opened, and she fell backwards into Taylor's legs.

"Are you kidding me?" Taylor asked. "You planned on sitting there eating chips and drinking DP until I came out?"

Grace grinned at her. "I like looking at you from this perspective. I can see right up your skirt. By the way, why are you wearing a skirt?"

"Good grief, Grace. Get up." Taylor stepped over her partner and went back to her desk.

Grace turned onto her stomach and looked at Taylor sitting with her back to her, typing feverishly on her laptop.

"You're in a wonderful mood today," she said. Taylor shrugged but didn't turn to look at her or say anything. "Did something happen at school or the library?"

Taylor shrugged again, which Grace knew was an affirmative answer. She stood, went and wrapped her arms around Taylor, and rested her head on Taylor's head.

"I'm sorry you had a bad day, and I'm sorry I inadvertently made it worse. You wanna talk?"

Taylor moved Grace's arms from her shoulders and went back to typing. She said nothing, so Grace squatted and tried to read what Taylor was typing, but Taylor typed too fast for Grace to keep up. She went back to the hall, retrieved her snacks and drinks, and settled in on the sofa, tucking her legs up under her, getting comfortable to wait Taylor out. An hour later, the chip bag was empty, and Grace was opening her second drink. She was still waiting for Taylor to be ready to talk.

"Are you okay?" she asked. All she got as an answer was another shrug. "Well, I've got to get to Mom's to stay with Grams so Mom and Mudda can go bowling. Do you want to go with me?"

Taylor's headshake surprised her. Taylor usually beat her to the car when they were going to visit Evie.

"Okay." She kissed Taylor on top of her head. "I love you. It'll probably be late when I get home."

Taylor waved over her shoulder with one hand and went back to typing without saying anything.

†

"When can we go see Freddy again?" Evie asked as Grace helped her into bed. "I miss her more now that I know she's alive than I did before."

"I'll call Pepper tomorrow and see when a good time would be." Grace tucked an extra pillow behind her great-grandmother's back. "Do you want to watch *Jeopardy* or something else?"

"Oh, I have to have my Ken Jennings fix," Evie said with a laugh.

Grace laughed and turned the TV on before settling into the chair next to Evie's bed. "I keep telling Taylor she should try out for *Jeopardy*, but she doesn't think she's smart enough."

"Where is she tonight? More research?"

Grace took a deep breath and let it out with a whoosh. "She's in a bad mood for some reason and isn't talking to me."

"Did you do or say something to upset her?"

Grace turned and looked to see if Evie was serious. "Why do you think her bad mood's my fault? Can't it be something else?"

"By the way you've got your panties in a wad, I expect it is your fault. What did you do?"

Grace shook her head, crossed her arms, and turned her attention back to the TV.

"Gonna give me the silent treatment, huh?" Evie said. "Well, two can play that game."

She, too, crossed her arms and stared at the TV. But it was only a moment before she shouted an answer at the program. "The Mason-Dixon line, you idiot!"

Grace couldn't help but laugh. "Your silent treatment didn't last long."

"Neither did yours. Now, what happened 'tween you and Taylor?"

"You're persistent if nothing else," Grace said. "It's not something I can talk about right now, Grams. For now, it has to stay between me and Taylor."

Evie held her hand out, and Grace took it. Evie was about to kiss it when she stopped and looked closer at the hand she held.

"When did this happen?" she asked, holding Grace's hand closer to her face. She looked up. "And when did you plan on telling us? Or are y'all planning on eloping?"

Grace laughed. "We'd planned on telling y'all right away, but, well, other things happened, and we just kept putting it off."

"Other things, such as Eleanor passing?"

"Yes, ma'am. We weren't comfortable dropping this on everyone while we're all still grieving."

"Maybe this news would be just what we need to start recovering." Evie kissed the ring. "I think Taylor has beautiful taste in jewelry. Tell me how she proposed."

"She didn't."

"But…you're wearing an engagement ring." Evie's eyebrows touched as she frowned in confusion.

Grace laughed again. "Yep. So is she. It was the day we went to see Freddy. On the way home, you said something about feeling you'd wasted a lot of time in your life. I decided I didn't ever want to feel that way. Ever since I picked up her ring the day before, I was trying to think of the best way to propose. I decided then was as good a time as ever. She was cooking supper, so I went into the kitchen, turned off the stove, and got on one knee and proposed. After she said yes, she ran out of the room, came back with this ring, and proposed to me. I also said yes."

Evie's eyes were wide as Grace spoke. She burst into laughter when Grace finished her story.

"Now, that's a proposal story to beat all proposal stories. Did y'all ever get to eat dinner?"

Grace shook her head, and her eyes filled with tears. "No. We met y'all at the hospital instead."

"Oh." Evie covered her mouth with her hands and then opened her arms. Grace went into them and finally cried over the loss of her grandmother.

†

"I told Grams we're engaged," Grace said as she climbed into bed beside Taylor.

Taylor frowned but didn't look up from her book.

"Am I still in your doghouse?" Grace ran a finger up Taylor's arm, but Taylor shook her off. "Fine. Good night."

Grace turned off her bedside lamp and lay on her side, her back to Taylor. She didn't think she'd be able to sleep, not knowing what was going on with Taylor, but she nodded off almost immediately. When she woke a few hours later, it took her a few seconds to figure out what had woken her. But then a soft hand slid down her torso and between her legs. She turned on her back, and Taylor smiled at her as she found Grace's tender spot.

The next morning, Grace slept longer than she usually did. The aroma of bacon and coffee finally drew her out of bed. She pulled her robe on over her nude body. Recalling the midnight rendezvous with Taylor, she smiled to herself. In the kitchen, she found Taylor at the stove. She kissed her on the neck, and Taylor turned her head with a smile.

"Good morning, sleepy head. I figured bacon would get you out of bed."

"Almost as good a way to wake up as what I experienced last night," Grace said. She ran her hands up Taylor's sides until they encountered her breasts.

Taylor groaned but shook Grace off. "Your bacon's about to burn. Sit down and eat breakfast."

Grace laughed and did as she was told. She watched as Taylor flipped an egg in the skillet and let it cook for the perfect amount of time. Taylor put the eggs on a plate and set them in front of Grace.

"Yum. Perfect as always. Almost as perfect as the chef." Grace pinched Taylor's butt cheek as Taylor turned back to the stove.

Taylor laughed and moved out of her way. She set her plate across from Grace's and sat down.

"How was your visit with Evie?" she asked. "How did you end up telling her we are engaged?"

"Oh, you did hear me say that, huh?" Grace grinned. "I wasn't sure since you didn't really react."

"I know. There are a lot of things on my mind. But tell me how you told Evie."

Grace tilted her head but left the first part of what Taylor said alone and told her about the conversation she and Evie had the night before.

"So, she approved of the dual proposal?" Taylor said. "Is she going to tell your mothers, or are we?"

"She promised not to tell, so we can have that honor. The question is, when are we going to do that? Mom's not going to be happy. She used to call herself the ‘Oh yeah’ mother since she felt she was always the last one to know anything.”

“Poor Cecelia. I love her to death, but she can be insecure sometimes. She comes from such a strong line of women that it’s uncharacteristic.”

Grace shrugged. “I don’t know. Sometimes it drives me nuts, but Mudda is always so patient with her. Like you are with me.”

Taylor smiled but didn’t look up from her plate. “I think that goes both ways. I’m sorry about yesterday.”

“You feel like telling me what was really going on? I know it was more than me nixing a story by the press about Evie and Freddy.”

A shadow of a frown crossed Taylor’s face. “That was part of it. When you asked me if I planned on telling Evie, I felt as though you didn’t trust me. As far as I’m concerned, trust is the most important thing in a relationship.”

“Oh, babe. It wasn’t that I don’t trust you. I was caught off guard. I’m sorry you felt that way.”

Taylor nodded. “I understand and thank you.”

“What else was going on?” Grace reached across the table and took Taylor’s hands. “Or is it ‘is going on’?”

Tears flowed down Taylor’s face. “It’s my fucking family. Why can’t they be like yours? They’re so damn hateful.”

Grace stood, rounded the table, and put her arms around her partner. “Oh, no, hon. I’m so sorry. What can I do to help?”

Taylor buried her face in Grace’s shoulder and shook with the sobs that racked her body. Grace rocked her and stroked her hair. After a few minutes, Taylor’s sobs turned to hiccups. Grace freed herself and went to the bedroom for a box of tissues. Back in the kitchen, Taylor had dampened a clean dishcloth and held it over her face.

"Are you okay?" Grace asked.

Taylor peeked at her over the top of the cloth. "I'm sorry."

"You feel like telling me what they did? You don't have to if you don't want to."

"I called Mom to tell her we're engaged," Taylor said. The look on her face broke Grace's heart. "She wouldn't even talk to me. She gave the phone to Dad, who proceeded to quote Leviticus and say ugly things about…about you and me. It made me so mad and hurt so bad."

"Damn their hides," Grace said. "I'm so sorry they did that to you. There's nothing I can say to fix it. I wish I knew what to do."

"I shouldn't have taken it out on you, but when I felt you didn't trust me about Evie's story, it all just came out."

"Your silence is harder to put up with than your yelling," Grace said. "I'm trying to learn to give you your space, but I always want to fix things."

Taylor stood up and opened her arms. Grace moved into her embrace.

"I'm sorry, Grace. My love for you is beyond what I thought possible. I know being married won't really change anything between us, but I can't wait to be your wife."

"I guess we need to start planning a wedding."

†

"What's that you're looking at, Cecelia?" Evie asked. "Reading my mail?"

Cecelia laughed and shook her head. "Not this time, Grams. This is a birth announcement from Marie's youngest nephew, Jose. His wife just had their fourth daughter. Want to see the picture?"

"Any boys?" Evie held out her hand for the picture. "Oh, my, look at that head of hair and those fat little cheeks. She's a cutie. What did they name her?"

"No boys," Cecelia said. "Her name is Angela. She looks just like her big sisters looked when they were born, and they all look like their mother. She's got some strong genes."

"What's he think of not having any sons?" Evie handed the photograph back to Cecelia. "Dean hated me for not giving him any."

"Jose loves his girls. I've never heard him say a word about being disappointed that he doesn't have any sons. He's a wonderful daddy and spoils those babies like no one else's business."

Grace looked up from her sketch pad. She was trying to catch Evie's aura, but today she felt her drawings were amateurish.

"What did Gramps do to make you think he hated you for not having sons?" she asked.

"Besides telling me, you mean?" Evie's laugh was bitter. "When poor little Christina was born, Dean made sure everyone around—the doctors, the nurses, my roommates, anyone who would listen—knew how worthless I was for not having a boy. He told the doctors to fix it where I couldn't have any more children, since all I could do was 'spit out girls.' My poor baby was dying, and he couldn't have cared less. He said she didn't deserve to live since she wasn't a boy."

"Oh, Grams. I never heard that story," Cecelia said. "I knew you had a baby that didn't live long, but I had no idea Gramps was so horrible about it."

"That was just the beginning of the horrible," Evie said, drying a tear from her face. "He didn't pay for Christina's funeral. My daddy did that, but she never had a headstone. Still doesn't."

"Where's she buried, Grams?" Grace asked. She set the drawing pad down and moved to sit beside her great-grandmother.

"In Gilead cemetery up in Keller, next to my parents and my grandmother. For a long time, I planted flowers there, but I haven't in twenty years or more. The last time I was up there was right after the cemetery was vandalized. It hurt so much to see my mother and father's tombstones lying on the ground that I never went back."

"I remember when that happened," Cecelia said. "Marie's brothers and dad helped clean it up and repair things. It's nice again, Grams. If you want to go out there, we can, whenever you feel like it."

Evie nodded. "We'll see."

"What else did Gramps do to make things horrible?" Grace asked. "You don't have to tell us if you don't want to."

"Eh, you need to know the history so it doesn't repeat itself. Not that you girls could ever be so cruel."

Evie tapped a finger against her lips for a moment before continuing, "Your grandfather belittled poor Eleanor and Betts so much. I tried to keep them out of his way as much as I could. I fed them their dinner before he came home, made sure they had their baths, and were at least in their rooms every evening before he sat down to read the paper or watch TV. He also made my life a living hell whenever someone we knew had a baby boy. That went on for a while, and then it stopped. He didn't turn nice, but he quit talking all the time about having a son. I never did figure out what changed."

Grace thought about the checks Taylor found and knew what had changed. She wondered if she should fill in the blanks for her Grams.

"Let's change the subject," Cecelia said. "This is too depressing. I hate knowing y'all were treated so badly. I don't remember Gramps treating us like that."

"He didn't treat his grands like that," Evie said. "He mostly ignored y'all, but I know he was as disappointed not to have any grandsons as he was not to have sons."

"I thought we were changing the subject," Grace said. "Taylor and I had dinner with Pepper and her wife, Sonya, the other day."

"They didn't leave Freddy alone, did they?" Evie asked.

"No, Grams. There's an organization that helps out so that caregivers can have a day or night off. Pepper and Sonya hadn't been able to celebrate their anniversary, so they stayed at a downtown hotel that night."

"I'm glad they got a break," Cecelia said. "I really like Pepper. She sure is sacrificing a lot of her life for a great-aunt. I hope she doesn't have nefarious motives."

"Nefarious, Mom?" Grace laughed. "You've been working crossword puzzles again, haven't you?"

"You hush," Cecelia said with a grin. "Just 'cause you're the only one in the room with a college education doesn't mean you're the only one with a big vocabulary."

"Someone needs to tell me what nefarious means," Evie said.

"Bad, wrong, horrible," Cecelia said.

"Oh, no. I don't think Pepper takes care of Freddy for the wrong reasons," Evie said. "She strikes me as an upstanding young woman."

Grace nodded. “I agree. Especially after visiting with her and Sonya the other day. I think she truly loves her aunt.”

“When can we go see them again?” Evie asked. “Even though Freddy didn’t know who I was, I enjoyed our visit. We talked a lot about her family. Pepper is one of Gary’s great-grandkids. I didn’t know he’d been killed in the war.”

“I’ll give them a call,” Grace said. “I know they would love for you to visit again.”

Chapter Ten

1948

"Another girl?"

Evie could hear Dean coming down the hall long before he entered the room she shared with three other new mothers. He burst through the door with a nurse and the doctor fast on his heels.

"Mr. Creech, please lower your voice," the nurse pleaded, to no avail.

"You spit out another girl?" Dean said. He looked around at the other three mothers and noticed the blue ribbons tied on each of their beds. "These ladies managed to give their man a boy. Why can't you?"

The doctor put a hand on Dean's arm as the nurse pulled the curtain around them, as though that would give them any privacy.

"Please, Mr. Creech," he said. "Your daughter was born quite ill, and we don't think she has long to live. We're going to move Mrs. Creech to a private room so that you can spend some time with the infant while she still has life."

Dean's face did not change. Evie's tears flowed freely down her face as she wadded the blanket covering her in her fists.

"I don't care what happens to that baby," Dean said. "And you can fix her," he pointed at Evie, "so that she can't spit out any more kids since she's only able to birth girls."

He threw the curtain back and stormed out of the room. The room was so quiet that Evie could hear the breaths the other mothers had been holding let out as they began to breathe. The nurse pulled the curtain around her again.

"I'm so sorry, Mrs. Creech," the doctor said. "I just came from examining your daughter. Her heart is very weak. I don't think it can sustain her for more than a few more hours. A couple of orderlies will come to move you to a private room, and then the nurse will bring you your baby. Is there someone we can call to come sit with you?"

Evie shook her head but then changed her mind. "Yes. Please call my parents. My daddy is the preacher at Gilead. He may be at the church, but Momma will be home."

The doctor patted her on the shoulder. "I'll personally go call them for you. Again, I am so sorry."

He and the nurse exited the room but left the curtain pulled around her. A moment later, the curtain moved, and one of the other ladies peeked around it.

"Mrs. Creech, I'm Amanda Holding. May I sit with you until your parents get here or until the orderlies come to move you?"

Evie nodded. She didn't trust herself to speak. She was afraid that if she opened her mouth, she would wail and never stop. Mrs. Holding pulled a chair close to the bed and took her hand. One of the other ladies pulled a chair to the other side of the bed and put her hand on Evie's shoulder, while the third woman perched on the end of the bed. No one said anything for the ten minutes it took for the orderlies to come for Evie, but their presence brought her a bit of peace.

The private room was quiet, too quiet. Evie wanted to go back to the other room, but she knew that wouldn't be fair to the other ladies. They deserved this time to be a blessed, joyful time. The door opened, and a nurse came in with the baby in her arms. The bundle was so still, Evie wondered if she had already died.

"Here's your sweet baby, Mrs. Creech," the nurse said. She laid the baby gently in Evie's arms. She traced the sign of the cross on the baby's forehead and turned to leave.

"Thank you," Evie whispered. "Thank you."

The nurse turned back to her. To Evie's surprise, tears streamed down the nurse's face.

"I heard what your husband said to you," she said. "You don't deserve that. There are people who can help you escape that situation if you need to. I'll bring you their phone number."

She was gone before Evie could say anything. She gazed down into her baby's face. The baby's cheeks had a blue tinge, unlike the rosy pink cheeks of Eleanor and Betts.

"Hello, Christina," she said. She held the baby to her breast, but the baby wouldn't suckle. "I'm not ready to say good-bye to you, sweetie. Please nurse. Please breathe. Please stay here with me. Your big sisters want to meet you so bad."

Her tears dripped off her nose and onto the baby's swaddling. She put her cheek against her daughter's and was taken aback at how clammy the baby felt. With her eyes closed, she prayed more fervently than ever before. She heard the door open, but didn't look up, even when she felt someone sit on the edge of the bed and put a hand on her shoulder. She knew it was her mother without looking.

"Dear Father in heaven," her mother prayed, "please spare this little lamb and give her a chance to live, to know the love her mother and all of us have for her. Give her little heart the strength to beat and her little lungs the strength to breathe. Give us all the peace and faith to accept whatever your will for this child is. Amen."

Evie nodded throughout the prayer. She looked up into her mother's wet eyes.

"Meet Christina, Gran'ma," she said. "Isn't she beautiful?"

"She is. Her hair is dark like yours was." Mrs. Harden stroked Evie's upper arm. "The doctor told me what Dean said to you. He had no right, no business to be so ugly to you in front of all those other people."

Evie leaned back to get a better look at her mother.

"He had no right to say that to me, regardless of if there were other people around," she said.

"Now is not the time to discuss this. May I hold Christina, please?"

Evie put the baby in her grandmother's arms. She watched as Mrs. Harden stroked the infant's cheek, humming a tuneless lullaby under her breath.

"Where is Daddy?" Evie asked.

"Mr. Montgomery is on his deathbed. Your father has been at their house since early this morning. I called over there and told whoever answered the phone, but I don't know if he got the message. I called your brother, and he said he'd go over and make sure your daddy knows what is going on."

She handed Christina back to Evie.

"I don't think she has much longer, dear."

Evie watched as her daughter's breaths came further and further apart. She slid her hand inside the baby's swaddling so that she could feel her little heart. Christina took one more breath, and Evie felt the little heart flutter and then stop. She hugged Christina close as she rocked and rocked and finally allowed herself to wail.

†

Present day

"Oh, Grams." Grace pulled another handful of tissues from the box, wiped her face, and blew her nose. "I'm so sorry. I can't believe he treated you so badly. He should have been with you when Christina died."

Evie nodded. "Yes, he should have been. And he should have paid for a funeral and a gravestone, but he didn't do that either. He even threatened not to pay the hospital bill simply because I didn't give him a son."

"Good grief. He was a true son of a bitch, wasn't he?"

Evie threw her head back and roared with laughter. "You have no idea, my dear. No idea. But you know what? You're the first one who ever said what everyone else was thinking. Thank you."

"Why didn't you leave him, Grams? Did that nurse bring you the information she told you about?"

"She did. In fact, you may find the card tucked away in some of my paperwork." Evie took a deep breath. "I didn't leave him because I didn't have a Biblical reason to. In my family, the only reason for a marriage to split up is adultery.

Unless you count kissing, that didn't happen, on either of our parts."

Grace looked down at her hands and wondered again if she should tell her great-grandmother what she and Taylor had found out as they sifted through the history of her marriage to Dean Creech.

"What are you thinking about?" Evie asked. "You're frowning so hard you only have one eyebrow."

"Just how hard things must have been for you," Grace said. "You told us earlier that Gramps was horrible to you and the girls after that. How did you manage to come through that, be sane, and have two girls who weren't permanently damaged?"

"Who's to say my girls weren't permanently damaged?" Evie shook her head. "Your great-aunt and your grandmother suffered with self-esteem issues right up 'til they died. They just kept that from your mother and you. Eleanor should have won an award for her acting. I don't think anyone but me and Mike knew how bad she hurt all the time. And I believe Betts died at such a young age for the same reason. I blame all of that on Dean. All of it."

"Damn it, Grams." Grace stood up and walked to the window. She looked out at the bluebird house and watched as both of the parents took turns feeding the clutch of chicks in the nest. "It's too bad we can't be like the bluebirds. They both take equal care of those babies, protect them, and keep them safe."

"But they can't think and reason like we can," Evie said. "Turn on the TV. It's time for *Jeopardy*."

†

"You want something to drink or eat?" Grace asked her mother as they settled in the living room after helping Evie to bed for a nap. "You look really tired."

"I am tired. My sleep has been poor since Mom died. I thought going bowling the other night would tire me out enough to sleep, but I still tossed and turned."

"Do you want to go lie down? I can stay as long as you need me to."

Cecelia shook her head. "No, sweetie, but thank you. I do have a question for you though."

"Sure. What's up?"

"When did you plan on telling me that Taylor gave you a ring?"

Grace looked at the ring on her hand, and feelings of guilt flooded her chest.

"I planned on it a lot sooner than now," she said. "So much has been going on that there just didn't seem to be a good time. I'm sorry. I really didn't mean for you to have to ask me. When did you notice the ring?"

"That night at the hospital." Cecelia had a wry smile on her face. "I noticed Taylor's too, but then things got kind of wild and then sad. I kept waiting and waiting, and you haven't said anything."

"Are you afraid you're the 'oh, yeah' mom again?"

Cecelia nodded. "That is kind of how I'm feeling. Who else knows?"

Grace blushed. "Grams figured it out the other day, and Pepper and Sonya noticed the rings the other night. But we haven't officially announced it to anyone."

"Have you set a date?"

"Not yet. Taylor's so busy with her research, and when she tried to talk to her folks, they were so nasty, she needed a few days to recuperate. We talked a bit. We think we'd like to try to get married close to Grams' birthday, but that's flexible."

Cecelia took Grace's hands. "I'm happy for you, baby. Taylor is a special young woman. You're both blessed."

Grace leaned into Cecelia's hug. "Thanks, Mom. I've had wonderful role models in you and Mudda. I love y'all so much."

CHAPTER ELEVEN

"Oh, we'd love to have y'all come out again," Pepper said on the phone later that evening. "That's all Aunt Freddy's talked about. My brother and his partner came over, and Aunt Freddy talked their ears off about Evie and the 'old woman' that came to see her. She was so impressed that the 'old woman' knew where all the pieces in the puzzle went."

Grace laughed. "Grams said she kind of surprised herself. It's been decades since she looked at that puzzle, but it came back to her. Here's the best part—she asked me to bring her a sketch pad and some pencils. I almost cried. It seems the visit did both of them a lot of good."

"Why don't you see if your moms want to come too? I'll make sure Sonya's home. We can have Easter dinner together. Do y'all celebrate Easter? I guess I should have asked that first."

Grace laughed again. "We don't really celebrate any of the holidays except Christmas and birthdays, and that's just because we like to get gifts."

"Don't we all?" Pepper laughed too. "Let me know how many are coming, and we'll celebrate Easter together."

†

"Easter?" Taylor raised her eyebrows. "My family used to celebrate with the baskets, hidden eggs, and chocolate bunnies, and always church and new clothes."

†

"Easter?" Cecelia's voice was full of surprise. Grace heard Mudda say something in the background. "We never celebrated Easter. Mom said they sat through long, boring church services on Easter, went to sunrise services, and then were lectured if they asked for baskets or candy. I'm sure it was Gramps giving those lectures, not Grams. Anyway, Mom had a bad taste in her mouth and eschewed the holidays."

"Eschewed?" Grace laughed. "I think you've been reading a dictionary."

"You hush." Cecelia laughed along with her. "I guess I should admit I've been taking a vocabulary class online. I got tired of feeling left out of you intelligent people's conversations."

"I love it, Mom. So, what do you think of going out to Weatherford for Easter? No lectures, I promise."

"I think it's an awesome idea. Did you ask what we could bring?"

†

Easter Sunday found the family piled into Cecelia's minivan and headed west on the interstate. Every church they passed had packed parking lots. Evie hmphed at the sight.

"How do they know this is the day Jesus rose from the grave? I don't understand how he can be resurrected on a different date every year."

Marie laughed and leaned forward to pat Evie on the shoulder. "I agree. That's still a note of contention between me and my folks. They're such devout Catholics. It was hard enough for them to accept I'm a lesbian, but when I questioned some of their beliefs, well, they drew the line there. We don't discuss religion or politics when we go visit."

"That's a good policy almost anywhere these days," Cecelia said. "I was at the gym the other day, and there was almost a fight in the yoga room. I thought it was over who got to use which mat or ball or whatever, but it was because someone badmouthed the president, and someone else disagreed."

"The gym?" Grace said. "When did you start going to the gym?"

"When my doctor said my blood pressure was high, and my cholesterol was higher, and that I needed to lose weight before the weight made me sick."

"And at the same time, she started taking vocabulary lessons online," Marie added.

Everyone laughed, except Cecelia.

"Well, I figured if I was going to get my physical body in shape, I should get my mental one in shape too."

"I think it's a good plan, Cecelia," Taylor said. "Maybe I'll start using the gym privileges at the school. I noticed my britches are getting tight."

"And I'm pretty sure that's not 'cause you're with child, huh?" Evie said.

There was a moment of silence before everyone in the van roared with laughter. By the time they calmed down, they were pulling into the driveway of the Queen Anne cottage. Pepper opened the front door and came to meet them even before Cecelia turned the engine off.

"Hey, y'all," Pepper called. "I'm so glad y'all could make it. Can I help carry anything in?"

Grace helped Evie out of the car and stayed by her side up the sidewalk to the house. Sonya held the door open as they approached.

"Evie, this is Sonya, Pepper's partner," Grace said.

Evie wrapped her arms around Sonya, who reciprocated with a surprised embrace.

"It's so good to finally meet the famous Evie," Sonya said.

Evie chuckled. "Famous? I'm not so sure about that."

Sonya took her elbow and led her into the sitting room. "Aunt Freddy's still in her room. I'll go see if she's ready to come out and see everyone. If y'all will excuse me?"

Evie took a deep breath and let it out in one long swoosh.

"You okay, Grams?" Grace asked, putting an arm around the older woman's shoulders.

"I'm nervous for some reason," Evie said. "I just have a feeling today is going to be special in ways we can't even fathom right now."

"Freddy wants to make a grand entrance and wants all of us to wait for her in the dining room," Sonya said when she returned from Freddy's room. She offered her elbow to Evie, who smiled as she accepted it. "She wants you to sit at the head of the table. Is that okay with you?"

"Now, let's be clear," Evie said. "Does she want the 'old lady' to sit at the head of the table, or Evie?"

"She was quite specific that 'the old lady who thinks she's Evie' sits at the head of the table."

Evie laughed and nodded. "In that case, 'the old lady who thinks she's Evie' will sit at the head of the table. I wonder if she'll ever realize I really am Evie."

Sonya pulled the chair out for Evie to sit in and patted Evie's shoulder as she bent over and said, "That might not happen, sweetie. I'm sorry."

Evie bowed her head in response but didn't say anything. Everyone else found seats around the table, Grace to Evie's right and Cecelia to her left. As soon as they were settled, Sonya went to get Freddy.

A stunned silence fell over everyone as the sound of a violin filled the house. Evie's mouth fell open, and her eyes filled with tears. Freddy entered the dining room, her violin on her shoulder, the bow effortlessly moving over the strings. Sonya stood behind her, her hand on her mouth. Her face mirrored Grace's surprise.

Freddy rounded the table to stand between Evie and Grace and finished her performance with a flourish of her bow. She turned to look at Grace and said, "Do you recognize it, Evie? I've added a lot more to it since I played it for you last. Do you like it?"

Grace glanced at Evie, who smiled and nodded. Grace followed her lead. "It's beautiful, Freddy."

Freddy turned to Evie. "Did Momma ever tell you I write music? She was so proud of me. Sometimes Daddy used what I wrote when we performed as a band. People always asked him what the song was, and he'd point to me and tell them they had to talk to me about that."

"I remember that," Evie said. "I was there sometimes when it happened. You would turn bright red, but you were always polite and told them."

Freddy's eyebrows came together. "I don't remember you being there," she said. "Were you Momma's guest?"

Evie looked down, and Grace saw a tear slide down her nose. She couldn't reach Evie since Freddy was standing between them, but she saw Cecelia reach over and squeeze Evie's hand. Evie smiled and looked up at Freddy.

"I was a guest of yours, Freddy. You just don't remember, but that's okay because I do. Do you still call this 'Evie's Opus'?"

Freddy grinned. "Yes, I do. There's more to it than I played today, but this is my favorite part."

"Mine too," Evie said. She looked at Grace. "Can you all move down a seat so Freddy can sit here?"

After a few moments of controlled chaos, Freddy sat next to Evie. Sonya took the violin and bow and laid them on the buffet behind them.

"Wow, Aunt Freddy. That was awesome," Pepper said. She stood at the far end of the table from Evie and Freddy. She looked around at everyone. "I used to spend Easter with Mom, Dad, and my brother, but for some reason, I feel this is more my family now. Thank you for coming today to share our feast."

With that, she and Sonya went through the swinging door to the kitchen. Pepper came back carrying a platter with a large ham garnished with pineapple slices and cherries. Sonya carried a casserole of sweet potatoes topped with marshmallows and another filled with green-bean casserole. Marie jumped up, took one of the casserole dishes, and set it in the middle of the table.

"Anymore in there y'all need help with?" she asked.

"Thank you. There's a few more things," Sonya said. She tilted her head and grinned. "I'll be glad to accept your help."

A few minutes later, plates were being passed, and laughter filled the room. Freddy sat smiling as Evie helped her decide what and how much she wanted on her plate. Grace watched the two of them and wondered if she and Taylor would be so happy to help each other out at that advanced age. She looked at Taylor, who sat on the other side of her from Freddy. Taylor smiled at her, leaned over, and kissed her on the cheek.

"I love you," she whispered. "Let's make it official today."

Grace nodded and tried to swallow the lump in her throat. "I love you too. Thank you."

It wasn't long before the group had enough to eat. Pepper leaned back in her chair and patted her stomach.

"I'm so full, and we still have dessert waiting," she said. "Cecelia, that cobbler you brought is calling my name, but I think it's going to have to wait a while."

Cecelia laughed. "I completely understand. I think I'm fuller than I've been since last Thanksgiving."

"Why don't we go to the sitting room and let our food settle for a few minutes?" Pepper said. "You can bring your drinks with you, or I can get everyone fresh ones."

"Before we do that, Grace and I have something we'd like to tell everyone," Taylor said. She reached out and took Grace's hand. Together, they stood up. "Y'all already know that Grace and I are engaged. We're sorry that we didn't tell you sooner and in a better way than we did. It was never our intention to make y'all guess and bring it up to us."

"We understand," Cecelia said. She took Marie's hand. "Things were kind of odd and cockamamie for a few weeks."

"Thank you," Grace said. "Our announcement is that we finally settled on a date for the wedding."

"Wonderful!" Evie clapped her hands. "When's the big day?"

Taylor and Grace smiled at each other and, in unison, said, "June twenty-fourth."

"The week after our birthday," Evie said. "Why don't you get married on the seventeenth?"

This time, Cecelia, Marie, Pepper, and Sonya exchanged glances.

"Uhm, well, we kinda, sorta have other plans," Cecelia said.

Evie frowned at her. "What do you all have up your sleeves?"

The women exchanged glances again.

Freddy leaned over to Evie and put her hand up like she had a secret, but she spoke out loud. "I think they're planning some kind of surprise for someone."

Everyone laughed except Evie.

"I think so too, Freddy. And at least four of them know how much I hate surprises, so I hope you're wrong."

Freddy sat back and frowned. "Why do you hate surprises? You had a surprise birthday party once, and you had fun."

Evie's mouth fell open. "You remember my surprise party?"

Freddy looked confused. She put her thumb to her mouth and chewed on the nail. "I don't know. I want to go work on my puzzle." She stood up so fast her chair fell over.

Evie reached up and put her hand on Freddy's elbow. "It's okay, Freddy. You don't have to remember. I'll be in to work on the puzzle with you in a few minutes, okay?"

Pepper stood and held her hand out. Freddy took it and allowed Pepper to lead her from the dining room.

"I'm sorry, girls," Evie said. "I think I took the air from y'all's balloon. Tell us more about your plans."

CHAPTER TWELVE

That evening, Taylor and Grace lay in each other's arms, their skin glistening with the sheen of sex-induced sweat.

"Today was interesting," Grace said. She traced Taylor's jawline with her finger. "I hate that Grams figured out that we planned to give her a surprise birthday party, but I'm glad we finally let everyone know about our wedding plans."

Taylor playfully snapped at Grace's finger when it came within range of her mouth. "That tickles, and you know it," she said. "I hate that we're the reason Evie figured out about her party."

Grace moved her finger from Taylor's face to her shoulder, drew it down her arm, and over to her breast. She grinned when Taylor's nipple hardened once again. Taylor grabbed her hand and removed it from her breast.

"You've already worn me out," she said. "Let's go to sleep. I've got a meeting with my facilitator tomorrow, and I'd like to be halfway conscious for it."

Grace nodded. "Okay, but only on the condition we can take up where we left off tomorrow night."

Taylor kissed her. "You have a deal. Good night."

†

"Hey, Mom," Grace said when Cecelia answered her cell phone the next morning. "I'm not going to be able to come over this afternoon to sit with Grams. I just got a call from the city of Lewisville. They want me to come and talk to them about painting a mural somewhere in town. Do you want me to see if I can find someone to sit with her?"

"No, but thank you for asking. Congratulations on another commission."

"I don't have it yet," Grace said. "I have a preliminary meeting to see what they're looking for, and we'll go from there. It's hard missing my time with Grams, and I know you need a break for a bit every day."

"I'll be fine. Grams is over-tired from yesterday, and I doubt she'll get out of bed today. I was worried this would happen."

"Oh, dear. Is she okay? I forget how old she is sometimes. She doesn't act her age."

Cecelia laughed. "That's true. Sometimes I feel like I'm older than she is. What are you and Taylor doing to plan your wedding? Guest list? Flowers? Et cetera?"

Grace took a deep breath. "We haven't really had much time to talk about it, but we do know we want to try to get married at the labyrinth at the MCC in South Fort Worth."

"Will they let you if you're not a member?"

"I don't know. I'd planned on getting hold of someone there this afternoon, but then this meeting in Lewisville came up. And Taylor has meetings today with her facilitators at the school."

"Has she actually started writing that dissertation, or is she hung up on research?" Cecelia asked.

"You know, I'm not sure. Something seems to be holding her back, but I don't know what or why. If I bring it up, she either shuts down or changes the subject. Hopefully she'll get some direction today." She checked her watch. "I gotta go, Mom. Give Grams my love and tell her I'll see her tomorrow."

"Good luck, sweetie."

†

"A train mural?" Taylor asked. "That sounds interesting. I've always loved trains."

"Me too. I love riding the train from the Stock Yards up to Grapevine and back. I'll probably go out there to make some preliminary sketches of the engine. How did your meeting go?"

Grace watched Taylor's face change and was afraid the usual shutdown or subject change was about to happen. Taylor turned to the stove, effectively turning her back on Grace. Grace didn't push and was surprised when Taylor turned off the stove and came to sit at the table. She took both of Grace's hands in her own.

CHAPTER THIRTEEN

"Quit?" Cecelia's mouth fell open. "Why?"

"She's so far behind researching for the paper she committed to write that she and her facilitator felt it was in her best interest to put off completing it," Grace said. "I was—am—so confused about it all. I don't know if she'll be able to keep her job since she got it because she was a doctoral candidate."

"Why is she so far behind?"

"Grams and Freddy."

Cecelia frowned. "What does Grams and Freddy have to do with this?"

"Taylor is totally enamored with them and their longevity. That, and Freddy seeming to come out of some of her dementia fog whenever she and Evie are together."

"But does she really?" Cecelia asked. "Freddy still thinks you're Evie, and Grams is some old woman that knew her mother."

"I know. But she's making sense now. And she's playing her violin. Pepper told us that Freddy hasn't picked it up in over six years. Even her doctor agrees that some of her signs of dementia are easing up."

"I didn't think dementia was curable."

"Me either. Taylor tried to explain the difference between dementia and Alzheimer's, but I'm not sure I really understood it all. Alzheimer's is not reversible or curable, but if the dementia is caused by psychological issues rather than physical ones, a lot of it can be reversed, and in some cases, cured. Pepper told Taylor that the doctor hasn't been able to definitively put a finger on what is causing Freddy's dementia. She thinks a lot of it has been brought on by grief—losing Evie, losing her parents, losing her career. Now that Evie is back in her life, some of that grief is relieved, and some of her dementia has let up."

"Is this all going against patient-client privilege?" Cecelia put her hands over her face. "Besides that, it's all confusing. What is Taylor going to do with all of this knowledge?"

"She wants to write a book and make a short film or documentary about Freddy and Evie. She wants to talk to Evie about it in the next few days, but she wants to make sure you're cool with the idea first."

"And she sent you to do her dirty work?"

Grace laughed. "I guess you could say that. Actually, she'd planned on coming today, but she decided it was more important to go talk to her boss about keeping her job. She also said something about meeting someone from one of the TV stations that might help her with the film."

Cecelia sat up straight and put one hand out to stop Grace. "TV? I'm not cool with my grandmother and her best friend being on TV. Won't that out them? I'm not sure that's a good idea."

Grace shook her head. "I don't think that's the plan," she said. "But I'll make sure she knows how you feel about it."

"My ears are burning," Evie called from her end of the intercom. "Someone come help me to the bathroom and then tell me what y'all are saying about me."

"How does she do that?" Grace asked. "Every time we talk about her, she wakes up."

Cecelia laughed as she stood up and went down the hall toward Evie's room.

Fifteen minutes later, Evie settled into the reclining chair in the living room. Grace set a glass of water and a plate of sugar cookies on the table at her elbow.

"Now, I know you girls were talking about me. What were y'all talking about?" Evie chose a cookie and nibbled on it.

"All I can tell you is that Taylor wants to talk to you about something she's working on the next time she comes over," Grace said.

Evie cocked her head. "For that report she's writing?"

"Something like that."

"Well now, I've already told her she can use my name and some things I've told her, so this must be something else."

Grace exchanged glances with Cecelia.

"I saw that look," Evie said. "Y'all are keeping secrets from me. And y'all know I don't like surprises, such as surprise parties."

Another look flew between the other two.

"And I don't think Freddy likes surprises either. In fact, I don't think surprises are a good idea for her," Evie added.

"Grams, please just stop," Grace said. "You've figured out we're planning you and Freddy a birthday party. Let us plan it, and you just relax, okay?"

Evie grinned. "Finally got you to admit to that. Now, what's Taylor up to?"

"That's for Taylor to tell you," Cecelia said. "*Price Is Right* is coming on. Do you want to watch it or not?"

†

"So, she got you to tell her we're planning her a party," Taylor said with a grin. "You didn't tell her why I want to talk to her, did you?"

"No. But it was hard not to. She should have been a detective or a lawyer. She can cross-examine a person until they want to spill the beans about every secret they ever had. She kept asking when you plan to talk to her. I told her when you're ready, and I didn't know when that would be."

Taylor leaned over and hugged Grace. "Thank you for understanding, babe."

"I love you. You know I'm going to support you in whatever you decide to do. But tell me what happened at work today."

"Well, I still have a job, but it's even more part-time now than it was before. I'm going to have to find something else so that you're not having to pay all the bills by yourself."

"Any leads?" Grace found she was holding her breath. While they lived frugally, not having a steady income was a scary thought. They still had a comfortable savings account balance from her last commission, but she hadn't yet heard if Lewisville had accepted her bid on their mural. The last installment from the store in Grapevine wasn't due until the end of the month.

Taylor grinned at her and nudged her with her elbow. "Breathe, silly. You do that every time you're worried about money. We're going to be okay and, yes, I do have a lead, a good one."

"Do you plan on letting me know what it is?" Grace rubbed her side where Taylor's elbow made contact.

"Remember Lois from the TV station and the newspaper I told you about?"

"Lois? A reporter for the newspaper? You are kidding, right?"

Taylor laughed. "That was what I thought too, but before I could say anything about it, she told me she'd already married her Superman. She's got a great sense of humor about it."

"That's good. So what's she going to do for you concerning a job?"

"The TV station wants to do a special series about the elderly and the challenges they face in today's society. From getting home care, to outliving their friends and families, to what they do for fun. Lois thinks that my background and my contacts make me the perfect person to write the stories. Tomorrow I'm meeting with her boss to talk about exactly what they are looking for. I've written a couple of articles about Evie and Freddy—don't worry, I'm not using their real names—that I'm going to give them. I don't know how much they pay or anything, but I think this is a great opportunity, especially since I'll get paid for doing the research for the book I want to write."

"Take a breath, Taylor," Grace said. "The series sounds interesting, and I think it's right up your alley. I don't see how they can turn you down. But I do think you need to let Grams know."

†

"Go out for dinner? On a Tuesday?" Evie's voice was full of worry. "That sounds like you're going to tell me something you don't want me to blow a gasket about, and you're taking me out so I have to speak in civilized tones."

Grace laughed. "You're exactly right, Grams. We don't want you screaming at us, so we're taking you into public where you'll have to continue to use your indoor voice."

Evie joined her in laughing. "I promise to be good. What time do you want me to be ready for my carriage to pick me up?"

"Mom and Mudda will bring you, silly. Meet us at the steakhouse about seven. Love you. See you tonight."

Later that evening, the five women sat in a round booth near the front of the restaurant, so Evie wouldn't have to walk far. Once the waiter had taken their orders and brought their drinks, Evie looked at Taylor.

"Okay, you. Spill it. What's this all about?"

"Good grief, Grams. Can't you at least wait until after we've eaten?" Cecelia asked.

Evie frowned at her. "I'm old. I don't have the luxury of being patient. Who knows when I'll kick the bucket?"

"Grams! Don't talk like that. You're going to outlive us all, and you know it," Grace said.

"Nope. I'm not burying anyone else. Now, Miss Taylor, what is going on?"

Taylor explained to the group about her opportunities and the series proposal the TV station had suggested, and how Evie and Freddy would be a part of it all.

"People aren't interested in how old people live," Evie said, shaking her head. "Living to be ninety-five years old isn't all it's cracked up to be."

"Grams, I think you'd be surprised at how many people look up to you and wonder how you've made it this long," Grace said. "And there are people who are looking for ways to help the community and don't know how. This series will help them find ways to help."

"Pffft." Evie shook her head again, but before she could say any more, their food was served. The conversation turned to lighter fare while they ate.

Later, over after-dinner coffee, Taylor once again asked for Evie's permission to use her story for the series. "I won't use your name, and I'll change things enough that people would have a hard time knowing it's you we're talking about."

"But what if I want the notoriety?" Evie asked with a grin. "Besides, all my contemporaries are long dead. It won't matter 'cause no one will know who I am."

Everyone laughed.

"Thank you, Evie," Taylor said. "You don't know how much this means to me."

"What about Freddy?" Evie asked. "Are you going to use her name?"

Taylor shook her head. "I can't, since she's not lucid enough to understand what I'm doing. Just as you have to sign a release form, she would too, and I don't think she would know what it all meant."

"Pepper is her power of attorney," Grace said. "Can she sign the release on Freddy's behalf?"

Taylor shook her head again. "Not for something like this. Using her name and image is a lot different than okaying medical procedures or taking care of her finances and house."

"Oh, my," Evie said. Tears filled her eyes. "I think Freddy's and my story is important. People need to know not to waste time with their lives. Our story could be that warning. Look at what I missed out on because I allowed my father and my husband to control me and my actions. I don't want anyone else to find themselves in the same place when they're in their nineties."

Cecelia took Evie's hand as Grace handed her a napkin to dry her tears.

"Grams, I understand what you're saying. Your support and acceptance have been a true blessing; you never tried to shame me or hold me back from being myself and loving the person I love." Cecelia looked at Marie and smiled, her eyes full of adoration. "I hate that you and Freddy lost out on loving each other into your old age."

"I never stopped loving her," Evie said. "But she doesn't know that."

"I think she does know," Grace said. "She played the violin for you the other day, and she played 'Evie's Opus'. Even though her mind can't wrap itself around the fact that you grew old along with her, her heart does seem to know."

"That's true," Evie said. "I was so surprised and full of gratitude when she came into the dining room playing her violin. My heart sang a song I thought it had forgotten."

"I don't think something like that can be forgotten," Marie said. "Love. That's what your heart has sung for her for all these years. Even though you thought she was dead, a part of your heart knew it wasn't true. As long as either of you are alive, that song will not die."

"I'm tired," Evie said. "I think it's time to go home. Taylor, bring me that paperwork, and I'll sign it."

Chapter Fourteen

"Pepper called while you were with Evie," Taylor said as Grace walked into the house a few days later. "She asked if we could bring Evie to visit Freddy. She said Freddy won't stop pacing and checking the front door, looking for us."

"Let me check with Mom and Grams." Grace flopped into the armchair and put her feet up on the ottoman. "I'm exhausted. Grams was in a rare mood and bitched all day about Gramps. I can't believe everything he put her, Grandma, and Aunt Betts through."

Taylor picked Grace's feet up and sat down on the ottoman. She removed Grace's sandals and massaged her feet. Grace groaned her appreciation.

"Did you eat with her?" Taylor asked. "Or are you hungry?"

Grace shrugged. "I didn't eat, but I'm so depressed I don't know if I can."

Taylor nudged Grace over and squeezed into the chair beside her. Grace laid her head on her partner's shoulder. She willed the tears not to start, but she wasn't successful.

"Is this all because of what your Grams told you today?" Taylor asked.

Grace shook her head but didn't say anything. She didn't trust her voice and hated to give Taylor bad news.

"Are you going to make me fish or are you going to tell me?"

Grace shrugged. "I don't know, Taylor. I'm just tired, discouraged, and disheartened to find out all this stuff about Gramps. We weren't all that close, but I always looked up to him."

"I can understand that," Taylor said. "But why are you discouraged? Oh. Wait a minute. You were supposed to hear from Lewisville about your bid today, weren't you?"

Grace nodded. "I didn't get it. And I don't have any other commissions lined up. I'm afraid we're going to go through our savings and not have anything left for the wedding or a honeymoon."

Taylor was quiet for a long time. She ran her fingers through Grace's hair, and Grace relaxed.

"Do you think I should find an actual job?" Taylor asked.

Grace sat up and looked at her. "I don't want you to have to do that, hon. Let me see if I can scare up a showing or two. Mayfest is coming up, and I usually do fairly well selling my work there, especially the pictures of bluebonnets and longhorns—"

"The two things you hate the most to paint," Taylor said with a strained laugh.

"Yup, but they pay the bills."

†

Freddy stood on the stoop, clapping her hands. Grace had a feeling she would have been jumping up and down if Pepper hadn't been holding on to her elbow. Grace guided the SUV into the driveway beside Pepper's Ram. Evie had her hand on the door handle.

"Don't open the door until I've cut off the engine, Grams," Grace said.

"I'm not a child," Evie said, even as she pulled on the handle.

Grace grinned and turned off the car. Pepper and Freddy met them at the side of the car. Freddy threw her arms around Evie even before Evie had her seatbelt off.

"I think she's glad to see y'all," Pepper said. "Back up, Aunt Freddy, so she can get out."

As soon as Evie was out of the car and on her feet, Freddy linked her arm through Evie's.

"I'm so glad you're here, old lady," she said. "I want to play my violin for you. I've added to 'Evie's Opus,' and I got a new puzzle."

Grace raised her eyebrows at Pepper.

"Yep, a new puzzle," Pepper said. "This one has musical instruments on it."

"Oh, wow. A real new puzzle," Grace said. "That's a huge step forward."

"At least a step forward. She still doesn't seem to realize you're not Evie and who Evie really is. She insists on calling her 'old lady.'"

"I have some important things I need to talk to you about today." Grace held the door and then followed Pepper into the sitting room. Evie and Freddy were in the puzzle room, looking at the new puzzle.

"Good important or bad important?" Pepper asked. She handed Grace a glass of sweet tea.

"Interesting important." Grace leaned back and took a deep breath. She explained Taylor's ideas and desire to make the documentary film about Evie and other octo and nonagenarians, and the hurdles they faced on a day-to-day basis.

"So, Evie is going to allow Taylor to use her name and situation?"

"Evie may actually be in the film," Grace said. She laughed as she added, "She's excited to get her new career as an actress started."

"What does all this have to do with Freddy?" Pepper frowned. "I'm almost afraid to hear your answer."

"Taylor isn't sure how to tell Evie's story without telling Freddy's. The thing is, since Freddy isn't lucid enough to give her permission to use her story and her name, Taylor can't do it."

"Well, I'm her power of attorney. Can't I give permission?"

"Taylor can explain why that won't work better than I can. Basically, it's because if Freddy ever regained full use of her faculties and found out you had done that and she didn't approve, well, it could cause a lot of people a lot of trouble, including you and Taylor."

"Freddy is having longer and longer times of being here than she is being off in her own world. Let me talk to her doctor and lawyer and see what they think. Maybe we can explain things to Freddy in a way she'll understand and can make a somewhat educated decision—"

"Guess what? Guess what?" Freddy rushed into the living room, sat down beside Pepper, and pulled on her arm. "The old lady is going to be a movie star."

Evie followed a little slower, her cane on the wood floor announcing her approach.

"Grams! You weren't supposed to say anything." Grace jumped up and took her elbow, then led her to a chair on the other side of the sofa.

"I hadn't intended to," Evie said. She accepted a glass of tea from Pepper. "I'm not even sure how it came up."

"I want to help her," Freddy said. "She told me part of it could be about me and my violin and 'Evie's Opus.'"

"Grace and I were just talking about that, Aunt Freddy. I'm going to call Dr. Leonard and Mr. Burger tomorrow and see if we can get them together and talk about this. I don't know if they'll think it's a good idea."

Freddy's face fell, and she turned to Evie. "I can't make my own decisions anymore," she said. "I've been out of my head and not sure of anything for a long time, but I'm better since you and Evie Grace came back to me."

Evie Grace? Grace mouthed at Pepper, who shrugged her shoulders.

Freddy looked back at Pepper. "I'm better now. I want to do this."

"I know you do, but I still want us to talk to the doctor and our lawyer to make sure all the T's are crossed and the I's are dotted. Now, let's drop this for now. Would y'all like some lunch? I made some tuna salad this morning."

†

"Is she really that lucid?" Taylor asked that night when Grace told her about their day.

"At times, it seems she's as normal as any of us. But then there are other times she's so childlike I'm not sure. I tried to talk to Grams about it on the way back to town, but she shut down and waved me off. I don't think she said three words all the way home."

"Is she upset about something, about the documentary?"

"I don't know, hon. I just don't know."

They sat in silence for a few minutes before Grace stood up and stretched.

"I'm going to go paint some bluebonnets and longhorns," she said. "I've been offered a place in ArtWalk's tent at MayFest. I need to get busy if I'm going to have much to offer."

"Don't work too late," Taylor said. "I love you."

CHAPTER FIFTEEN

"Did I ever tell you about Freddy's kittens?" Evie asked Grace a few days later.

Grace shook her head. "Not that I remember. Do you mind if I keep sketching while you talk?"

"No, that's fine. But only on the condition you show it to me when you're done. Oh, and I want to show you some of my own sketches too."

"It's a deal." Grace put her pencil back to the paper and began filling in the details of her great-grandmother's face.

†

1932

"Come over and see the new kittens," Freddy said as she and Evie walked home from school. They stood on the corner where they went their separate ways to their own houses. "There's six of them, and they're all so cute."

"I'll ask," Evie promised. "If it's up to Momma, I'll probably be right over. If Daddy's home, he'll think up something for me to do."

They laughed and exchanged hugs before Evie turned right, and Freddy continued across the street.

"Hi, Mom. I'm home," Evie called as she came in the front door.

"I'm in the kitchen, sweetie."

Evie went to the kitchen and put her books on the table before giving her mother a hug.

"Did you have a good day at school? There's some milk in the icebox if you want a glass."

"Thanks. School was okay." Evie poured herself some milk and helped herself to some fresh-baked cookies cooling on the counter. "Freddy's cat had kittens last night, and she wants me to come over and see them. May I go, please?"

"Do you have homework?"

Evie shook her head. "Mrs. Maclean gave us time at the end of class to work on it, and I finished mine."

"Okay, then. Just be back by five-thirty. Your daddy's due home at six. I want you home and cleaned up and the table set by the time he sets foot in this house."

"Thank you, thank you, thank you. I'll be home in time, I promise."

"Change your clothes first, young lady."

"Yes, ma'am." Evie raced up the stairs and changed into a pair of dungarees and a checkered shirt. Five minutes later, she flew out the front door and down the street. It wasn't long before she was sitting under Freddy's back porch with Freddy and six newborn kittens.

"Oh, they're adorable," she said. "I wish I could have one."

"Ask your mom. Maybe she'll let you. Tell her they're good for catching mice and lizards, things like that."

Evie shook her head. "No. I know what that answer will be. Daddy says God didn't mean for us to have pets. God made animals to serve us, not the other way around."

"But if the kitty is earning her keep by catching mice and stuff, she will be serving you," Freddy argued.

Evie shrugged. "I'm not even going to ask. If I do, he might make me memorize all of Genesis, and I don't want to have to do that. And he might spank me; last time he used his belt."

Freddy's eyes filled with tears, and she reached over the kittens and hugged her best friend. "I hate that he treats you like that. I wish we could adopt you."

†

Present day

"Did Great-Great-Grandpa really believe animals shouldn't be pets?" Gracie asked, appalled.

Evie nodded. "I only remember us having animals that served us. We had chickens, both for their eggs and their meat, a cow and a goat for their milk, and once we had a pig that Daddy slaughtered. Freddy and I loved that pig. Knowing we were going to eat it made me so sad that I was sick every time Momma served pork."

"Is that why Grandma and Mom never had pets?"

"I don't know about your mother, but that's the case with Eleanor. Dean thought my daddy walked on water, and he did his best to be just like him, except he didn't beat us, which I guess is a blessing."

"Verbal and emotional abuse are just as bad as physical abuse," Grace said. "You just can't see the bruises. And all of it lasts a lifetime."

"I tried to protect Eleanor and Betts the best I could," Evie said, a tear streaking its way through the creases on her face.

"It seems like Grandma was able to break the chain."

"She did a wonderful job raising Cecelia. Your gramps didn't think so when Cecelia came out as a lesbian. But your grandma and grandpa accepted it without so much as a blink of an eye. And they loved Marie. She was their daughter as much as Cecelia is. I love her too. She's so good for Cecelia, and she loves you with all she is. I'm glad they decided to have you, even if it was in a rather unorthodox way."

"And I love her," Grace said. "I was in third grade before I realized we were a special kind of family. I thought kids with a man and a woman for parents were in the weird situation."

Evie laughed. "Sometimes I think you were more right than you realized. How's your sketch coming?"

Grace stood up and went to sit beside her great-grandmother. She handed her the sketch pad and heard Evie's sharp intake of breath.

"I didn't know you were drawing me," she said. "I think you left off a few wrinkles."

"Ran out of room," Grace deadpanned. Evie looked at her out of the corner of her eye and roared with laughter.

†

"You're earlier getting home than I thought you would be," Taylor said, hugging Grace as she came in the door.

"Is that good or bad?" Grace asked as she looked over Taylor's shoulder. "Your other girlfriend still here?"

Taylor playfully pushed Grace's shoulder. "Nope. She snuck out the back window when we heard you drive up."

Grace laughed and pulled Taylor into her arms. She kissed her partner until she felt her melt in her arms.

"What do you think about us getting comfortable?" she asked as she walked Taylor backward toward the bedroom. "It's been a while since we had some afternoon delight."

"Mmhm," was all Taylor could get out before Grace kissed her again and bent her over backward onto the bed.

It wasn't long before they lay in each other's arms, enjoying the rare break from their normal, hectic routines.

"We should do this more often," Taylor said a bit later. "I've missed this."

"Me too." Grace kissed Taylor's cheek. "But I don't think we'll be able to for a while. I've got ArtWalk, Mayfair, and taking care of Grams, and you have the documentary. Sometimes I feel like we live on different planets that just happen to pass each other."

"I'm sorry," Taylor said. "Have you got any more leads for murals?"

Grace nodded. "I don't know if I'll be able to take advantage of them though."

"Why not?" Taylor leaned up on her elbow so she could look down at Grace.

"One's from a new hotel being built in Las Vegas, and the other is for a hospital being remodeled in Seattle. I'd have to fly up to see the places, find out what they want, make some sketches, make a bid, wait for only God knows how long to hear, and then go back and spend weeks painting."

"Do you want to do that?" Taylor asked.

Grace shrugged. "I don't know. We need the money, and the challenge sounds like fun. But I don't like the idea of being away from you, Mom, Mudda, and Grams for that length of time. Especially Grams. Even though she seems okay, she's so old and fragile. I'd hate to be away and chance something happening."

Taylor leaned down and kissed Grace gently on her lips. "I understand," she said. "We'll be okay if you choose not to make those bids."

†

"Meet Evie and Freddy," the narrator said as the two old women sat on the Queen Anne cottage porch, holding hands and smiling at each other. "They will turn ninety-five on June seventeenth of this year. They have literally known each other from birth. Their mothers gave birth within minutes of each other and shared a hospital room. Over the years, Evie and Freddy became fast friends and set in motion ninety-five years of friendship, separation, heartache, and the miracle of reconnection."

"What do you think?" Taylor asked. Grace could tell how nervous she was since she was chewing on the cuticles of her fingers.

"It's a good start," Grace said. "How are you going to do this if Freddy's lawyer and doctor won't agree to her signing her release?"

Taylor put her hands over her ears, shook her head, and said, "La, la, la, la. Bite your tongue."

Grace grinned and pulled Taylor's hands away from her ears. "I know that's a scary thought, but it's something you realistically have to think about."

"I know, and it is scary." Taylor rubbed her face with her hands. "It's a thought that's keeping me awake at night."

Grace wrapped her arms around her partner. "It's going to work out, sweets. I love you, and I only want the best for you."

"Thank you." Taylor returned the hug, along with a kiss. "How are your own endeavors going?"

"I delivered twenty-five paintings to ArtWalk this morning. Sandra was overly effusive with her compliments, as usual. I can never tell if she's serious or just being nice. Anyway, she's going to display them in the gallery and then take them to Mayfest. She also suggested I do some medieval-themed paintings for the Renaissance Festival in Waxahachie. This is her first year to set up down there, and she's excited about it."

"Medieval themed? What will you paint?"

Grace shrugged. "I'm going to have to do some research. I'm not sure, but we need the money, so I'm going to do it. The paintings have to be relatively small so the buyers can carry them around and enjoy the rest of the festival."

Taylor laid her head on Grace's shoulder. "Are you sure I shouldn't find a real job?"

"Let's wait and see how the sales go at Mayfest and the first week at the Renaissance fair. If they go well, you won't have to worry about it. If they don't, well, we'll revisit the subject then. Okay?"

Taylor nodded but didn't say anything.

"I can hear your wheels turning," Grace said. "What are you thinking about?"

Taylor took a deep breath. "I just get so angry that my trust has been frozen, and I can't access the money my grandparents meant for me. We wouldn't have anything to worry about if my damn father wasn't so homophobic."

Grace tightened her arms around Taylor. “I’m so sorry. I don’t understand that way of thinking.”

“I know. You’re lucky—blessed—to have such an understanding family.”

Grace laughed. “It would be kind of awkward if they weren’t, since Mom and Mudda have been together since this side of forever.”

Taylor grinned. “That’s true. I was telling Lois about the situation with my trust. She gave me the card for an attorney that she thinks can help me get my money.”

“Oh, that sounds expensive.” Grace wrinkled her nose.

“My thoughts exactly. But she said the lawyer doesn’t get paid unless he’s successful. She didn’t know how much he would charge, but she thinks I should at least call and talk to him. What do you think?”

“If it doesn’t cost to talk to him, I don’t think it’s a bad idea.”

“I’ll call him tomorrow. Thank you.”

Chapter Sixteen

"Pepper and Sonya said I can get another cat," Freddy said. "They're going to take me to the animal shelter to pick one out. Will you come with me?"

Evie and Grace exchanged a look.

"It's so funny you're bringing this up now," Evie said. "I told Grace about the kittens your cat had when we were in seventh grade—"

"It was eighth grade. Your daddy wouldn't let you have one 'cause it wouldn't do your family any service." Freddy frowned. "I still don't understand that. Our cats kept rats, snakes, and bugs out of our house. That was being of service."

Grace looked over at Pepper, whose eyes were big.

"Aunt Freddy, you remember taking Evie to see your kittens?" she asked.

Freddy's face registered confusion. She looked first at Evie and then at Grace. "I didn't take her to see them. She came to see them."

Pepper laughed. "Okay. But you remember her coming to see them, right?"

"Yes. Why does that surprise you?"

"Show me who Evie is," Pepper said. "Is it her or her?" She pointed first at Evie and then at Grace.

Freddy looked at each of them, frowning so hard her eyebrows met above her nose. "Can't it be both of them?" she asked. She pointed at Evie and said, "She's the old lady Evie," and then she pointed at Grace, "and she's the young Evie, Evie Grace."

Evie took her hand and smiled at her. "I like that, Freddy. I am your old Evie. It's good that you know that."

Freddy swiped at a tear as it crept its way down her face. "I'm glad I know that too."

Pepper motioned to Grace, and the two younger women left the two old friends and went to the kitchen. Pepper slumped into a kitchen chair.

"Wow. I didn't see that coming," she said. She took a deep breath and dug her phone from her pants pocket. "I'm sorry, but Dr. Leonard asked me to call her if there are any significant breakthroughs. I think this could be considered that."

Grace helped herself to a soda pop from the refrigerator and sat at the table. *Wow, indeed. It looks like Taylor will get her release after all*, Grace thought.

Pepper came back and sat down across from Grace. "I have an appointment to take Freddy to the doctor tomorrow morning. She agreed to include Mr. Burger in the meeting as well if he's free. Will you ask Taylor to email the release to me? I can't guarantee it will get signed, but it looks like there's hope."

†

"She knew who was who," Grace said for the umpteenth time. "It looks good about getting your release signed."

Taylor beamed. "You have no idea what good news that is," she said. "Thank you, thank you, thank you."

Grace tapped her cheek with her forefinger. "Plant one right here, darlin'."

Taylor grabbed Grace and danced her around the living room, then kissed her on the mouth.

"That good enough?" she asked.

"Ummm, I can think of some other things you can do to show your appreciation." Grace slid her hand down Taylor's back and squeezed her butt cheek.

Taylor squealed. "Hold that thought for a few hours. I have work to do, and I have a feeling you probably do too."

"You're right." Grace released her partner. She let her bottom lip droop. "I'd rather play than work though."

Taylor was already at the door of the study. She waved her fingers over her shoulders. "I love you. Get some work done."

Grace went to her studio over the garage and looked around. Grace had tacked Evie's sketches to the bulletin board. She went and looked them over. She chose her favorite one and studied it. After a few moments, she set a large canvas on her easel and grabbed her favorite pencil. By the time Taylor called to tell her dinner was ready, she had transferred the sketch to her canvas. She stepped back and smiled at her progress.

"I'll be back soon, Grams," she said.

The next morning, Grace could barely eat breakfast for wanting to get back to her studio. Just as she laid down her first layer of oil paint, her cell phone rang. She thought about letting the call go to voicemail, but changed her mind as she looked again at the painting she was working on. She dug her phone out of her back pocket and checked the caller ID.

"Hey, Pepper. What's up?"

"Did I catch you in the middle of something?" Pepper asked. "I was beginning to think your phone was going to voicemail."

"I just started a new painting." Grace studied the work she had already done and was mentally deciding which pigment to go to next. "How're things on your end?"

"We just got back from seeing the doctor and the lawyer. Aunt Freddy was the most lucid I've seen her in the last seven years. She answered every question correctly, and she got mad when she felt the questions were being repeated, only in different words. She kept reminding us that she is not stupid and can make up her own mind, and to just sign the damn release."

Grace laughed. "Oh, Taylor will be so glad to hear this. What did the doctor and lawyer say?"

"I talked to Dr. Leonard privately for a few minutes after the appointment. She reminded me she'd never found a true medical reason for Aunt Freddy's dementia, and that she'd felt it was psychological from the very beginning. She thinks having Evie come back into her life was just what was needed to bring her out of it."

"Wow."

"That's about how I feel," Pepper said.

"So, what happens now?"

"The lawyer wants to talk to Taylor and the filmmaker, to learn more about the motives behind the documentary, before he'll sign off on Aunt Freddy signing the release. I've got his phone number." She rattled off a string of numbers as Grace used her sketching pencil to copy them onto a piece of scrap paper. “I think they should call him as soon as possible.”

“I’ll call her as soon as we hang up,” Grace said. “She’s going to be stoked.”

“I’ve got to go. Aunt Freddy is tuning up her violin and just screamed some obscenities. I need to go see what’s going on.”

“Give her a hug for me, and I’ll talk to you later.”

†

“Lois and I are going to Weatherford to meet with Mr. Burger the day after tomorrow,” Taylor told Grace as they cooked dinner together. “I’m so excited I can barely stand myself.”

“I’m excited for you. Do I put the pasta in now or wait ’til the water is boiling?”

“You go sit at the table and let me do this,” Taylor said with a laugh. “I think I’ve told you how to cook pasta a dozen times, and you still don’t know how.”

“I know. I guess I’d rather be doing other things than cooking,” Grace said. She wrapped her arms around Taylor’s waist and kissed her on the neck.

“Down, girl.” Taylor loosened Grace’s arms. “You need some sustenance if you’re going to keep this up. You are insatiable lately.”

Grace sat down at the table and grinned. “I don’t hear you complaining.”

Taylor shook her head. “I’m not,” she said. “I can always tell when your painting is going well. You’re hornier than usual.”

"Really?" Grace hadn't put the two together until now. When she thought back, she saw that Taylor was right. "I hadn't thought about that. Is it a bad thing?"

Taylor turned and put the sauce and noodles on the table and sat down. She reached over and took Grace's hands. "No, sweets, it is definitely not a bad thing. But it can be a bit tiring. I take it that the paintings of longhorns and bluebonnets are going well?"

Grace laughed. "I'm done with them for a while. I hope for a long time. No, I'm working on something personal right now—Grams' birthday present. And I'm really proud of how well it's going."

"Speaking of her birthday, we really need to sit down with your mother and Marie and make some hard and fast decisions about both Evie's birthday party and our wedding. They're not that far away, and we have hardly done any planning."

"I'll call them in the morning and see when it's best for us to get together. You're not still set on me wearing a dress, are you? I think I was about eight the last time I wore one."

"We'll discuss it later. Right now, eat your dinner. We have a date for some fun, remember?"

Chapter Seventeen

"I am not wearing a dress," Grace repeated for the umpteenth time. "It's not going to happen. I'll wear a tux. I'll even wear a white tux. But I'm not wearing a dress."

"I don't think she wants to wear a dress," Marie said with a grin.

"Okay. Let's move on from what y'all are going to wear," Cecelia said. "Are you going to carry a bouquet with your tux?"

"A bouquet? Of flowers?" Grace made a face.

"Yes, silly. Of flowers. Bouquets are made of flowers." Taylor shook her head. "I'm going to carry a bouquet. But I think a boutonniere will be best for her."

Cecelia made a note on the tablet in front of her. Grace put her head in her hands and shook her head. Cecelia was on page ten or eleven of notes, and all Grace could see were dollar signs. Taylor rubbed her back.

"What's wrong, sweets?" she asked.

"How much is all this going to cost? I keep thinking about our already dwindling bank account." Grace stood up and paced the room. "Look, y'all. I want us to have a nice wedding, but is all this hoopla really necessary? The only way we can afford it is if I put in a bid in Seattle or Vegas and get it, or if Taylor gets what she calls a 'real' job. I don't want it to come to that. Can't we keep this simple?"

Cecelia and Marie exchanged a glance and a grin.

"What's so funny?" Grace demanded, her hands balled into fists on her hips.

"Well, it's something like this," Marie said. "When you were born, Cecelia and I started a savings account to pay for your college and/or your wedding. We've put money in that account every month since then. I have a direct deposit from my paycheck to the account. And anytime we got bonuses or extra, we socked it away for you."

"When you got your full scholarship to the art school, it kept us from having to dip into the account," Cecelia took up the story. "We decided we'd use the money to help you out when you graduated and were getting on your feet. But you were already on your feet when you graduated."

"Okay, okay," Grace said, raising her hands. "Are you telling me that I have a nest egg? Or were you going to leave it for me to inherit when you guys kick the bucket?"

Cecelia's eyes narrowed, and she shook her finger at Grace. "You may be an adult and out on your own, but you will treat me and Marie with respect, especially in our own home. We don't have to give you a cent of that money or anything else. Don't act like an entitled brat."

Grace stood staring at her mother, her mouth hanging open. Taylor stood up so fast she knocked her chair over and rushed out of the kitchen.

"I didn't realize that's how I was acting," Grace said, her voice low. "I'm sorry. I really am. I know you don't like apologies to come with excuses, but I've been under a lot of stress lately and, well, I'm sorry."

Cecelia stood up and drew her daughter into an embrace. "I know you're under a lot of stress, sweetheart. And I know you weren't meaning to be rude and disrespectful. And that's why I said something. If I hadn't, it would have become easier and easier for you to talk like that without realizing you were."

"Should I go check on Taylor?" Marie asked.

Grace nodded as she buried her face in Cecelia's shoulder. The tears that had been so close to the surface for a while finally surfaced. Cecelia held her as she sobbed.

"This is more than just stress, isn't it?" Cecelia said as she led Grace back to the table and lowered her into a chair. "Is everything okay between you and Taylor? Are y'all strapped right now?"

"Taylor and I are fine, probably better than we've ever been, but we are strapped right now," Grace said between hiccups.

Cecelia got a glass from the cabinet and filled it with water from the refrigerator dispenser. She set it in front of Grace, along with some Tylenol.

"Take those before your headache gets any worse," she said.

Grace looked up at her mother. "How do you know I have a headache?"

"'Cause I'm your mom." Cecelia laughed and patted Grace on the shoulder as she sat down. "You always have a headache after a good cry. Now, what's going on with Taylor? Why'd she scuttle out of here so fast?"

Grace shook her head. "I'm not sure why she did that. She has been making overtures to her family, and they're still rejecting her. I think seeing you mad at me caught her as off guard as it caught me. Maybe it made her think about how her family raised her."

"I'm sorry, sweetie." Cecelia leaned over and hugged Grace. "Marie either found her, and they're having a good heart-to-heart, or Marie can't find her and is scared to let us know."

"It was the first option," Marie said as she and Taylor came back into the kitchen. Taylor had a fistful of tissues that she deposited in the trashcan.

"I'm sorry, y'all," Taylor said.

Cecelia held a hand up. "There's an awful lot of 'I'm sorry' going on here," she said. "This was supposed to be fun."

"Well, now that I know there's enough money to pay for our wedding, I can start to have fun with this," Grace said with a grin. "But I'm still not going to wear a dress.

Chapter Eighteen

"I want to go help Freddy and Pepper pick out their new cat," Evie told Grace a few days later. "I talked to her on the phone—"

"Who did you talk to on the phone?"

"If you wouldn't interrupt me, you would know," Evie scolded. "Your momma told me your manners have been slipping lately."

Grace laughed. "Momma's got a big mouth. I'm sorry I interrupted. Please continue."

"Thank you for your permission." Evie huffed and looked at Grace. "You sure you're interested? When you've got your face buried in that sketch pad. I don't know whether you're really listening or not."

"Grams, are you PMSing? You're in a bad mood." Grace set the tablet down and crossed the room to sit next to her great-grandmother.

"Ha. PMSing. I didn't even know what that meant until a few years ago. I didn't have the luxury to PMS when I was growing up or as long as Dean was breathing."

"What do you mean?" Grace took Evie's hand and traced the veins on the back of the wrinkled hand. *I want to draw these hands someday.* Grace's mind raced with the idea of a series of pictures, and she had to force her attention back to Evie.

"One time, about a year after Christina died, I had horrible menstrual cramps…"

†

1949

"Where is everyone?"

Evie cringed when Dean's voice echoed through the house.

"We're in the bathroom, dear," she called. "I'm giving the girls a bath."

She tried to pull her skirt down over the commode so he couldn't tell she was using it. The door opened, and the girls crouched below the edge of the tub.

"Didn't you do that this morning?" he asked. He looked at her, then at the girls. "Have you sat on that commode the whole day? Get those girls out of the tub and get to the kitchen and make me some dinner."

He slammed the door so hard that the cabinet door flew open. Betts started crying.

"Hush, sister," Eleanor said. "He'll get even madder if he hears you crying."

Eleanor pulled the plug so the tub could drain and slithered over the edge. She reached around Evie, pulled a towel off the rack, and held it out.

"Come on, Betts."

The little girls held hands while Eleanor helped Betts out of the tub and then wrapped the towel around her.

"Thank you, Eleanor. Y'all turn around so I can clean myself up and get off this toilet."

"Yes, ma'am." Eleanor put Betts in front of her and turned her back on her mother.

Evie fixed her menstrual pads and wiped herself as clean as she could before pulling her underwear up and her dress down. She washed her hands of the blood that had dripped on them and then hurried the girls down the hall to their bedroom. Before she could pull their pajamas from the chest, her cramps had her doubled over again. She sat on the edge of Eleanor's bed and prayed for release. Eleanor brought her their sleepwear, and while Evie helped Betts put hers on, Eleanor pulled hers on. Evie's heart broke because her five-year-old daughter had to grow up so fast.

"I'm hungry, woman," Dean yelled. "Get out here and fix me some dinner. Now."

"I'm coming," Evie called. Then to the girls, "It's early yet, so you don't have to go to bed. But play quietly so you don't disturb Daddy. I'll be back to tuck you in. I love you."

"Love you too, Momma," the girls said in unison.

Evie stood up and tried to walk as upright as possible, even though the cramps in her mid-section were so severe she felt sick to her stomach. Once in the kitchen, she pulled the pork chops from the icebox and started them cooking in the cast-iron skillet. It wasn't long before she could set a plate full of food in front of her husband.

"Where's yours?" he asked.

"I ate with the girls," she said. "But I'll sit with you if you'd like."

"Sit." He pointed at her chair.

She had hoped he would excuse her, but when he didn't, she obediently sat down. The cramps were threatening to double her over again, but she willed herself to continue to sit up straight.

"I've been gone all day," he said as he cut up his pork chop. "We had three fires to fight, and when I get home, I shouldn't have to wait for my dinner. I don't want this to happen again. Do you understand that?"

"Yes, dear. I let the girls play in the tub and lost track of time. I'm sorry. It won't happen again. I promise."

"Why were you sitting on the commode when I got home? You were there when I left, and by the way this house looks, I'd wager you sat there all day."

"I didn't sit there all day, Dean." Evie took a deep breath to keep the anger from her voice. "I'm having cramps and a heavy flow—"

"Do not talk about that stuff at the table." Dean shook his knife at her. "Don't talk to me of it at all. I don't care. If you ate right and at the right times, you wouldn't have these problems."

Evie bowed her head and didn't say anything. She knew she needed to get back to the bathroom, or there would be hell to pay for the mess that she would leave in the chair. She counted to ten, taking a deep breath between each number.

"I need to go check on the girls," she said. "I promised them a bedtime story."

Dean waved his hand at her. "Go. You're not good company anyway."

†

Present day

“My God, Grams.” Grace wiped the tears from her face. “Why was he so horrible?”

Evie shrugged. “I don’t know. I tried everything I could to make him happy, to be the dutiful wife he wanted me to be, but he made sure to let me know regularly how badly I failed. The fact that the girls grew up to be the women they were had nothing to do with his fathering skills.”

“No, but it had everything to do with the wonderful mothering you did.” Grace hugged her. “I wish things could have been different for you when you were younger.”

“If they had been, I wouldn’t be the person I am today,” Evie said. She sat up straight. “And I kind of like who I am now.”

“I kind of like you too,” Grace said with a laugh.

CHAPTER NINETEEN

Freddy clapped her hands as Grace pulled the SUV into the shelter parking lot. "Gonna get a kitty," she said. "I've missed having a kitty."

"How long has it been since you had one?" Evie asked. She opened her door but waited for Grace to come and assist her out of the vehicle.

"I'm not sure," Freddy said. "Pepper, when did Red go over that bridge you talked about?"

"The Rainbow Bridge. Red went over the bridge about a year and a half ago." Pepper shook her head. "The house has been quiet since he left us."

Freddy tucked her hand in the crook of Pepper's elbow. "Are we going to get another red cat?" she asked.

"I don't know. Let's look at all of them and see if one is more special than another, okay?"

Freddy stopped and put her hands on her hips.

"What's wrong?" Pepper asked. Grace and Evie turned to see what was going on.

"Stop speaking to me like I'm a child," Freddy said. "I'm not acting like one, and I don't deserve to be spoken to like one."

"I'm sorry, Aunt Freddy." Pepper put a hand on the older woman's shoulder. "I've been in the habit for so long, trying to help you understand what I was saying and trying to understand what you needed. It's great to have you back. I love you, and I'll be more careful. Okay?"

Freddy nodded. "Thank you." She put her arms around Pepper, and they shared a hug. "Now, let's go see if one cat is more special than another."

Pepper laughed and tucked Freddy's arm back around her elbow. Evie smiled at Freddy, and Freddy smiled and winked back at her.

Inside, Pepper spoke to the attendant behind the desk. He pulled a key from under the counter and motioned for them to follow.

"Hi, ladies. Welcome to our shelter. We're a no-kill shelter, which means every animal here has a home and will never be euthanized."

Freddy stopped in her tracks. "I thought we would be rescuing a cat," she said. She looked up at Pepper. "Should we go to one of the other shelters?"

Pepper shook her head. "It's okay, Aunt Freddy. John told me that almost all the cats at the other shelters have been rescued and brought to this shelter and a couple of others. We're still rescuing one, I promise."

"Who is John, and is he trustworthy?"

"I'm John," the young man said with a laugh, "and I promise I'm trustworthy. You're rescuing a cat from having to live its life in a cage. None of our animals will be put down, but that means some may have to live in a cage for a long time.

We're always looking for foster homes too, if you think you'd like to try that."

"No." Pepper shook her head so hard her glasses almost flew off. "One cat. We're giving one cat a forever home, but we're not being fosters."

"Are you aware that cats do much better in pairs?" John asked as he slid the key into the knob of a door with frosted glass. "When they have a companion, they're less likely to be destructive or have behavioral problems."

"Oh, two kitties." Freddy smiled up at Pepper. "We can afford two cats."

"Financially, yes," Pepper agreed. "But—"

"Give in," Freddy said. "You know you're going to."

Evie threw her head back and laughed. "Oh, my goodness. You used to say that all the time to your mother and father, and they almost always did. You even tried it on me, but I was a lot stronger than they were."

Freddy had a sly grin on her face. "Most of the time," she said. "I can remember a time or two I got my way."

Evie's face turned so red that Grace was afraid her blood pressure was sky high. But then, a little slower than everyone else, she realized what Freddy meant. Then she also turned red. John had moved on up the aisle as the women all cracked up, laughing.

"Mind your manners," Evie said as she took Freddy's hand. "You embarrassed that poor young man."

"I think I embarrassed Evie, uh, I mean Grace, even more." Freddy grinned at Grace, who shook her head in exasperation.

"Let's go look at cats," Pepper said. "That's what we're here for, right?"

John waited for them at the door of a room full of cages, most of them occupied by one, or sometimes two, cats. He pointed to the rear of the room, where there were a few cages set apart from the rest. "The cages back there house our geriatric cats. It sounds as though you're interested in kittens, or at least young cats, but I'd like to encourage you to at least visit the old guys. They are overlooked most of the time."

"You know how to change that?" Evie asked.

"How?" John looked at the cages and then back at Evie. "What would you suggest?"

"Move them out of the shadows. Put their cages up here where they're the first ones anyone sees. Us old folks get shoved to the back so much when we still have an awful lot to offer. Old cats probably do too. Bring them up here in the light."

Grace put an arm around Evie's shoulder but didn't say anything. Evie's words brought tears to her eyes. Although she knew Evie received the best treatment at home, she'd seen sales and service staff ignore and neglect Evie.

"Ma'am, I think you have a good point," John said. "I'm going to bring that up with the director when she comes in this afternoon."

"I hope you're not just saying that to shut an old woman up," Evie said. She pulled Grace's arm. "Let's go look at the old guys."

"Uhm, we're not adopting any cats today," Grace said.

Evie looked at her out of the corner of her eye. "I didn't say we were, but if I want to, you and what army will stop me?"

"Mom and Mudda?" Grace said. "It's their house. Don't you think they should have some say in the matter, especially since they—and me—will be the ones feeding it and cleaning up after it?"

Evie stopped short and turned to Grace. She shook a finger in the younger woman's face. "Have you forgotten that the house was mine before I gave it to Cecelia and Marie, on the condition that I can live there until I cross over? And have you forgotten that I wiped not only your mother's ass, but also yours? You can clean up after one measly cat."

The room was so quiet, Grace felt she could hear her eyelids move over her eyeballs. Even the cats were quiet.

"Now. Are you going to help me go look at those cats, or should I ask that nice young man to help me?"

"Damn, Grams. What bee got in your bonnet?" Grace took her great-grandmother's elbow and led her toward the back of the room. "You and Freddy are both in high spirits."

"'High spirits.' Humph." Grace looked over to see a smile cross Evie's face. "Been a long time since I was in the kind of high spirits I wish I was."

Grace grinned and shook her head but didn't say anything.

An hour later, after phone calls to Cecelia and Marie, Evie sat with a cardboard crate on her lap, cooing to the black and white tuxedo cat inside, who went by the name of James Bond, JB for short. And Freddy's crate held two orange tabby cats that looked as though they were siblings. One was solid orange, while the other wore a necklace of white. Someone had found them together during a severe thunderstorm, and the two cats were inseparable. The shelter personnel dubbed them Prince and Gene.

"What's Sonya going to think of y'all bringing home two cats?" Grace asked Pepper in an undertone she hoped the elderly women couldn't hear.

Pepper shrugged. "I have no idea. But you see how stubborn Aunt Freddy can be. And that orange fellow fell in love with her the minute they laid eyes on each other. We couldn't leave his buddy behind."

"I think you're the one who fell in love with him," Grace said with a grin.

"Shhh. Don't tell anyone," Pepper said with a finger to her lips.

†

Later that evening, Grace leaned against Taylor, who lounged on the sofa with her feet on the ottoman. "I wish you could have seen the look on Mom's face when we got home. She tried to act mad, but I could tell she was over- the-top happy about Grams adopting JB. She'd already gone to the store and bought food, litter, a box, and a boatload of toys. I tried to remind her JB was elderly, but she waved me off."

"At least you didn't bring one home," Taylor said as she smoothed Grace's hair off her forehead. "You need a haircut. You want me to do it, or you want me to call the salon."

"Last time you did it, I believe Marvin threatened to cut your fingers off if you did it again. I'll call him tomorrow and make an appointment."

"Just don't make it too close to the wedding."

"Why not?" Grace ran her hand through her hair. "I'd think you'd want it fresh cut."

"Fresh cut doesn't always look the best," Taylor said. "Make sure there's at least ten days between the haircut and the 'I do's.'"

†

"So, how did the first night with a cat in the house go?" Grace asked Cecelia on the phone the next morning.

"I wouldn't know. I haven't seen more than a blur of that cat since you left yesterday. It stays up on the bed with Evie or in the chair with Evie, but if either me or Marie so much as move, it darts under the covers or the nearest piece of furniture. I know it's eating and using the potty, but it's like having a spirit cat."

"John said he might be a bit skittish at first. Apparently, he had a rough time before he came to the shelter."

"Grams told me something about that." Cecelia paused, and Grace could picture her mom running her hand through her hair. "I can't imagine what that poor kitty must have gone through."

"I know. John said his owner had been dead about four days before anyone found him. JB hadn't had anything to eat in at least three days. Thankfully, the man left the toilet seat up, so JB had water."

"Well, he's claimed Grams. He actually growled at me when I went in to check on her this morning."

Grace chuckled. "I read his history while Grams did all the paperwork. The coroner wrote that he waited until animal control arrived before he examined the man's body because JB growled whenever he approached. He's her new watch cat."

"I guess. I gotta go. Grams is beeping the intercom."

"Okay. I'll be there this afternoon. Call me and remind me. I'm working on a new project. You know how I get."

Cecelia laughed. "Yes, I do know how you get. Make sure there's nothing cooking on the stove before you get started. Love you, girl."

"Love you more. And, no, there's nothing cooking."

Grace disconnected the phone and wandered into the kitchen. She retrieved a soda pop and a bottle of water from the refrigerator before going out to her studio. Evie's portrait stared at her from its easel. Grace smiled to herself as she realized it was one of her best paintings ever. It still needed a few details, but it was mostly finished. Instead of working on it, Grace sat at her table, pulled the smaller canvas to her, and chose a charcoal pencil.

Grams' hands were proving to be more of a challenge than she had anticipated. Grace had surreptitiously taken photos of Grams' hands from several angles. She chose a photo of the hands relaxed on Grams' lap, one on top of the other. The skin was so thin that the veins and blood vessels formed an intricate map of red and blue just below the surface. Grace could get the outline right, while the finer details were more difficult to capture. But Grace wasn't about to give up.

When her phone rang, Grace jumped so hard she tumbled off her stool. She looked up and shook her head when she saw how long she had been in her studio. She pulled the phone from her pocket and grimaced when she saw her mother's caller ID.

"Yes, I lost track of time," she said as soon as she answered the phone.

Cecelia laughed. "I figured you had, but the reason I'm calling is to tell you that you don't need to come over unless you want. Marie came home early, and my boss told me I could take the afternoon off. Everything's slow right now."

"Oh, Okay. Are you guys going to be okay, not working your hours like that?"

"We're fine, Miss Worrywart. In fact, we've been talking about retiring."

"Retiring? Y'all aren't old enough to retire."

Cecelia laughed again. “It would be an early retirement for me since I’m only sixty, but Marie will be sixty-seven in August, and that’s the normal retirement age.”

“Can y’all afford to though?”

“You have always been such a worrier,” Cecelia said. “For your information, yes, we can afford to retire. We’ve saved and invested wisely. We’ll be fine. In fact, that’s something we’d like to discuss with you and Taylor.”

“What? What do you want to discuss?” Grace’s voice cracked as it rose a couple of octaves.

“Calm down, Dauda,” Cecelia said. Grace could tell she was laughing at her but trying not to let her hear it. “Why don’t we plan on having dinner in a couple of days? I’ll get someone to stay with Grams, and we can go to the steakhouse. On us.”

“Well, if you put it that way, who am I to say no to a free steak?”

Chapter Twenty

A few days later, Taylor and Grace met Grace's mothers at the steakhouse. After hugs all around, they waited for their turn to be seated.

"Y'all want something to drink from the bar?" Marie asked. "I'm going to get me a beer."

"Mmm, that sounds good," Taylor said. "A lite beer would be wonderful."

"I'm driving, so I'll just have a Dr. Pepper," Grace said.

"Make that two DPs." Cecelia put an arm around Grace. "You have such good taste in beverages, Dauda."

"Yeah, well," Grace said. "I'd rather have a margarita, but it's my turn to be the designated driver."

"Poor baby." Taylor pouted at her. "Can't have an adult beverage and has to feel sorry for herself."

"Hush." Marie handed Taylor her beer. "I seem to remember the same conversation last time we were out, but you were the 'poor baby' that time."

Grace wagged her finger at Taylor. "Nah, nah, nah."

"Act your age, Dauda," Marie said as she nudged Grace and laughed.

The hostess called them to be seated, cutting their conversation short. Once the waiter took their orders, Grace put her elbows on the table and rested her head in her palms.

"Alright, spill the beans," she said. "What's with this retiring early and needing our permission to do so?"

Marie and Cecelia looked at each other and grinned.

"First of all, your permission is the last thing we need," Cecelia said. "It's like I told you on the phone the other day, Mudda and I have been saving money and making some wise investments for a long time now. And with the inheritance I got from Mom, well, let's just say our retirement fund is a comfortable pillow. And the way both of our jobs are going, it would be prudent for us to retire before we're jobless for whatever reason."

"What are your plans?" Taylor asked. She linked her arm through Grace's. "I wish we were at a point that we could just quit."

"Humph." Grace set back and crossed her arms, tucking Taylor's hand in the crook of her elbow. "That's a long way off unless we start playing the lottery and get remarkably lucky."

"Marie and I had those exact thoughts thirty-five years ago." Cecelia smiled at Marie. "Remember? We lived in that teeny-tiny trailer barely big enough for us, and then we brought this one home. And we thought we were stuck."

Marie nodded. "We've come a long way, babe."

Cecelia laughed. "We certainly have."

"So, what happened that changed things?" Taylor asked.

"It's partly her fault." Cecelia pointed at Grace. "We suddenly realized we were responsible for this one's future and our own. While Charlie and Bob, Grace's father and his partner, were willing to help, we knew we had to do it on our own. Where I worked at the time, offered financial planning once a year, and I took advantage of it. We made a plan, started the savings account we told you about that we'll be turning over to you in the near future, and we learned how to budget in such a way that we lived comfortably then and now. Plus, we have enough to continue to live comfortably once we retire. Of course, it didn't hurt when Grams transferred the title of the house to us, and we didn't have to pay a mortgage or rent anymore. But instead of spending that money, we added it to our savings."

"Wow." Grace looked at Taylor. "I think it might be prudent of us to listen to their advice and do as they do."

"You're just now realizing that?" Cecelia said with a laugh.

Their food arrived just then, and they put the conversation on hold while they dug into their steaks and baked potatoes.

When the after-dinner coffee arrived, Grace once again asked why her parents wanted to talk to them about their pending retirement.

"You are a nosy soul. You know that, don't you?" Marie said.

"I've been told that a time or two," Grace said. "But look who I learned it from."

The women laughed.

"Yes, and you were an excellent student," Cecelia said. "Seriously though, there are some things we'd like to discuss with you two about all of this."

"Should we be worried?" Taylor asked.

"I don't think so," Cecelia said. "But there will be a bit of thinking things over and discussion between the two of you."

"Can y'all get to the point before the clock strikes midnight?" Grace pretended to look at her wrist to check the time.

"Your car will change into a pumpkin?" Marie asked.

Grace wrinkled her nose at the not-funny joke.

"Y'all stop," Cecelia said. "Okay, here it is in a nutshell. We want to travel. We plan to buy one of those RVs that looks like a bus on steroids and go to all the places we've talked about going. But, well, there's Grams. You've been a lifesaver for the past several years, and now we're about to ask you to do even more."

"We weren't too worried about it at first," Marie said. "But then y'all announced your engagement, and we've been having second thoughts."

"Why?" Grace asked. "I would do anything for Grams and y'all."

"But it's not just you anymore, sweets," Cecelia said. She smiled at Taylor and reached across the table for her hand. "This lovely lady is about to be your wife, and we already consider her much more than a daughter-in-law. I feel like we have two daughters now. The two of you need to make this decision together and not in the spur of the moment."

"Why do I have the feeling there's a lot more to this than taking on more of Grams' care?" Grace said.

"There is." Cecelia looked at Marie, who smiled at her in a way that always made Grace's heart jump. It was the smile she knew she gave Taylor and, more often than not, received from her. "Like I said, we want to travel. I'm not talking about quick jaunts down to San Antonio or Galveston. I'm talking about cross-country, three or four month-long trips."

"Whoa." Grace sat back, her mouth open. "That's some serious traveling. I don't mean to throw a wrench in it, but

Grams is about to be ninety-five years old. What if something happens while you're gone? What if you can't get back in time?"

Cecelia's eyes filled with tears. "Believe me, we've thought about that, incessantly. But Marie and I sat down with her last week and told her about our dreams. She told us to stop wasting time because that was one commodity in life that is irreplaceable. She told us that she and Freddy lost so much time because of one man's selfishness, and they're only beginning to realize how much they've actually lost."

Marie handed her a napkin. "Your grandmother is a wise, caring, and generous woman," she said to Cecelia. She looked over at Grace and Taylor. "She told us not to wait for her to die to begin to live the life we've dreamed of for so long. Of course, we argued, but she is a strong woman. And this is where the two of you come in."

Taylor nodded. "You don't even have to ask. I love Evie as though she's my own grandmother. And I know how Grace feels about her."

"How would y'all feel about moving into the house?" Cecelia asked, wiping the last tear from her cheek. "Someone needs to be with her twenty-four seven."

Grace and Taylor exchanged a glance before bursting into laughter.

"What's so funny?" Cecelia asked.

"Timing." Grace shook her head. "You've always had impeccable timing."

"We got a letter from our landlord yesterday letting us know that he is putting all his rental property up for sale in about three or four months. He is giving us rights of first refusal." Grace looked at Taylor again. "We were actually thinking of seeing if we could get financed for a mortgage, but our finances are so, well, unstable, we decided to just look for someplace else to live. And living in Grams' house and helping take care of her was one tick on our list to ask y'all about."

"Well, this is good timing then," Cecelia said. "I have to give a minimum of ninety days' notice that I intend to retire, and that will be up close to Labor Day. We were hoping to leave on our first trip the week after Labor Day. That should give y'all a chance to have a honeymoon and get moved in."

"Honeymoon?" Grace laughed a strangled laugh. "Y'all have taken the weight of the wedding off our shoulders, but a honeymoon is a pipe dream."

"Humph." Cecelia kicked Grace under the table as she huffed. "Even after I showed you the balance on your savings account, you don't think you girls can take a nice honeymoon? How expensive do you plan on making this wedding and honeymoon?"

"Ouch, Mom. Damn. I'm going to have a massive bruise."

"It would have been worse if I had more room to aim." Cecelia crossed her arms.

"Calm down, Cee," Marie said.

Cecelia's eyebrows rose to her hairline, and Grace started laughing. "Watch out, Mudda. But thanks for taking her ire off me."

"Cecelia, our wedding isn't all that expensive," Taylor said. "I think Grace's chief concern is more time-wise than money-wise. It looks like the documentary about the elderly community is going to be more about Evie and Freddy than the community in general. Which means it is going to take a lot more planning and preparation than we originally thought. And Grace has started a new project, but she's keeping it so under wraps that I'm not even allowed in her studio."

"Studio. Damn. If we move into Grams', where will I put my studio? I have to have a studio—" Grace had to take a deep breath to keep from panicking.

"With locks on the door," Taylor added.

"Okay, here's what I'm hearing," Marie said. "The documentary is about Freddy and Evie instead of the elderly community at large, so it is going to take more time. And Grace has her mind so much on her painting, she doesn't know which way is up. So, taking a honeymoon right after the wedding is not really feasible. Do I have the important details correct?"

Taylor grinned at her. "In a much more succinct manner than I could say it, yes, you have the important details right."

"Okay. Roughly, when do you think you'll be able to go on a honeymoon?"

Grace and Taylor looked at each other. Grace shrugged. "I don't know. I am working on a special project, but I hope to have it completed before Grams' birthday. When do you think the documentary will be done, Taylor?"

"We hope to have the filming done by early to mid-August, and editing done by the end of October, November at the latest, to air in the new year."

"It takes that long?" Marie asked. "I had no idea."

"Me, neither," Taylor admitted. "The behind-the-scenes stuff is a lot more complicated than I ever imagined, but I'm having a blast learning. I'm thinking I made the wrong career decision."

Grace turned in the booth to get a better look at her partner. "Do what? This is the first I heard about this."

"Down, Grace, down," Cecelia said. "It's okay to change directions mid-career. I wouldn't even be able to think about retiring if I hadn't done that and found something I truly love."

"That, and I can combine my social anthropology expertise with making documentaries," Taylor said. "The Discovery Station and several others are always looking for people like me."

"Sounds like you're really serious about this," Marie said.

Taylor nodded. "I am."

Grace looked at her mother. "I think I just realized what you mean and how you feel when you say you're an 'Oh, yeah, mom.'"

Taylor leaned over and kissed Grace on the cheek. "I'm sorry, sugar. I planned on discussing it with you, but you've been with Evie or sequestered in your studio, and now here we are."

"Back to a timeline on when you think you can go on your honeymoon," Cecelia said.

"I don't know," Grace said. "Can we get back to you about that?"

"I hate that our timeline might interfere with your timeline for your trip," Taylor said.

"Let's not worry about that right now, okay?" Cecelia said. "Our time is flexible, and it's important to us that you two have that special time."

"Excuse me, ladies?" The hostess interrupted their conversation. "It's eleven o'clock and time for us to close the restaurant. I hate to ask y'all to leave, but I don't have any choice."

Cecelia and Taylor checked their watches as Grace pulled out her phone and checked the time.

"Oh, my God," Cecelia said. "I'm so sorry. We lost all track of time."

The hostess laughed. "Y'all aren't the only ones." She motioned to a few other patrons straggling their way out.

Outside, the four women once again traded hugs. "Y'all discuss everything and let us know when you've made some decisions, including when y'all want to move," Cecelia said. "Talk to you tomorrow."

Grace and Taylor made the short drive back to their house in total silence. Grace stole occasional glances at Taylor, who sat with her elbow on the passenger door armrest, her fingers tapping on her lips. Even after the car was in the driveway and turned off, the two sat, neither making a move to exit the SUV. Grace reached over and took Taylor's hand.

"I know better than to ask what you're thinking about," she said. "I'm totally bamboozled by the way things have gone the past few months. Are you okay?"

Taylor nodded but didn't look over at Grace or say anything. A sniffle alerted Grace to something more.

"Honey? Why are you crying?" Grace gently turned Taylor to face her. "What's wrong? We don't have to move in with Grams or anything else if you're not comfortable with it."

Taylor shook her head. "It's not that." She sniffled again and wiped her face on her shoulder. "It's your family. I never experienced the kind of love y'all have for each other when I was growing up. Ever. Until I met you. You and your family are showing me what love is supposed to be like."

Grace tried to pull Taylor into an embrace, but the shifter and console were in the way. She jumped out of the car and ran around to the other side, where Taylor had already thrown her door open. Grace took Taylor in her arms.

"Oh, baby. Oh, sweetie. I'm so glad you're a part of my family. I can't imagine my life without you. It's a shame you didn't know this kind of love as a child, but I'm so glad I can provide it now."

†

"So, when are you girls moving in?" Evie asked as soon as Grace walked into her room the next day.

"Good afternoon to you too, Grams." Grace crossed the room to kiss her great-grandmother but stopped when an ominous growl emitted from under the blanket she had on her lap. "I was going to ask if you're cold, but I take it that's JB's hideout."

Evie nodded. "Yes. He's still rather skittish and likes to be under something. He thinks we won't know where he is."

"Mom told me he was rather protective of you. Is it safe for me to come kiss you?"

"Yes." Evie petted the lump on her lap. "He's more noise than anything."

Grace sidled up to Evie's chair and gave her a quick peck on the top of her head. JB growled some more but stopped as soon as Grace moved away from the chair.

"Why does he like you and none of the rest of us?" Grace sat in a chair safely away from Evie. "And how am I supposed to help you if he won't let me near you?"

"He's been through a lot lately. You can be in a pretty sour mood when you're stressed, you know. Give him a break. But he won't hurt you. I just let him know he's safe. He'll growl, but that's all. Now, back to my original question. When are you girls moving in?"

"Our landlord wants us out within the month so he can get the house ready to put on the market, so pretty soon. My biggest concern is studio space. I'm in the middle of a pretty big project that I need a place to work on. There's not enough room here."

Evie tapped a finger against one cheek. "Hmmm. Let me think about that for a bit. I'm sure that there's some place suitable close by. What is your project?"

Grace looked down at her hands and studied her nails so as not to look directly at her great-grandmother. "Well, it's under wraps right now, Grams. I haven't even let Taylor see it. I want it perfect first."

"Two big red flags are hanging over your head, girlie."

Grace looked up at Evie and flinched at the look on her face. "What? What did I say?"

Evie held up one finger. "First, you never keep secrets from the person you love. One secret leads to another and another, and suddenly no one knows who can be trusted." She held up a second finger. "And two, there is no such thing as perfection."

It was Grace's turn to hold up a finger. "Number one, it's not a secret. I'm just not ready to show it to anyone yet, even Taylor. Number two, I know there's no such thing as perfection, but there's nothing wrong with striving for it."

JB growled from under his blanket.

"He doesn't appreciate the tone in your voice any more than I do," Evie said with a huff.

Grace stood up. "I'm going to the kitchen. Would you like me to bring you anything?"

"Running away doesn't excuse your rudeness."

Grace took a deep breath and held back the comeback she wanted to make. "I'll bring you some tea and cookies," she said. "I'll be back shortly."

"You owe me an apology," Evie called after her.

Once in the kitchen, Grace sat down at the breakfast bar and lowered her head until her forehead rested on the cool granite. She shook her head from side to side. *I don't know if this is going to work. What have I gotten me and Taylor into?* She'd no more than formulated the thought when her phone rang, and the caller ID let her know Taylor was calling.

"Hey, beautiful," she said as she accepted the call. "What's up?"

"Nothing really. I just had a feeling you needed me to call, so I did."

"Wow. Are you becoming psychic?" Grace went to the cabinet and got two tea glasses and a plate.

"What happened?"

Grace filled Taylor in on the brief but frustrating conversation she'd had with Evie. "If she's going to be like this, I don't know if I can live here and keep some semblance of sanity."

"She's not usually like that though," Taylor said. "You might want to make sure she feels okay."

Grace sat back down. "You're right. I'm about to take her some tea and cookies. She says I owe her an apology, but I don't think I do."

"Apologize anyway. It won't kill you, and it might make it easier to find out if everything is okay."

Grace sighed. "I love you," she said. "You are always the voice of reason just when I need it. Thank you."

"Lois just came in. I'll talk to you later. Be nice to Evie, okay?"

Grace slid her phone back into her pocket. She found a tray and carried two glasses of tea and a plate of cookies back to Evie.

"Did I hear you talking to someone?" Evie asked. JB was sitting on top of the blanket, and Evie was stroking his sleek black and white coat. JB slit his eyes at Grace but didn't growl.

"Yes. Taylor called and asked me to give you her love. I'm sorry about the way I spoke to you a while ago."

Evie smiled up at her as she accepted the proffered glass of tea. "Thank you, but I think I owe you an apology too."

"We're okay," Grace said. "Are you feeling alright? You're awfully pale."

"I'm feeling my age today," Evie admitted. "Just blah. Nothing in particular. Just blah."

"Would you like me to make an appointment with Dr. Hanley? It's been a while since you saw her, hasn't it?"

Evie wrinkled her nose. "I like her, but I hate going to the doctor, especially when there isn't anything wrong that I can put my finger on."

"What if I asked her to come see you? Would that be better?"

Evie waved the words away. "Doctors don't make house calls anymore, child. They quit doing that a long time ago. I'm seventy-odd years older than you, and I know that."

Grace laughed. "That's true for the most part. But last time I took you, the doctor signed you up for a new program they were starting, where the doctors will come to you as long as there aren't any tests that need to be done. They can even take your blood without you going in, and I think she said they have a portable EKG machine too."

Evie shook her head. "I don't remember that. I hope I'm not losing my mind. I don't want to be like Freddy was."

Grace laid a hand on Evie's arm but promptly removed it when JB growled at her.

"You're not going to be like Freddy was, Grams. You can't be expected to remember everything, after all."

"That's sweet of you, Grace." Evie blinked back tears that threatened to overrun her rheumy eyes. "Both Daddy and

Dean expected me to remember everything and got mad if I didn't. Dean didn't even like it if I made a grocery list, but he got mad if I bought something we didn't need or forgot something we did need. I tried to put a calendar on the wall with all our appointments and stuff on it, and he tore it down and burned it."

"Why was he like that?" Grace asked, shaking her head. "I'd be willing to bet he couldn't remember squat."

Evie laughed as she wiped away a tear with the back of her hand. JB was watching every move she made, and when a second tear started down her cheek, he put a paw up and gently touched it.

"Oh, my," Evie said. She stroked his head as he patted her face.

"Wow. He's really in tune with how you feel. Have you ever had any other pet like that?"

Evie shook her head. "I thought I told you I never had a pet before now."

Grace grinned at her. "See? I can't remember much either."

Chapter Twenty-one

"So did she let you make her an appointment?" Taylor asked as she set a plate of tuna salad and crackers on the table. "Sorry there's not more for dinner. I didn't realize we were going to be so late."

"This is fine," Grace said as she put some tuna on a couple of crackers. "Amazingly enough, yes, she did let me make her an appointment. Dr. Hanley's nurse practitioner will be there tomorrow morning. I'm glad Mom's going to be there instead of me. I get so nervous when Grams is being examined. What if they find something wrong with her?"

Taylor took Grace's hand and kissed it. "I know it has to be scary. I'd be afraid too. I wish she could live forever."

Grace nodded but didn't trust her voice to say anything. Instead, she stuffed an overloaded cracker into her mouth and almost immediately started coughing. Taylor gave her a glass of water, but even a couple of drinks didn't settle the coughing. After a few minutes, Grace could breathe again and stopped coughing. Her face was wet with tears. She didn't know if it was from coughing or realizing Grams couldn't live forever.

"I was about to call 911," Taylor said. She handed Grace a damp cloth and a fresh glass of water. "Are you okay?"

"I think so." Grace was hoarse from her coughing bout. "I'm sorry."

"Don't apologize, just take smaller bites."

Grace started to laugh but thought better of it when she coughed again.

†

"How did things go with the doctor this morning?" Grace asked Evie the next afternoon.

"She said I'm terminal," Evie said with a straight face.

"What?" Grace felt all the blood drain from her face.

Evie and Cecelia burst into laughter.

"Sit down, Dauda, before you fall down," Cecelia said. "Ms. Cramer, the nurse practitioner, is so nice. This morning was the first time we met her."

"Okay. Y'all liked her. That's good. What did she really say?" Grace sat down and scowled at her mother and great-grandmother. "Y'all about gave me a coronary."

"In that case, I'm a lot healthier than you are," Evie said. "According to Miss Cramer, I'm in about the best health she's seen in a nonagenarian. And, in case you didn't know, a nonagenarian is a person who is between ninety and ninety-nine years old. And I definitely belong to that club."

"A nonagenarian, hmm? Did Ms. Cramer tell you that?" Grace looked at her mother even as she addressed Evie.

"No. As a matter of fact, Cecelia told me. She's taking some kind of talking class on the computer and learning a lot of two-thousand-dollar words."

"That's what I thought," Grace said, grinning. "You're having a lot of fun with that class, aren't you?"

"Yes, I am. Marie has even started taking it."

"Probably in self-defense," Grace said under her breath.

"I heard that. Stand up here and give me a hug. I need to get to work." Cecelia stood up and held her arms open. Grace embraced her and, for a moment, didn't want to let go. "I think that's one of the best hugs you've given me in a long time."

Grace nodded and tightened her hold again for a second. "I love you, Mom."

"Love you more. Walk me out."

Grace linked arms with her mother and escorted her to the front porch.

"Is everything really okay with Grams?" Grace asked once they were out of Evie's earshot.

"Yes, dear. She's going to be ninety-five in a few weeks, so she's not in the best of health, and that's to be expected. But nothing out of the ordinary or to really worry about. She still shouldn't be left alone for long periods of time since she's not steady on her feet."

"Okay. Mom, Taylor, and I are looking forward to moving over here. We're getting things packed up, but where am I going to put my studio? I need some place to work."

"I know, sweetie. Grams and I talked about that this morning. We have a couple of irons in the fire. Give us a few days. There's a good chance we'll have something lined up. I gotta go, and you need to get back inside to Grams."

CHAPTER TWENTY-TWO

"Hi, Mom? Grams?" Grace called. "Where are you?"

"On the back porch, Grace. Come join us," Cecelia answered.

Grace slid the screen door open and stepped out onto the porch.

"What are y'all doing out here?" she asked. "Isn't it kind of hot?"

"We're enjoying the sunshine," Evie said. She held out a hand. Grace took it, bent over, and planted a kiss on her forehead. "And we're letting JB explore the back yard."

"Is that a good idea? What if he wanders off?" Grace looked around the yard for the cat.

"He's wearing a harness and leash." Cecelia pointed at the cord attached to the porch banister. At its end, JB was sniffing along the bricks of the foundation of the house.

"It's hot out here." Sweat was already beading on Grace's face. "I'll wait inside where it's cool for y'all to come to your senses and come in too."

"Go ahead," Evie said. "But you'll miss out on what we've figured out for your studio."

"What?" Grace stopped and turned back around. "Okay. I'm listening."

"Pull up a chair and sit down like a civilized human being," Cecelia said.

Grace pulled a chair over and joined the other two ladies. "What do y'all have in mind? What's the light like?"

"Shhh," Grams said. "Let me tell you my idea. See that house back there?"

Evie pointed at the house behind hers. Grace nodded.

"It's on the market. What I'm thinking is we buy it and give it to you and Taylor. You can stay here with me when Cecelia and Marie are traveling and over there when they're home. It's got a lot of room. I think, with some remodeling, the upstairs would be a good studio for you."

Grace held her hand up. "Wait. What? Buy that house for me and Taylor?"

"Yes. It'll be your wedding gift," Evie said, grinning from ear to ear. "And I won't broker any argument from you about it. In fact, the realtor is on his way over right now for you to take a look at it."

As if on cue, the doorbell rang. Cecelia jumped up and put a hand on Grace's shoulder to keep her from getting up. Grace felt her mouth opening and closing as if she were a fish out of water. *What the hell is going on here?* she thought. It was only a minute before Cecelia and a handsome young man rejoined them. He bent over and kissed Evie on the cheek.

"Mrs. Creech, it's so good to see you again," he said. He then turned to Grace. She shook his extended hand. "Ms. Jenkins, I presume?"

Grace nodded but couldn't seem to form any words. Evie laughed.

"She's in shock, Zach," she said. "We just told her about our idea. She's been speechless ever since."

"If I'd known that was going to happen, I would have suggested it a long time ago," Cecelia said with a laugh.

"Well, I hope you find your voice by the time we visit the house," Zach said. "Your input will determine your grandmother's final decision."

"Great-grandmother," Evie, Cecelia, and Grace said in unison. After a split second of silence, everyone on the porch burst into laughter.

"My mistake," Zach said. "Your great-grandmother's decision."

He held his hand out to Grace and pulled her to her feet.

"Shall we cut through the yard and climb the fence, or would you rather have me drive?" he asked. It took a second for Grace to realize he was kidding with her.

"I think driving would afford us a bit more dignity," she said, trying hard to keep a straight face.

"You? Dignified? Ha!" Cecelia said.

"Would you like to come with us?" Zach asked Evie. "I drove my sensible car today just so you can accompany us if you like."

"Your sensible car?" Grace asked.

"Yes. My sensible car is my Lexus sedan," Zach explained.

"And your non-sensible car?" Cecelia helped Evie out of her chair as she spoke.

"He has a pick-up truck jacked up so high, I could walk under it," Evie said. "Cee, can you talk JB into coming inside?"

Cecelia followed the leash into the yard and picked JB up, even though the cat was anything but ready to stop his exploring. Zach took Evie by the elbow and escorted her through the house, Grace following close behind. It took several minutes for Cecelia to settle the cat in Evie's room, but finally, the small group was on their way.

Zach pulled up in front of a nondescript house with no curb appeal whatsoever and a huge live oak tree looming over it. Because of its size, the live oak's roots filled the front yard, leaving almost no room for grass. The house's faded paint had once been a medium brown. The screen in the door was ripped and hanging down.

"Uhm, I think the back of the house looks better than the front," Grace said.

"I've talked to a tree doctor," Zach said. "He said this tree is on its last leg and he recommends taking it down and removing the roots. It'll be a mess for a while, but eventually the front yard can be tastefully landscaped. A new front door and some paint will help spruce up the front. But it's what's inside that counts, right?"

"Yeah," Grace said, dollar signs flashing in front of her face. *Take the tree down? Remove the roots? Landscape? Paint? Oh, shit.*

She climbed out of the car and turned to assist Evie. Tree roots had cracked the driveway cement, and she feared Evie would trip. "Be careful, Grams. This driveway is like a minefield."

Zach went ahead of them and punched a code into the key box hanging from the doorknob. He withdrew the house key and, after a bit of jiggling, unlocked the front door, holding it for the ladies to enter.

"Wow," Grace said as they stepped into a bright room that stretched from the front of the house to the back, with the kitchen to one side at the back of the house. The kitchen had a large island with a double farmhouse sink. Stainless steel appliances sparkled, still with the stickers announcing they were brand new. A family room stretched out across from the kitchen. The floors were some kind of hardwood, shiny and unmarked.

"This is sure not what I expected from what the outside looked like," Cecelia said.

Evie and Zach were grinning from ear to ear.

"Isn't this beautiful, Grace?" Evie asked. "Do you think Taylor will like that kitchen?"

Grace ran her hand along the granite countertops. She felt tears sting her eyes. She buried her face in her hands.

"What's wrong, sweetie?" Cecelia said as she slipped an arm around Grace's waist. She turned, laid her forehead on her mother's shoulder, and shook her head.

"This is too much, Mom. Too much. How can Grams afford to do this?"

"You worry too much, Dauda. This is something Grams wants to do for you and Taylor. You need to learn to let us spoil you."

"You've spoiled me all my life," Grace said with a sniffle and a snort. "And so has Grams. I want to spoil y'all."

"Your turn will come, child." Evie had joined them and put her arm around Grace from the other side. "For now, let us spoil you. Zach went to get a chair from his car so I can sit while you explore."

Zach came back inside with a folded canvas chair. He opened it and helped Evie settle into it. Once she was comfortable, he turned his attention back to Grace.

"Let me show you the bedrooms," he said. "The master suite is at the end of the hall. Although it's in the same hallway as the guest rooms, it has a great deal of privacy. Upstairs, in what used to be the attic, is a bonus room. Mrs. Creech told me you're an artist and need a studio."

Grace nodded. "I'm more interested in that than the bedrooms, to tell you the truth. Does the bonus room have good lighting?"

"Not really," Zach admitted. "But the remodeling plans show that the owner had planned on installing a number of skylights up there. If you finish the remodeling, along his plans, I think you'll find it will have great lighting."

"That leads me to another question," Grace said as she followed him to the base of the staircase. "What happened to the owner? Why didn't he finish the remodeling? What's been done is beautiful."

"Unfortunately, his wife was diagnosed with metastatic breast cancer. She fought for three years but lost her battle about seven or eight months ago. He couldn't move out of here fast enough after she passed away."

"Oh, dear." Cecelia wiped the tears from her face. "Did she die in this house? If so, we'll have to get Marie's sister to come smudge for you. Well, we should do that anyway."

"Mom." Grace put a hand on her elbow. "We haven't decided to buy the house yet. Don't jump the gun."

Evie cleared her throat but said nothing when they turned to look at her. She motioned for them to get on with the showing.

Upstairs, Grace took in the large room. It stretched the length of the house with a couple of doors on the far side of the room from the staircase.

"There's a full bath and a closet over there," Zach said, pointing at the two doors. "I'm not sure what their thoughts were for this room, but I think they had hoped to make it the master suite. I think if you put in those skylights, there, there, and there," he pointed at three places on the ceiling equidistant apart, "then the light up here would be amazing."

Grace ran her fingers along the wall as she walked the perimeter of the room. At each end of the room were new windows, but they were both shaded by large trees. Removing the tree in the front yard would improve the light at that end of the room. She looked up at the vaulted ceiling, where Zach suggested putting in the skylights.

"This is more than perfect," she said in awe. A thought occurred to her. She turned to Zach. "We're pretty close to the arts district here. Do you know what the zoning is? Could I turn part of the house into a gallery?"

"That's something I can look into for you," he said. "Will your decision whether to buy or not depend on the answer to that question?"

Grace shook her head. "No. I've fallen in love with this house. I guess we ought to let Grams know so she can talk the price down."

Zach laughed and half-bowed from the waist as he motioned to the staircase. "After you, ladies."

†

"You're kidding me?" Taylor's mouth fell open, and if Grace hadn't moved fast, the bowl of pasta she held would have hit the floor. Grace set the pasta on the table and eased her partner into a chair.

"Nope. We're now the owners of a house that we'll only live in part-time," Grace said.

Taylor's eyes filled with tears. "And you made this decision without me, without even asking me what I thought?"

"Uhm, yeah, kind of?" Grace slid her chair over next to Taylor's, but Taylor pushed away from her. "Wait a minute. I don't think you understand. The decision was made for us before I even knew it was in the wind. Going and looking at the house was merely a formality. Grams had already signed the paperwork and paid the mortgage—in full."

"In full?" Taylor stood up and leaned against the counter. "I wish she had spoken to us first."

Grace went to her and put a hand on each of Taylor's shoulders. "I felt that way too," she said. "But once I saw the house—oh, hon. It's like the man who remodeled it knew us. Wait 'til you see the kitchen. It's more than fabulous. The house still needs some work. The front of the house is hideous. You'll hate the front of the house, but it's fixable. Please. Try to keep an open mind until you see it."

"And if I hate it?"

"I'll tell Grams to use it as a rental property. We'll live in Grams' house with her, and I'll rent studio space at the artists' co-op downtown."

"You'd do that?"

Grace pulled Taylor into an embrace. "Yes, I will. I love you with all my heart, and your happiness is more important to me than any house or studio."

The next day, Grace took Taylor to see the house.

"Well, you're right about one thing," Taylor said as she climbed out of the SUV. "The front of this house is hideous."

Grace laughed. "Isn't it? But Zach gave me the phone numbers for a tree man, landscaper, and house painter. They'll make it much worse and then much better."

"Who pays for that though, Grace?" Taylor leaned against the car and crossed her arms. "I don't see how we can afford it. Is this place going to be a money pit?"

"I wondered the same thing," Grace said. "Grams made provisions in the mortgage settlement to cover all of that, as well as put skylights upstairs and some to put into an account for anything else we want or need."

"Where did your grandmother get all this money?"

"Great-grandmother," Grace said. She laughed when she realized Taylor had corrected herself in unison with her. "She won't tell me. All she would do was assure me she hadn't robbed a bank. Mom thinks it's from an insurance settlement Gramps had when she was a kid and from his old pension plans. Come on. Let's go inside."

It was only a matter of days before workers were taking the live oak tree out of the front yard and digging out the roots. Grace and Taylor stood across the street, watching workers load the final stump onto a truck and haul it away. The yard looked much larger without the tree, but it was still a maze of roots that a backhoe was digging up.

"Geesh," Taylor said. "What a mess. Are you sure taking the tree down was a good idea?"

Grace nodded. "The tree man told me the tree was dying from the inside out, and most of the trunk was already hollow. It would have taken only one strong wind to bring it down on the house."

"Okay. I just have to wonder what the yard will look like without it."

"The landscaper is supposed to have drawings ready for us tomorrow or the next day." Grace took Taylor by the hand. "I'm kind of nervous about all this, you know?"

"I am too," Taylor said, hugging Grace's arm. "I still can't help but wonder where the money is coming from."

"If I ask Grams that question one more time, she might take the house away from us. She just says to be happy with the gifts that come our way."

"Are you girls moving in over there?"

Grace and Taylor dropped hands and moved a step apart as a woman who looked old enough to be their grandmother joined them on the sidewalk.

"Yes, ma'am," Grace said. "We're going to finish some of the remodeling that the previous owner started, and then we'll live there part-time."

"Part-time? Where will you live the rest of the time?" The woman put her hand over her mouth. "Oh, I'm sorry. That's none of my business, is it?"

Grace laughed. "It's okay, Mrs.—uhm, I'm sorry. What is your name?"

"I'm Dorothy Amos. I've lived here for over fifty years." She pointed at the house behind them.

"I'm Grace Jenkins, and this is Taylor Bradford."

"It's good to meet you. Do you girls have children?"

Grace and Taylor exchanged a glance. "No, ma'am. We haven't decided if we want kids or not," Taylor said, a note of hesitation in her voice.

"Make sure you're sure before you do," Mrs. Amos said.

"That makes good sense," Grace said. She checked her watch. "I don't mean to be rude, but I have to be someplace in ten minutes. It was good to meet you. I hope we'll be good neighbors."

"As long as you don't play that horrible rap music at ear-bursting levels, we'll get along just fine." Mrs. Amos slapped her knee as she laughed. "I'll see you girls another time."

CHAPTER TWENTY-THREE

"Dorothy Amos? That old hag?" Cecelia said when Grace told her and Evie about their encounter. "I didn't know she was still alive. She used to put toothbrushes in our trick-or-treat bags at Halloween."

Grace laughed. "She seemed harmless enough. And she seemed to realize that Taylor and I are a couple. She asked if we were planning on having kids."

"Nosy old thing," Evie said. She yawned. JB sat up from where he was lying on her lap and also yawned. "Grace, come help me lie down. I'm pooped out."

Grace assisted Evie to her feet. She gave her mother a look of alarm when Evie stumbled and then leaned heavily on Grace's arm.

"You okay, Grams?" she asked.

"For an almost ninety-five-year-old woman, I'm doing about as okay as you can expect," Evie retorted. "What kind of question is that?"

Cecelia rolled her eyes and shook her head as she shrugged when Grace glanced over at her.

Grace moved at Evie's slow pace to her bedroom, JB right on their heels. Once in Evie's bedroom, the cat jumped up on the bed and began to bathe.

"He's made himself right at home," Grace said as she eased Evie down to the edge of the bed. She kneeled in front of her and untied her shoes. "At least he's quit growling at me."

"I think he realizes it won't make you go away, so he tolerates your presence," Evie said as she leaned back on her pillows. "Close the door behind you, please."

Back in the living room, Grace found Cecelia staring out the window. She slipped an arm around her mother's waist and leaned her head on her shoulder.

"What's wrong, Mom?"

Cecelia shook her head but didn't say anything. When she sniffled, Grace knew she was crying. She retrieved the tissue box from the coffee table and offered Cecelia a tissue.

"What's going on? Is everything okay with Mudda and the retirement?"

Cecelia laughed a tear-filled laugh. "Yes, Marie is fine, and the retirement is in process. I'm just missing Mom. Mrs. Amos and she are about the same age and were friends when they were kids. I played with her son a lot. He's the one who taught me how to throw a football."

"I'm sorry. I miss Grandma too. There have been so many times I've started to pick up the phone to tell her about Grams and Freddy, and everything else."

As if on cue, Grace's phone rang. Cecelia and Grace looked at each other for a split second before laughing. Grace dug the phone from her pocket and checked the caller ID.

"Hey, Pepper. Long time no talk. How are you all doing?"

"Oh, my God, Grace. If we don't get Aunt Freddy and Evie together soon, I'm going to have to be admitted to someplace that has a rubber room. Did you know they've figured out how to call each other? On my phone?"

"They're talking on the phone? Grams hates talking on the phone."

"Not anymore. I just now rescued my phone from Aunt Freddy. They've been talking for almost half an hour."

"I just put Grams down for a nap," Grace said. She checked her watch. "Yep, about half an hour ago. I didn't even know she had a phone."

Cecelia retrieved her purse from the side table at the front door and turned it upside down on the sofa. No phone. Grace started laughing.

"Grams lifted Mom's phone from her purse," Grace said.

"I have to go to work," Cecelia said. "I'm going to get my phone from the petty thief among us and take off."

Grace grinned and nodded at her as she went to Evie's room.

"Is it possible for Freddy to take a field trip and y'all come to town to Grams' house? Or is that too much sensory overload?"

"She's been doing a lot better," Pepper said. "She went grocery shopping with us the other day and, for all practical purposes, she did okay. We didn't get everything we needed before she started getting agitated, but that was her first time ever in a super Wal-Mart, and it was a bit overwhelming."

"I get sensory overload at Wal-Mart," Grace said. "But it's good that she got out for a while."

"Let me talk to her and see what she thinks about coming to town to see y'all. How are things going for you guys?"

Cecelia stopped on her way out and kissed Grace on the top of her head. "Later, Pepper," she called toward Grace's phone.

Pepper laughed. "I take it your mom's on her way out of the house."

"Yep. On her way to work. You won't believe what's been happening since we visited last." Grace leaned back into the sofa, propped her feet up on the coffee table, and filled Pepper in.

"She bought y'all a house? I'll be damned. Where did she get the money?"

Grace shrugged, even though she knew Pepper couldn't see her. "I've asked, but the subject is taboo. She won't even hint where it came from."

"But you're only going to live there part-time?"

"When Mom and Mudda are traveling, we'll stay here, but when they're home, we'll stay at our house. We're still doing some work at the house, including putting skylights in the attic for my studio. And Zach, our real estate agent, is checking into zoning. We might turn part of the house into a small gallery."

"That's cool. Oh, shit. Aunt Freddy's yelling for me. I'll let you know when—if we can come into town. Give Evie a kiss for me."

"Talk to you later."

CHAPTER TWENTY-FOUR

"I hear we need to get you a phone of your own," Grace said when she responded to Evie's call for help an hour later.

Evie frowned at her. "Pepper's a tattletale. She interrupted our phone call, then called you, and told on us. And she said she had to call clients."

"I'm sure she did make the phone calls to her clients, but, yes, she did tell me about your calls to Freddy. You don't like telephones."

"I didn't when I didn't have anyone to talk to," Evie said as the two went back to the living room. "Is it time for *Jeopardy* yet?"

Grace checked the time. "In about fifteen minutes. How would you like for Freddy to come see you instead of us having to drive all the way out to Weatherford?"

"Is she up to that?" Evie tried but failed to keep a smile from her face. "I'd love for her to come see where I live. I've tried to describe it to her, but she has a hard time visualizing things. She always has. That's why she keeps the puzzle box top in front of her while she's working on the puzzle. When are they coming?"

"I don't know for sure that they are yet," Grace said. "I suggested it to Pepper, and she promised to talk to Freddy about it."

"Well, tell me what's going on at your house," Evie said.

"I told you all that before you lay down." Grace sat down beside her and took her hand. "Are you feeling okay, Grams? Please don't make light of it if you aren't."

Evie patted Grace's hand with her free hand. "I'm old, honey. I don't know how much longer I'll be blessed to walk on this earth. Despite some recent memory lapses and a bit of weakness, I'm fine, I promise. In fact, in a lot of ways, I feel better now than I have in decades. I have my Freddy back. And that's all thanks to you and our lovely Taylor. Where is she anyway? I haven't seen her for a few days." Evie hesitated a moment and then, with a grin and an elbow nudge, she added, "Have I?"

Grace laughed. "No, you haven't. Taylor's been pretty busy working on the documentary and packing up our house."

"Are you helping with the packing, or are you making her do all the work?"

"I'm helping," Grace said, mentally crossing her fingers against the white lie. Taylor was doing most of the work because Grace was busy with her new paintings.

"I know she told me when she and that nice lady that's working with her are going to come talk to me," Evie said, tapping her chin with a forefinger. "I think Cecelia wrote it down, but I can't remember when she said. Wouldn't it be good if they came when Freddy is here?"

"That's a good idea, Grams. I'll mention it to her this evening. I know she's excited about this film, but I think she's finding there's a lot more to it than she anticipated. Between that, packing, and planning our wedding, I'm afraid she's overdoing it. I'm thinking of suggesting putting off the wedding until after the documentary is done."

Evie's mouth fell open. "You can't do that, Grace Marie. Y'all have too much already invested in it, especially emotions. You'll break her heart, and I'm pretty sure that's not what you want to do. Is it?"

"Of course not. You don't believe that I would want to hurt Taylor, do you?" Grace stood up and shoved her fists into the pockets of her pants. "I love her more than I knew it was possible to love someone. I want to spend all the time we can together. I grieve the years you and Freddy missed, and each time I see you, I'm more convinced that I don't want to lose a day with Taylor."

Evie nodded. "Good. That's what I wanted to hear. Dean forced me and Freddy to waste decades of our lives and almost stole Freddy's sanity. I never liked him, but now I hate him. With a purple passion, as you used to say. The only thing that man was good for was giving me Eleanor and Betts."

Tears trickled through the wrinkles on her face. Grace sat down on the coffee table directly in front of her great-grandmother and handed her some tissues.

"I'm sorry, Grams. I'm so sorry. You were worth so much more than that. I can't imagine what you went through, but I think it made you the strong woman you are now."

Evie nodded. "Yes, and I tried to instill that strength in my girls, in your mom, and in you. I see you stumble once in a while, but you have a support system in your mother, Marie, and Taylor. You are surrounded by so much love. Never forget that."

Grace shifted to sit on the sofa next to her and pulled her into a tight embrace.

Chapter Twenty-five

"Good news, Grace," Zach said when she answered the phone a few days later. "Your street is on the very edge of the arts district, and it is zoned for artistic home business."

"Does that mean I can make the living room a gallery?" Grace asked.

"That's what that means. I'll send you the paperwork for the pertinent permits, et cetera. How's the landscaping and studio renos going?"

"Messy." Grace laughed. "Taylor's afraid our neighbors are going to hate us by the time all of this is done."

"Have you met any of them? I've only had good vibes from them," Zach said.

"We met Mrs. Amos from across the street. Turns out my grandmother and she were friends in high school."

"Small world." Zach said something to someone in the background. "I have to go, Grace. Let me know if there's anything else I can do."

†

Grace and Taylor stood in the middle of the wide-open living area of the new house.

"How will we separate the gallery from our private area?" Taylor asked.

Grace held a catalog in one hand. She pointed at the page it was open to. "These rice paper screens," she said. "They're light and pretty and, at the same time, they'll block off the rest of the area."

She went to the wall next to where the kitchen started and walked across the room to the side of the staircase. "If I measured right, we'll need six screens. I can get blank screens and decorate them myself, or we can get them with a design already painted on them. There are so many choices available."

Taylor stood with one arm crossed across her body and the other elbow resting on her wrist, tapping her mouth with a forefinger.

"I have a feeling you want to get the blank ones, right?" she asked with a grin.

Grace grinned and nodded. "I can already see in my head what I want to paint on them."

"I bet you can. Are you going to leave the staircase and your studio open to the public?"

"No, not really, at least for the most part," Grace said. She sat down on the staircase. "We'll put a chain across here to keep the nosy people out. We can invite our customers who order custom work to see where I do my planning and do the work."

Taylor walked over and linked their arms. “Tell me again what this gallery is going to be like.”

Grace’s eyes lit up. “It will be minimalist,” she said. “My work, the series I’m working on now, and then later, more series I have planned will be the main art we show and sell. But I want to invite some other artists who work in other mediums to show here too. Sculpture, folk art, fiber arts, things like that. I want to keep it as simple and open as possible so we can have events here. I picture doing Grams’ and Freddy’s birthday party here if we can get things done by then. And,” she took both of Taylor’s hands, “what would you think of having our wedding here?”

Taylor looked around the house. Grace couldn’t read her face and worried she may have stepped over an unknown, invisible line.

“Do I get to decorate for the wedding?” Taylor asked.

Grace laughed as she pulled Taylor to her and kissed her. “Of course. I wouldn’t have it any other way.”

CHAPTER TWENTY-SIX

"Freddy and Pepper will be here any minute," Evie said for the umpteenth time. "Is the tea ready? Did you buy her favorite cookies?"

She struggled to stand up, but Grace put a hand on her shoulder and kept her in her chair.

"Grams, please calm down. Pepper said about one, and it's still a quarter till. Do you want a glass of tea to sip on until they get here?"

Evie shook her head. Grace saw the tears welling up in her eyes. She kneeled beside Evie's chair and put her arms around her great-grandmother. "What's wrong, Grams?"

Evie shrugged. "I don't know, but I feel as nervous as a cat in a room full of rocking chairs. I keep thinking about what if she doesn't like coming to visit here since Dean once lived here? Or if she doesn't like the way we make our tea? Or if we got the wrong brand of pecan sandies?"

"I think you're worrying for no good reason," Cecelia said as she entered the room with a tray of cookies and a pitcher of tea. "Too late now anyway. They just pulled into the driveway."

"Oh, my." Evie smoothed her hair down and straightened the collar of her blouse. "Help me up, Grace."

Grace assisted Evie to her feet, and together they went to the front door. Evie waved as they watched Pepper open the door for Freddy to climb out of their sedan. Freddy was grinning from ear to ear and waved back. Pepper grabbed her by the elbow to slow her down. She said something, but Freddy shook her head and pulled away from Pepper. Grace opened the storm door.

"Hi, y'all," she said. "Come in out of the heat. We've got sweet tea and pecan sandies waiting for you."

"And my Evie," Freddy said. "She's waiting for me."

She wrapped her arms around Evie and swayed. Grace and Pepper stood ready to catch them if they swayed too far. Finally, Evie stepped back and took Freddy by the hand.

"Let's go sit on the sofa," she said. "We're too old to stand here for too long."

"Okay. I could use some iced tea. And did I hear pecan sandies?"

"Yes, you did."

Grace and Pepper got the two old women settled on the sofa with their tea and cookies, and then left them to visit.

"We'll be in the family room if you need us," Grace told them, but wondered if they'd even heard her. They were sitting with their heads together, chattering like teenagers.

"How was the drive?" Grace asked as she settled on the opposite end of the sofa from Pepper. She waved as Cecelia went by with her purse on her shoulder. "See you later, Mom."

She laughed when Cecelia stuck her head into the living room and told the old women to behave themselves.

"Aunt Freddy doesn't know how to behave since she came back to reality," Pepper said. "She didn't shut up all the way here. I was ready to put a gag in her mouth, but I was afraid she'd turn me in for elder abuse."

"We took Grams to the mobile store and bought her a phone. I'll give you her number before y'all leave. Are you going to get Freddy a phone?"

"I don't have a choice. She has hidden mine in her bedroom somewhere, and neither Sonya nor I can find it, yet we hear her talking on it all the time. She has been mentally away for almost seven years, but she's had no trouble figuring out today's technology."

Grace laughed. "Grams isn't quite as tech-savvy. We got her the simplest phone the store had, and it still took me and Taylor almost two hours to teach her how to use it. I just wish she hadn't figured out how to take pictures and selfies."

"Are you afraid she'll start sexting Aunt Freddy?" Pepper asked with a grin.

"Oh, gawd. I hadn't even thought of that. I'm not sure if I'd put it past her though. Whatever you do, don't give them any ideas."

"How are things going at the new house?" Pepper asked. She pointed out the glass doors. "Is that it back there?"

"That's the one," Grace said. "We're going to put a new fence up back there with a gate in it so we don't have to drive over. It's almost two miles to drive from there to here and about a hundred yards to walk from here to there."

"That's a good idea. Do we get to see the inside anytime soon?"

"Actually, I wanted to talk to you about that. We're turning the front part of the house into a gallery, mostly to use for private events and for special artists to do private shows. Our goal is to have the first event be Grams' and Freddy's birthday party. Do you think that would be too much sensory overload for her?"

Pepper shook her head with a laugh. "She doesn't seem to have too much trouble with sensory overload anymore. In fact, she seems to need more and more stimulation. She's discovered game shows on TV and games on Facebook. She lifted Sonya's iPad and figured out how to use it. Thankfully, we have unlimited data."

"Is she still working her puzzles?" Grace asked.

"Oh, yes. Only now I have to buy new ones on a regular basis. An online club I found sends a new puzzle each month. I dread her figuring out that the postman delivers them. I have a feeling she'd hound him unmercifully."

"Girls? Can y'all come in here, please?" Evie called from the living room.

"We're coming, Grams," Grace called back. Pepper pretended to pull her hair out, and Grace laughed.

Evie and Freddy sat close together on the sofa, Freddy's arm around Evie's shoulders. They both had wide smiles on their faces.

"Uh, oh," Pepper said. "What are you two up to? You've got shit-eating grins on your faces."

"Shit-eating grins?" Freddy said, furrowing her brow. "Oh, I like that. Evie, let me see your shit-eating grin."

Evie grinned an exaggerated grin, and the two women burst into laughter.

Grace and Pepper shook their heads and waited for them to settle down.

"Seriously, what do you need?" Grace asked when the women finally stopped laughing.

Evie looked at Freddy, and the smile they shared was so full of love that Grace felt her heart leap.

"We want to get married on our birthday," Evie said. "We want you to take us shopping to choose wedding bands. Can we do that now?"

Grace looked at Pepper and knew their faces mirrored each other's, eyes wide and mouths open.

"And I think we have to get a marriage license," Freddy said. "And choose where to live once we are married."

"Uh, whoa. Wait a minute." Pepper put her hand up. "Just wait a minute."

"Married?" Grace said at the same time. "Wow. Just wow."

Evie laughed and looked at Freddy. "I told you that's what she would say. 'Wow. Just wow.'"

"Yes, you did," Freddy agreed. "And I told you Pepper would say, 'Just wait a minute.'"

"I think they've been around us too long if we know what they're going to say next," Evie said. "What do you think they'll say now?"

"Be quiet for a minute, Grams," Grace said. "I have to have a minute to process all of this."

"Well, at least we're telling y'all instead of making you guess like you did when you and Taylor got engaged," Evie said. "And it would do you good to remember I have seven decades on you and you need to be respectful of that."

"Hush, Evie," Freddy said, putting two fingers on Evie's mouth. "Let the poor girl think. We did catch them off guard."

†

"Oh, my gawd," Cecelia, Marie, and Taylor said in unison.

"Getting married and turning ninety-five on the same day," Cecelia said. "I wish Mom were here to see this. Damn."

Marie grinned. "It's really got your goat if you're cussing," she said, nudging Cecelia with her elbow. "Watch your language in front of the kids."

Grace shook her head. "If I remember correctly, you're the one who taught me to cuss."

"That's neither here nor there," Cecelia said. "We now have to figure out how to incorporate a wedding into their birthday party."

"That, and we have to make sure they get their marriage license. The logistics of all this is mind-boggling," Grace said. "They've twisted Pepper's and my arms into taking them shopping for wedding rings next week."

Taylor groaned. "We already have so much to do. We have to be out of the house by next weekend."

"What if I call my brothers and see if they can help?" Marie said. "Are y'all mostly packed up and just need things moved?"

"Everything except my studio," Grace said.

"And it would be done if you'd let me in there," Taylor said. "She put a lock on the door and won't let me have a key."

"Why not, Dauda?" Marie asked. "What are you hiding in there?"

"My new collection. I don't want anyone to see it until I reveal it in the new gallery."

"And that will be when?" Taylor asked.

"At Gram's and Freddy's birthday party and wedding."

CHAPTER TWENTY-SEVEN

"Are you sure I can't help?" Taylor asked as Grace lugged boxes to her studio. "Can't you throw sheets over the paintings?"

Grace took a deep breath. "You know, that's not a bad idea," she said. "I do need your help. I'm not good at packing, and I always end up with a mess."

"I figured as much. I'll go get some sheets."

Ten minutes later, Grace had draped the sheets over the pictures of Evie and her hands, and Freddy and her violin. She smiled as she thought about them.

"Can I come in now?" Taylor called.

"Yeah, come on in," Grace said.

Taylor came through the door and groaned. "Have you done anything in here at all?"

"Paint," Grace answered.

"Okay. Where do you want me to start?"

Grace pointed at the worktable on the far side of the room. "Over there, I guess."

Grace and Taylor filled, labeled, and taped the boxes. Taylor kept asking, “Are you sure you need this? You have three others.” And Grace repeatedly answered in the affirmative.

After packing the studio, they moved the boxes to the living room, where most of their life together filled the boxes stacked to the ceiling.

“I’m glad Jose and Julian are going to help us move this stuff,” Grace said. “Otherwise, we’d probably have to hire movers. Now all we have to do is pay them with a good lunch.”

“Which will probably cost as much as hiring movers,” Taylor said with a laugh.

“I hate having to put our furniture in Grams’ garage instead of taking it to the house.” Grace ran her hand along the arm of the sofa. “We had so much fun shopping for all this stuff.”

Taylor nodded and took Grace in her arms. “We’ve had a lot of fun together,” she said. “I’m so glad we’ve decided to get married. A piece of paper shouldn’t make a difference, but I think it does.”

“I know. It feels like we’re starting so many new chapters at once.” Grace rested her head on Taylor’s shoulder. “Do you feel as overwhelmed as I do?”

Taylor stroked Grace’s back and hummed. They danced in place for a moment or two until Grace broke away and led Taylor to their bedroom.

CHAPTER TWENTY-EIGHT

"Uhm. You want what?" The clerk at the courthouse raised her eyebrows almost to her hairline.

"A marriage license," Evie said. "You do know what those are, right? Maybe you should get someone to help you." She held onto the counter and stood on her tiptoes to look over the clerk's shoulder. "Maybe that young man over there can help you," she said.

"No, ma'am. I know what a marriage license is. I was just surprised because…" The clerk's voice trailed off as she pretended to find something in a drawer below the counter.

"Because what?" Evie tilted her head. "Because we're both women?"

"Uh, no, ma'am. Not that. Not that at all." The poor clerk blushed so deeply that Grace was afraid she'd burst a vein.

"Then what, pray tell, is the problem?"

Grace could tell Evie was having far too much fun at the clerk's expense. She stepped up to stand beside her great-grandmother.

"Don't pay her any mind," she told the clerk. "You don't dare show weakness around her, or she'll take full advantage of it and never let you forget."

The clerk, whose name tag identified her as Anita Tyler, gave her a sheepish smile. "I, well, uh, they're so much older than most of the people applying for marriage licenses."

"We both have excellent hearing for our advanced age," Evie said, placing a hand on her hip. Freddy stood in silence beside her, a grin spread across her face.

"I'm, whoa. I'm so sorry," Ms. Tyler said. "Any chance we can start over? I honestly didn't mean to offend either one of you."

Evie reached across the counter and patted her hand. "You're fine, dear. I guess I should apologize as well."

"Yes, you should," Grace said at the same time Ms. Tyler said, "No, not at all."

Everyone laughed as the clerk pushed the paperwork across the counter. "You need to fill this out and bring it back to me once you have. I'll need to see a valid ID—"

"ID?" Freddy said. She turned so pale that Grace was afraid she was going to pass out. "I don't know if I have an ID. Oh, dear."

Grace put a hand on her shoulder. "Pepper gave me your ID, a letter from your lawyer, and your Social Security card."

"She has to know her Social Security number," Ms. Tyler said.

Grace nodded. "The lawyer's letter will explain why she may not know it," she said. "The letter includes an exemption by the court justice of the peace in Weatherford."

Ms. Tyler frowned and once again seemed unsure of herself. "May I see the letter?"

Grace pulled it out of her bag and handed it over.

"Y'all fill out that paperwork, and I'll go show this letter to my supervisor," Ms. Tyler said. "I'll do my best to make sure you get your marriage license today."

Evie took Grace's elbow and Freddy's hand, and together the three of them went to a small table. Grace watched as Evie meticulously filled out each blank and colored in the appropriate boxes with concentrated precision. Freddy, on the other hand, scrawled her information in almost illegible handwriting. Once or twice, she asked Grace to interpret what something meant. By the time the ladies finished, Ms. Tyler was back at the window, motioning for them to join her.

"My supervisor says everything is in order with this letter and exemption," she said. She took the paperwork and looked it over, raising her eyebrows when she looked at Freddy's. She asked the women a couple of questions to verify some of the information as she typed it into the computer. Grace paid the fee, and within a short time, they left with the marriage license safely stowed in Grace's bag.

"Well, now, that wasn't nearly as hard as I expected it to be," Evie said as Grace settled her in the front passenger seat and helped Freddy into the backseat. "I think we deserve a banana split from Dairy Queen. Don't you agree, Freddy?"

Freddy leaned forward and put a hand on Evie's shoulder. "I think that sounds wonderful, especially if we can share it."

"I guess we need to shop for wedding clothes now," Evie said a little while later as they enjoyed their ice cream at the Dairy Queen around the corner from the courthouse. "I can't decide if I want to get a wedding gown or just a simple dress."

Grace almost choked on her sundae. "A wedding gown? Grams, do you have any idea how much those things cost? And, really, don't you think you're a bit old to wear a wedding dress?"

She and Freddy both jumped when Evie slapped the table with her hand.

"That's the second time today our age has been thrown in our faces. Is this what they're talking about when they talk about age discrimination on the news? I think too old only applies if you're putting me in the ground. Then I'll be too old for a wedding dress."

The fast-food sitting area was completely silent when she finished speaking. She looked around and blushed.

"I'm sorry," she said. "I didn't mean to disrupt everyone's lunch."

"You just never mind about that," a woman who looked to be in her seventies said. "You tell them. We're never too old unless we decide we're too old."

"Yeah. What she said," a burly construction worker added. "You take her to find her the prettiest wedding dress in town."

Grace's mouth fell open when he reached into his back pocket and retrieved his wallet. He opened it as he approached their table, pulled a one-hundred-dollar bill out, and laid it in front of Evie.

"I know that won't buy a wedding dress these days," he said, "but put it toward whatever you want when you get married."

Before any of them could respond, he was out the door. The restaurant stayed quiet for an instant before it went back to its normal decibel level. Evie fingered the money.

"I don't need this," she said. "I have plenty of money to buy a dress. What should we do with it?"

Grace and Freddy shrugged. Grace was still speechless. They sat in silence for a moment before Evie reached for her cane and struggled to stand up. Grace jumped up and helped her to her feet.

"What are you doing?" Freddy asked.

"I'm going to give this to the manager," Evie said. "I'm going to tell her to use it to pay for however many orders this will cover."

Freddy grinned. "That's one reason I love you so much. You are always thinking of others, and you're so generous."

"I can do this myself," Evie said when Grace took her elbow.

Grace sat back down and watched as her great-grandmother went to the counter and asked for the manager. The young woman came around the counter, led Evie to a nearby table, and sat with her, listening intently to what Evie was telling her. She accepted the one-hundred-dollar bill with a sweet smile. She helped Evie to her feet and gently gave her a hug before escorting her back to their table.

"Thank you again, Evie," she said as Evie slid into the booth next to Freddy. She extended her hand to Freddy. "I understand congratulations are in order."

Freddy grinned as she shook the young woman's hand. "Thank you."

"I'd like to give y'all a nice wedding gift," the manager said. "If you'll get in touch with me the day before, I'll bring you an ice cream cake as your wedding cake, if that's okay."

"That is so nice of you," Evie said. "Grace is my great-granddaughter, and she's doing most of the planning. The wedding is going to be in her gallery."

"You own a gallery?" The manager's eyes grew big. "Wow. That's so cool."

Grace smiled. "Thank you. It's not really that much of a big deal. I have a feeling Grams neglected to tell you the whole story. The wedding and these two love birds' ninety-fifth birthdays are on the same day."

The manager put her hand on her chest. "Ninety-fifth? Wow. Now I know I'd like to do something special for you. Please, Grace, call me or come by the night before so I can assist with the refreshments."

"That's really generous. Thank you." Grace took the manager's business card and tucked it in with the marriage license.

†

"He gave her a hundred dollars?" Taylor stopped organizing their closet in the bedroom at Evie's house and turned to face Grace, who was arranging books on a bookshelf.

Grace nodded. "Yep. That surprised me as much as Grams wanting to go wedding dress shopping. I'm glad I talked her out of that. I hate to shop in the first place, but the thought of having to do it with two *noctogenerians* just made me cringe."

Taylor laughed. "*Noctogenerians*? I think you mean nonagenarians. Maybe you should take the vocabulary class your mother is taking on the internet."

"No thanks." Grace stood up and stretched. "I had no idea we owned so much stuff. Even with most of it over at the house or in storage, I feel this room is a bit overstuffed."

Taylor looked around. "Yeah, it is kind of crowded. Maybe once we get some of our own pictures and artwork on the walls, it will feel more like ours."

Grace crossed the room and wrapped her arms around Taylor. She kissed her lightly on the lips as Taylor's arms encircled her.

"I think once we make love in here, this will feel more like home."

An hour later, they lay entangled in the sheets, a fine film of perspiration covering their bodies.

"You know, there's nothing like making love in a bedroom that shares a wall on one side with Grams and on the other side with Mom and Mudda," Grace said. She rested her chin on top of Taylor's head, which rested on Grace's shoulder. "Makes me wonder if this is such a great idea after all."

Taylor chuckled. "I know. I had to keep reminding myself not to moan too loud."

"Me too. And neither of us is exactly quiet when we're in the throes of making love."

Taylor tilted her head to look up at Grace. "'Throes of making love?' I think you are taking your mother's vocabulary class."

"No. I'm really not. But listening to her has made me realize how much I've dumbed down since I graduated from college. I guess that's made me step up my vocabulary. Am I being too ostentatious?"

Taylor cracked up laughing.

"What? What did I say?"

Chapter Twenty-nine

The next day, Grace inspected the completed studio. Despite the overcast sky and sprinkles, the new skylights let in amazing light.

"Wow. Just wow."

"Is that a good wow or a bad wow?" the contractor's representative, Ms. Boswell, asked.

Grace grinned and looked at her. "It's an amazing wow. Y'all have done a bang-up job. It's beautiful up here. The skylights really were exactly what this room needed. And the floor—this whitewashed pine is stunning. I love everything."

Ms. Boswell smiled and held a clipboard out to her. "In that case, I know you won't mind signing off on the work we did, and then I'll get out of your hair. On the condition I get invited to your first public showing."

Grace laughed as she signed the numerous pages with a big red X marking each place that needed her signature. "Ms. Boswell, you can count on an invitation. Thanks again."

"You're more than welcome. I'll see myself out. I look forward to seeing you again soon."

Grace stood under the center skylight, spread her arms out, and turned in a full circle, spinning until she was dizzy, a grin on her face.

"This is the best studio ever!" she yelled at the top of her lungs.

"Glad you like it."

Grace jumped when she heard her mother's voice at the top of the stairs. She threw her arms around Cecelia and spun her around too.

"Let me go, you hyena," Cecelia said with a laugh, pushing away from her daughter. "Now I'm dizzy. I just wanted to see your studio. I haven't been over here since they first started the work. It's beautiful in here."

"Isn't it?" Grace was breathless, both from her exertion and from her excitement. "I don't have any lights on up here, and look at all this light. I've never had such a beautiful place to work."

"So, what now?"

"I start hauling all those boxes up and here and unpack." Grace grimaced when she thought of the sheer number of boxes she had to lug up the staircase.

"Can I help?" Cecelia asked. "I'll bring all those canvases wrapped in sheets up here."

Grace laughed. "Absolutely not. I should have known you had an ulterior motive for offering. You're trying to get a sneak peek at my new collection."

Cecelia hung her head. "Guilty as charged. My curiosity is absolutely killing me."

"Mom, I love you, but you have to wait just like everyone else. Taylor hasn't even seen it. I'll reveal everything at Grams' and Freddy's birthday party and wedding."

"Speaking of, I hear you wouldn't take Grams shopping for a wedding dress. I don't understand why not?"

Grace looked at her mother to see if she was serious. The mischievous look told Grace all she needed to know.

"I haven't even gone shopping for my own wedding outfit," Grace said. "I'm not taking Grams shopping. You and Mudda or Taylor can take her. Y'all have a lot more patience for that sort of thing than I do."

"And taste." This time, it was Taylor's voice that made Grace jump. She crossed the room and hugged her partner.

"And taste," she agreed. "If it wasn't for you, there's little chance I'd even wear matched socks."

Cecelia laughed. "I can remember many times when you were young that you headed out of the house dressed in the most peculiar ways. I thought for a long time that you just had eclectic taste. It finally dawned on me when you went off to art camp for the first time that you had no idea how to put outfits together."

"I remember that." Grace laughed. "You actually safety pinned matching shorts, shirts, and socks together so I'd know what to wear with what."

"Oh, my gawd." Taylor was laughing so hard her face was red. "You've never told me that story. That explains a lot."

"You are not going to pin my clothes together," Grace said. She wagged her finger at her partner. "Don't even think of it."

"Have you decided what you're going to wear for the wedding?" Cecelia asked Taylor.

Taylor turned a beautiful shade of pink as she nodded.

"You have?" Grace asked. "I haven't seen it."

"And you're not going to," Taylor said. "You're not supposed to see it until the wedding day."

"So, where are you hiding it? I haven't seen anything new in our closet."

"You are a nosy nelly," Cecelia said. "I'm sure Taylor has a safe place, out of your sight. And I'm sure she'll tell me later. Right, Taylor?"

Taylor laughed, nodded, and hugged Cecelia. "You bet. I've got to go now. I told Lois I'd be back. I'm sure she's wondering where I am."

She gave Grace a quick peck and hug and was gone again.

CHAPTER THIRTY

"Where are they going to live?" Grace asked the next time she spoke to Pepper on the phone.

"I was going to ask you the same thing. Aunt Freddy hasn't said anything about it. I asked her the other day. She just shrugged and went back to her puzzle."

"I haven't had the courage to ask Grams. She is so touchy lately. Seems everything I say has to be questioned to the nth degree. Next question, has Freddy said anything about what she wants to wear on the big day?"

Pepper sighed. "Well, she told me something I need to run by you 'cause I'm not sure she's got it right."

"Uh, oh. That sounds ominous."

"She said you agreed to take her shopping."

Grace's mouth fell open, and she couldn't speak for a long moment. "Uh, no. I never said that. In fact, I thought I made it abundantly clear I hate to shop, and I don't want to shop, even for what I'm going to wear to my own wedding. Good grief. Where in the hell did she get that idea?"

"I don't know." Pepper laughed. "You sound like Sonya when it comes to shopping. I have an idea though. What if I take you and Aunt Freddy shopping? I like to shop, and I think I've got fairly good taste."

"Would you really do that?" Grace sighed a long sigh of relief. "I'd appreciate that so much. Mom and Mudda both think I should wear a dress even though I keep telling them that's not going to happen."

"I bet we can find you something snazzy. Aunt Freddy's the same way. She hates dresses. Let's make a date to hit the stores in a couple of days."

"We do need to figure out where they're going to live," Grace said. "Maybe Mom and Taylor can broach the subject with Grams. I'll let you know if we find anything out. Thanks again for offering to go shopping with me."

Grace disconnected the phone and shoved it in her pocket. She did a three-sixty and looked around her studio with a satisfied smile. Everything had a place and was in it. Neatly folded drop cloths lay on the table, ready to protect the new floor for her next project. Blank canvases waited on the worktable or against a wall for her next brainstorm. The new collection sat in the corner, each canvas individually wrapped. The show easels were clean and ready to be set up once the gallery was ready for them. Grace crossed the room to her favorite table, the table where her pencils, charcoal, and tablets had a home, and where she would sketch each new idea before transferring it to canvas.

"I love this room," she said as she sat down and pulled some paper toward her. She chose a pencil and began to sketch her soon-to-be wife's wedding present.

†

"Did you find anything out?" Grace sat across the table from her two mothers. Cecelia poured herself another cup of coffee and raised the carafe in Marie's direction, who shook her head even though she was yawning.

"No. Grams got touchy when I asked her. She's been almost bitchy lately." Cecelia shook her head.

"I noticed that too," Marie said. "She about took my head off this morning when I went in to help her to the bathroom. She wanted to know what took me so long and why Grace wasn't there to help her."

"Good grief. I'm sorry, Mudda. If I'd known she was going to get angry, I wouldn't have asked for your help."

"No problem, kiddo. She showered, went right back to bed, and fell asleep. If I didn't know better, I would think she was keeping some late hours."

Cecelia had her laptop out, paying bills. "Well, that might not be a bad assumption. Look at how many minutes she's using on that phone of hers."

She turned the computer so that Grace and Marie could see what she was talking about.

"Oh, my gawd," Grace said. "She's had the phone for how long? That's more minutes than I use in a month."

"But you don't live a county away from the person you love," Marie said as she took Cecelia's hand. "I'd bet our minutes would have looked like that, or even double that, if we'd had phones when I had to take Momma to Mexico for Abuelito's funeral."

"Our long-distance bill was bad enough." Cecelia kissed Marie's hand. "How about you, Grace? Do yours and Taylor's minutes hit astronomical heights when you're not together?"

Grace nodded. "I see so little of her here lately, between moving, her working on the documentary, me getting the studio set up, and all the permits and shit for the gallery. We talk on the phone every minute we can, but that's not many right now."

"You look tired. Is that why you asked Marie to take care of Grams this morning?"

"I am tired. And I'm cramping on top of that. I took some ibuprofen and went back to bed for a couple of hours. Shouldn't Grams be up by now? I think I'll go check on her."

Before Grace could move, the intercom crackled. "Where is everyone?" Evie asked. "Have I been deserted?"

"I'm on the way," Grace called when Cecelia pressed the button to respond.

Evie was sitting on the edge of her bed, her phone in hand, when Grace got to her bedroom. Grace watched as Evie typed on the screen, her arthritic fingers moving faster than Grace imagined they could.

"Sending your sweetheart a message?" she asked as she pushed the door open and entered the room.

Evie looked up and smiled. She held the phone up so Grace could see the screen. "Have you seen these funny emojis you can get? Freddy and I have so much fun sending them back and forth."

Grace sat down next to Evie and chuckled. "Those are fun. You'll have to show me where you found them. How did you find them?"

Evie shrugged. "I'm not quite sure. Freddy put them on here when we were out there the other day. Pepper and Sonya show her how to do all this stuff, and then she tries to show me how. But I just don't understand these new-fangled things."

"Ha," Grace said as she put her arm around Evie's shoulders. "I think you've done a fine job of figuring it out. Mom was paying bills a while ago and saw how many minutes you and Freddy are on the phone together. Do you even sleep at night anymore?"

"I don't like the idea that Cecelia can know when I'm on the phone," Evie said, her lips pressed into a thin line. "Isn't that an invasion of privacy?"

Grace scooted away from her. "Grams, Mom pays the bill. Because of that, she can see how much data and how many minutes you use, Mudda uses, and she uses. If she were paying for my phone, she'd be able to see that too. It's not an invasion of privacy. She doesn't know what you're saying."

Evie said nothing, but Grace could tell she still wasn't happy. Grace took a deep breath.

"Grams, what's going on? You've been so angry with everyone lately. Are you feeling okay? Are you having second thoughts about something? We're all worried about you."

Evie shook her head. "I'm fine. There's just a lot on my mind."

"Talk to me, Grams. You've always been here for me. Let me be here for you."

Grace watched as tears filled Evie's eyes and spilled out onto her wrinkled cheeks. Grace reached past her and pulled some tissue from the box on the bedside table. She put them in her great-grandmother's hands, but Evie didn't move to wipe the tears away.

"What's up, Grams?" Grace whispered. Evie put her head on Grace's shoulder but didn't say anything. Grace put her arms around her and hugged her. "Are you afraid of something?"

Grace felt an almost imperceptible nod against her shoulder.

"What are you afraid of?"

"Turning ninety-five," Evie said. "And marrying Freddy. What if she loses her mind again? I can't take care of myself, much less her."

"Oh, Grammy." Grace kissed her on the forehead. "I don't know what to tell you. The fact that you're turning ninety-five does scare me. I want you to live forever and…"

"I sorta want to live forever," Evie said. "I lost so much time to live, and I feel like life is finally within reach, except that I'm turning ninety-five."

"But you have Freddy in your life now," Grace said.

"And that kind of scares me too. I love her so much. I've always loved her, more than I know how to describe. More than there are words. But now, we have a chance to spend the rest of our lives together, and realistically, we know that can't be too much longer."

Grace didn't know what to say. She knew that neither Evie nor Freddy would probably still be around even a few years down the road.

"Do you still want to marry Freddy?"

Evie looked up at Grace, shock in her eyes. "Of course I do. We've already lost so much time."

"Grams, we need to know where you and Freddy want to live after y'all get married."

Evie shrugged. "I don't know. I don't want to leave here, and I've been scared to ask Freddy. What if she wants to stay in Weatherford? What will we do then?"

"I think we all need to sit down together and talk about it. You might be surprised. Maybe Freddy wants to live here. Do you think that would work?"

"I don't know," Evie said again. "We're already a bit overcrowded, aren't we?"

"For now. Once Mom and Mudda head off on their adventures, it won't be so bad."

"I'm having second thoughts," Evie said.

"Second thoughts?"

"I don't think I thought all this out as well as I should have."

"What do you mean?" Grace frowned.

"Your mothers have the right to retire and go on their way, but I feel that asking you to stay here with me is going to stifle your painting and delay starting your gallery. I know Taylor will help, but how long will she want to be saddled with an old lady? Maybe two old ladies? Especially with the two of you being newlyweds. I feel like I'm being so selfish."

"You're not being selfish," Grace said. "I think you're being very giving and generous."

A tap on the door frame got their attention. "Are y'all okay?" Cecelia asked. "You've been in here for a long time."

"Just discussing things," Evie said. She struggled to her feet. Grace steadied her until she had her cane and her balance. "Such as where Freddy and I want to live. The answer is I don't know. I want to stay here, but we're already bursting the seams of this house. And I don't want to live in Weatherford. So, there's that. I'm hungry. What's for breakfast?"

"It's lunch time," Cecelia said as she took Evie's elbow and guided her out of the room.

†

"Well, I might have a solution," Pepper said after Grace relayed the conversation she had with Evie when they met for lunch a few days later.

"Oh? Thank God. What is it?"

"Sonya is being transferred to Arlington, and I have an interview with the Fort Worth Historical Society. We've been worried about what to do about Freddy, and I think your dilemma might actually be our salvation."

Grace tilted her head in confusion. "Do what?"

"I know you need to be closer to your studio than across two backyards, and I also know you and Taylor are going to want more privacy than you'll have living in that house with Evie, and maybe Aunt Freddy, and your moms when they're in town."

"Yes, and?"

"Sonya and I need a place to live so she doesn't have to get up at the crack of dawn to be in Arlington by nine every morning. And while I can do my job from just about anywhere that has internet access, it would be a lot easier to do it in closer proximity to who I work for."

"Do I have to pull teeth to figure out what you're getting at?" Grace asked. She wanted to reach across the table and shake the words out of Pepper.

Pepper grinned. "It's just such fun to watch you wriggle," she said.

Grace rolled her eyes. "Please. Out with it. What are you saying?"

"What if Sonya and I move in with Evie and Freddy in Evie's house? That kills a whole bunch of birds with one stone. Aunt Freddy and Evie will be together, and we can take care of them when Cecelia and Marie are on the road. You'll be able to be in your studio and gallery, and you and Taylor will have your privacy."

Grace's eyes lit up. "I think you may have hit on the perfect solution. The only problem is what will happen to Freddy's house out in Weatherford?"

"My brother and his partner's lease is up on his apartment at the end of June, and they sort of like the idea of living rent-free in a house with a yard. They want a dog and to plant a garden. They'll take good care of the place, probably better care than we have. And they have agreed to keep Prince and Gene."

"You've got it all figured out. If you weren't married and I wasn't engaged, I'd kiss you."

CHAPTER THIRTY-ONE

Grace fell backwards onto the bed, her arms flung out to either side. She closed her eyes and shook her head. She heard the bedroom door open and close, but she didn't open her eyes or move, even when someone sat on the edge of the bed.

"Hard day?" Taylor asked, running a finger from Grace's wrist to her shoulder.

Grace shivered as goose bumps formed behind Taylor's finger.

"Stressful," Grace said. She opened one eye and looked at her partner. "I hate shopping as it is, but with Pepper and Freddy, it exhausted me."

"Was it a successful trip?"

"Yes. I bought my wedding outfit, and Pepper helped Freddy pick hers out. But it wasn't an easy trip. Pepper wouldn't let me buy the first thing I chose. She insisted we look at lots of stuff before making a decision."

"And did you buy the first outfit you looked at?"

The grin on Taylor's face made Grace want to throw something at her, but she refrained. She rubbed her face with both hands and shook her head.

"No. No, I ended up buying something altogether different."

"Will I like it?"

Grace sat up. "All I can say is you better."

Taylor laughed and put her arms around Grace and pulled her close for a kiss. Grace melted into her embrace and allowed one of her hands to find the curve of Taylor's breast, but Taylor leaned away from her touch.

"Not right now," Taylor said. "Everyone's waiting for us to go to dinner."

Grace groaned. "I forgot. Damn it all. Let me go get cleaned up, and I'll be right out. Where are we going anyway?"

"Bar-be-que House."

Grace groaned again. "Put some antacid in your purse, please."

The restaurant seated the group in a room to the side of the main dining area. Though surprised, Grace liked that they had the room and privacy.

"This is nice," she said. "I didn't even know this room was available."

"I asked for it," Marie said. "I know we've got a lot to discuss, and I felt we had a couple of choices. Either find a place where we could have a private dining area—such as here—or have some catering brought to the house. This was less expensive."

A bit of organized confusion reigned while everyone settled in, ordered drinks, and studied the menu. After everyone placed their orders, they made small talk until their food arrived. Laughter was abundant as they enjoyed their meals. Once the wait staff cleared their plates and served banana pudding and after-dinner coffee, Pepper stood and got everyone's attention.

"I know there's been a lot of concern about where Aunt Freddy and Evie would live once they are married."

Evie and Freddy smiled at each other as Freddy stretched her arm over the back of Evie's chair.

"Grace and I talked about it a few days ago, and I think we may have a solution." Pepper told the group her idea for her, Sonya, and Freddy to move into Evie's house.

"That way, Grace and Taylor can live in their new house, and Grace can concentrate on her painting, and Taylor can work on her documentary while they have some privacy as newlyweds. Evie and Aunt Freddy will be together, and Cecelia and Marie can travel without worrying about things being okay here."

"And Carter will live in my house," Freddy said. "He asked me if he can build a garden. I told him, only if he brings Evie some zucchini, because she makes the best zucchini bread in the world."

Evie laughed and slapped Freddy on the arm. "I haven't made zucchini bread in years."

Freddy's face fell. "Oh. But, well, uhm…"

"If Carter brings us some zucchini, if I can get someone to help me, I'll make you some zucchini bread," Evie said. She leaned over and kissed Freddy on the cheek. "Thank you for remembering that I used to make it. I hadn't thought about it for a long time."

Freddy's face turned pink, but the smile on her face warmed Grace's heart. She reached over and took Taylor's hand under the table.

"Mom," Grace said. "What do you think of this idea?"

Cecelia and Marie looked at each other. Grace didn't like the look on her mother's face.

"What's up, Mom?" she asked. "You look worried."

"What about when Marie and I aren't traveling? Where will we stay? We're not going to be on the road one hundred percent of the time."

"Oh, Cecelia," Pepper and Sonya said in unison. They looked at each other, and Pepper continued, "We're not going to take your home away from you. The house is yours and will always be your home. We're going to live there to look after these two lovebirds and to be closer to our new jobs. If it will make you feel better, when you're in town, we can find someplace else to stay."

"Mom, I don't think it will be that much different than me and Taylor staying there," Grace said.

Cecelia took a deep breath, and Marie patted her arm.

"I don't know why I'm having a hard time with this," Cecelia admitted. "It's a good idea and a perfect solution. But, for some reason, I feel displaced. I didn't expect…I don't quite know what I expected."

She pulled a napkin from the dispenser and dried her eyes. Grace stood up and walked around the table. She knelt beside her mother's chair and hugged her.

"A lot has happened in a short amount of time," Marie said. She had her arm across the back of Cecelia's chair and rubbed her shoulder. "We're picking up the RV in two days. It's suddenly making it real. A change of plans in any way just sort of throws a kink in the gears."

"I'm sorry," Pepper said. "I didn't mean to make things harder than they have to be."

"Oh, Pepper, you didn't," Cecelia said, still drying tears from her face. "I lay in bed last night worrying about all this. You just gave us a perfect solution. It hit me wrong for some reason. I guess I thought it was my responsibility to come up with a solution. I'm sorry."

Sonya laughed, and Pepper turned and gave her a strange look.

"Oh, don't play dumb," Sonya said to her. "I just heard your own words coming from her mouth. You're always telling me you feel it's your responsibility to take care of things."

Marie laughed as well. She patted Cecelia's shoulder. "Looks like you've met your match, hon. You got beat to the punch this time 'round."

"I guess I did." Cecelia grinned at Pepper. "I think your idea is a good one. My one question is this: Has anyone asked these two what they think of it?"

She motioned to Evie and Freddy, who had their heads together. They were so engrossed in each other that they didn't seem to realize they were the center of attention. Taylor reached across Grace's empty chair and tapped Evie on the shoulder. The older woman jumped and looked up. Everyone laughed at the startled look on her face.

"What?" she asked. "Do I have something on my face? Freddy, do I have something on my face?"

Freddy tilted Evie's chin up with a finger and studied her face. She shook her head. "Not that I can see, my dear."

Grace went back to her chair and took Evie's hand. "Grams, what do you and Freddy think of living at your house once y'all are married and having Pepper and Sonya living there with you instead of me and Taylor?"

"I think it's a good idea," she said. "I don't know why there has to be so much discussion about it."

"Then I guess it's settled," Freddy said. "Can I have some more banana pudding?"

†

Taylor sat on the end of the bed, taping the flaps of the box in front of her closed. "We just unpacked these boxes, and now we're repacking them."

"Yep. But once we unpack them again, that should be the last time," Grace said. "It will be nice to have our own place without worrying about it being taken away from us."

"There is that." Taylor stretched, yawned, and lay back on the bed. She flung one arm over her eyes. "I'm exhausted. Burning the candle at both ends and in the middle is catching up with me."

Grace stretched out beside her and put a hand on Taylor's midriff. "How much longer 'til the documentary is finished?"

"Evie and Freddy have given us permission to tape their wedding and part of their birthday party." Taylor sat up and put her hand over her mouth.

"What, babe? What's wrong?" Grace sat up beside her.

"It just dawned on me that I have to have your written permission before we can tape at the house and in the gallery."

"What are you worried about? You know I haven't got a problem with that."

"Oh, there's so many legal ramifications about taping in a business," Taylor said. "I've learned there is much more to this process than I ever knew. I love it and—oh, you're going to shoot me."

"Why?" Grace closed her eyes for a split second. *What is she up to?*

"I want to go back to school," Taylor said. "I want to take courses in cinematography and film and learn how to do what Lois does."

"Uhm, instead of finishing your doctorate?" Grace asked.

Taylor nodded, her eyes wide. Grace could tell she was close to crying. She wrapped her arms around her and hugged her.

"You know all I want for you is for you to be happy," she said. "If that means going back to school, then that's what you need to do."

"I love you," Taylor said. "Thank you for understanding. I love you so much."

Chapter Thirty-two

"So, where have y'all decided to go on your honeymoon?" Cecelia asked a few days later. She and Grace sat at the table in the new RV, which now had a place of honor in the driveway of Evie's house. They were folding freshly laundered kitchen and bathroom linens for the home away from home.

Grace shook her head. "I think it's going to have to be put off for a bit. Taylor and Lois will be in the final editing process on the documentary, and I've already got appointments to speak to some new up-and-coming artists whose sculptures I might be interested in showing in the gallery. And now Taylor wants to go back to school to study how to make films."

Cecelia stopped folding a cup towel, holding it up in mid-air.

"Back to undergraduate school?" She put the towel down and leaned on the table. "I know you and Taylor have been together for almost four years, but how well do you actually know her? Her family has never been part of your lives. It seems like you've been putting her through school since the two of you met."

Grace's mouth fell open. She also put down the towel she was folding. She blinked hard to keep tears from overflowing her eyes.

"Wow. Just wow. I can't believe that you think she's a gold digger. That's the last thing she is. Her family isn't part of our lives by their choice. As far as they're concerned, she's going straight to hell, as am I, and you and Mudda, and Pepper and…" She stopped and took a deep breath. "And as for school, she has student loans that are threatening to drown us, but I'm not going to stop her from pursuing something she loves. You encouraged my art, and you backed me when I chose art as a major instead of something that made more sense to survive in this world—"

Cecelia put a gentle hand over Grace's mouth to shut her up.

"I'm sorry, Grace. But I'm your mother. If I didn't worry and ask the hard questions, I'd be falling down on my job. I love Taylor, and you know that. I know you love her. I just want to make sure you're going to be okay."

Grace nodded, and Cecelia dropped her hand.

"I do love her, Mom. I've watched you and Mudda my whole life and have known what true love looks like since I was tiny. And now I see Pepper and Sonya, and see it again. And, oh, my God, the love Grams and Freddy share." Tears spilled over at the thought of the elderly women. "Ninety-five years old, lost seven decades together, overcame psychological dementia, and their love is stronger than ever. That's the kind of love I want the world to see when they look at me and Taylor."

Cecelia took Grace's hands in her own. "And they do, sweetheart. I'm sorry I questioned it. I love you so much."

"I love you more."

Chapter Thirty-three

Grace woke up when Taylor flopped down onto the bed beside her.

"You're home late," she said after they shared a kiss. "I was going to order Chinese, but I fixed a sandwich instead."

Taylor laughed. "I saw. You left the mayo on the counter."

Grace slapped her head. "Good grief. I'm sorry. Does it need to be thrown out?"

"No. It's okay. I put it up." Taylor sat up, pulled her T-shirt over her head. and turned so Grace could unhook her bra. She giggled and slapped Grace's hands away when they snuck their way around to her front. "I'm sorry I'm so late. You might want to check your phone 'cause every time I tried to call, it went straight to voicemail."

Grace turned over and plucked her phone off the bedside table. "Damn. I let the battery die. Good grief."

"Lois has one of these doohickies where you just lay your phone on it, and it charges—no wires or anything. I think we should see if we can get a few for around the house."

"It seems like you're spending more time with Lois than you are with me," Grace said.

Taylor turned and looked at her. "Do I hear a hint of jealousy?" she asked. "You know we're wrapping up as much of the filming and editing as we can before the party next week. And you have no reason to be jealous. Lois is happily married and told me today she just found out she's carrying their first baby. I don't think her feet touched the ground all day." She pulled her robe off the footboard of the bed. "I'm going to take a shower."

Grace sat with her dead phone in her hand, her mouth hanging open. She contemplated whether she should follow her partner and try to make things right or give Taylor some space. She knew from past experience that Taylor needed her space for a while after they had a disagreement. But she didn't think this counted as a disagreement. She plugged her phone in and went into the bathroom.

Steam filled the en suite and coated the mirror. Grace pulled a thick towel from the towel rack and leaned against the wall next to the shower. After a few minutes, her hair was limp, and she was sweating. By the time Grace considered giving up, Taylor turned off the water and opened the shower door. Grace smiled at the sight of her partner's glistening body and held the towel open for her. Taylor allowed her to wrap the towel around her and didn't struggle when Grace kept her in an embrace.

"I'm sorry I made you think I was jealous of Lois. I'm not jealous of her, but of the time this project is keeping us apart," Grace said. When Taylor stiffened and started to say something, Grace stopped her with a soft kiss to her lips. "Let me finish. Please?"

Taylor nodded but didn't relax.

"I'm almost certain I know what you were going to say," Grace said. She leaned her forehead against Taylor's. "I know my business has taken me away from home for weeks at a time, and this is different because you're home every night. Am I close?"

Taylor nodded again.

"Since Freddy has come back into Grams' life, I've been thinking about how much time they lost and how much time we lose every time I travel without you." Grace's eyes filled with tears. "I love you, Taylor Bradford. From now on, I will only travel if you come with me. I'll still do murals, but only if I can be home every night. I don't want us to chance losing any more time together."

Taylor wrapped her arms around Grace's neck, and the kiss she gave her made Grace's knees weak.

"I love you too, Grace Jenkins. You only take jobs that excite you, and I don't want you to refuse work you're excited about. I'm sorry I've spent so much time apart from you. I can't promise it will get any better until the documentary actually airs. Can we go into the bedroom to talk? I need to brush the tangles out of my hair while it's still wet."

Grace stepped back and held out her hand. Once in the bedroom, she retrieved Taylor's brush from their vanity and sat down on the bed. She scooted back, and Taylor sat between her outspread legs. Grace started brushing Taylor's hair, starting at the bottom, and working the tangles out a bit at a time.

"Umm." Taylor sighed, and Grace felt her relax some more. "It's been a long time since you brushed my hair. Until just now, I hadn't realized how much I missed it."

"I've missed brushing it for you. I love how thick it is and how long you've let it get." Grace pulled Taylor's hair away from her face and into a loose ponytail that she brushed until the sheen was almost too much to look at. "You've never let it get this long in all the time we've been together."

Taylor chuckled. "I'm letting it grow so I can put it up for the wedding. Can you believe our wedding is only a couple of weeks away?"

Grace arranged Taylor's hair over her shoulders so she could kiss the back of Taylor's neck. "I know. I think we should start our honeymoon right now."

Taylor bent her head forward to give Grace more skin to minister to. She let the towel drop, and this time didn't stop Grace when Grace reached around and cupped her breasts.

†

The next week was so busy that Grace and Taylor both just fell into bed and slept at the end of each long day. Grace finished up the last details to get the gallery up and running and ready for the weekend's festivities. The last inspection by the city to make sure everything was safe and up to code racked Grace's nerves, even though she knew everything was okay.

At the same time, Pepper and Sonya were helping Cecelia and Marie move a second bed into Evie's room. Grace knew Evie wanted a queen or king-sized bed and wasn't happy that a second hospital bed was being moved in instead.

"She's driving me nuts," Cecelia said as she came into Grace and Taylor's house through the back sliding doors.

"Do I assume you're talking about Grams?" Grace asked as she hugged her mother. "You want some coffee or iced tea?"

Cecelia flopped into the closest easy chair in the family area. She splayed her legs out in front of her and hung her arms over the side. “Sweet tea, please. And a cool cloth for my head, if you don’t mind.”

Grace complied and sat across from her mother once she served the tea. “What’s wrong, Mom?”

“Grams is driving me up the frickin’ ass wall,” Cecelia said. Sitting up, she buried her face in the damp washcloth. “She is so angry that we aren’t getting her and Freddy a big bed. She keeps reminding me that she’s not a child who needs a crib, and neither is Freddy. I even called her doctor and talked to her about it. She nixed that idea as soon as she heard it. Now, Grams is threatening not to come to her birthday party and is saying she and Freddy are going to elope.”

“Oh, good grief.” Grace stood up and paced around the room. “Is she serious about not coming to the party, et cetera?”

“I don’t know,” Cecelia admitted. “She’s become a grouchy old woman ever since Mom died.”

Cecelia’s voice caught, and Grace saw tears in her eyes before Cecelia once again pressed the cloth to her face. Grace went and sat on the edge of the chair and rubbed her mother’s back.

“I’ve noticed that too,” she said. “She ignored me when I tried to talk to her about it. I’m not sure what to do to help her or you. I miss Grandma too, so much, but I can’t imagine what you and Grams are feeling.”

Cecelia patted Grace’s leg. “Thanks, baby. I appreciate you saying that. Marie and Pepper were trying to talk to Grams and Freddy about the sleeping arrangements when I escaped and ran over here.”

“What is Freddy saying?”

"Nothing, and that's part of the problem. Grams wants her to speak up and take up for her, and Freddy just sits in a chair in the corner and grins. Pepper's afraid the stress is making her regress, but I don't think Grams understands that could be happening."

"Shit." Grace stood up and paced the room. "Do you think I should go over and see if there's anything I can do?"

Cecelia shrugged at the same time as she nodded. "I don't know if it will do any good, but I don't think it can do any harm. If nothing else, maybe you can get Freddy out of there and over here where it's quieter."

Grace took a deep breath and bent to hug her mother. "I'll be back, I hope."

At Evie's house, she found Marie in the kitchen, leaning against the refrigerator, and Pepper resting her head on the kitchen table.

"Y'all look like you've lost the battle," Grace said.

"Did your mom send you over as reinforcement?" Pepper asked without raising her head, her voice muffled.

"Sort of. Is Grams still in her room?"

Marie nodded but didn't say anything. Grace went and kissed her on the cheek and patted the back of Pepper's head before heading down the hall to Evie's bedroom. She tapped on the door and pushed it open. She smiled at the sight that met her eyes. Evie and Freddy were sitting side by side on Evie's bed, their backs against the raised head of the bed, their foreheads together and clasping hands in front of them.

"Can I come in?" she asked.

Evie looked up and nodded. Grace could see she had been crying.

"Are you okay, Grams?" she asked as she approached the bed. She took a few tissues from the box and handed them to her great-grandmother.

"Just tired. And frustrated. And disappointed. And worried," she said as she dabbed at her eyes. She offered a tissue to Freddy, who also dried the tears on her cheeks.

"Mom told me about the issue with the bed," Grace said. She held her breath for a moment, anticipating the anger from Evie. But all Evie did was nod.

"Yes. I understand everyone's concern about me falling again," she said. "But why does Freddy have to have a hospital bed? She doesn't back in Weatherford."

Grace perched on the edge of the bed and patted Evie's outstretched leg. "I know. Do you want me to ask them if they can move in a regular bed for her?"

"I already tried that," Freddy said, startling Grace. "They said they knew Evie would try to sleep with me, and she might fall off my bed. So, both of us have to sleep in a hospital bed."

"Humph." Evie shook her head. "They're cribs for adults, that's all they are."

"I know that's how you feel, Grams. And, in a way, you're right. But we love you so much, and we don't want to take a chance of you getting hurt again. You gave us such a scare when you broke your hip."

Evie sighed. "I know. It scared me too. I understand why y'all are insisting on this. And I know I'm not going to change anyone's mind." The tears started again, and she took Freddy's hand. "But I want us to be able to sleep together. And even as small as we both are, there's not room for both of us in this bed."

Grace bowed her head, unsure what to say to make her great-grandmother feel better. She jumped when she heard Taylor's voice at her shoulder.

"I wonder if they make bigger beds," Taylor said. "I think we should see if we can find a wider hospital bed."

"Finally," Freddy said. "Finally, a voice of reason."

The next day, Grace, Cecelia, and Pepper called every medical furniture dealer in the metroplex and beyond. Late in the afternoon, Pepper gave a thumbs-up before scribbling some information from the person she was speaking to on the tablet in front of her. She disconnected and looked up with a grin.

"A medical supply store in Austin carries an extra-wide hospital bed meant for obese patients. They will deliver one to us on Wednesday of next week. I explained we need it by Saturday and why. The manager promised he'd try to expedite the order but couldn't make any hard and fast promises."

The three women high-fived each other.

"What's going on in there?" Evie called from the front room. She and Freddy were working on a jigsaw puzzle spread on a card table set up just for that purpose.

Grace, Cecelia, and Pepper joined them, and Pepper repeated the information she had about the bed.

"I hope they can get it here by Saturday," Evie said. She took Freddy's hand. "I don't want us to have to spend our wedding night sleeping in separate beds."

The three younger women laughed when Freddy turned bright red and bowed her head.

"What?" Evie said, nudging Freddy. "What are you so embarrassed about? They're all lesbians and either married or about to be married. They know what happens on wedding nights."

It was Grace's turn to blush. Looking at Cecelia and Pepper, she was gratified to see that they too, were blushing.

"Now, look at them." Evie pointed. Freddy started laughing, and after a moment, all five women were laughing so hard that they were holding their sides.

"What's going on in here?" Sonya stood in the doorway, and when the others saw her, they once again dissolved into almost hysterical laughter.

CHAPTER THIRTY-FOUR

Thursday afternoon, Grace called the manager at the Dairy Queen.

"I've already designed a big ice cream cake," the manager said. "I just need to know what flavor the two of them like best."

"Gee. Now that's a good question," Grace said. "I've never seen Grams eat anything but vanilla. She loves banana splits and hot fudge sundaes, if that helps. As for Freddy, I hate to admit I don't know her that well."

"I'll stick with vanilla, in that case. What time should I bring it by? The party and wedding are going to be at the gallery, right?"

"Right."

They discussed the best time for delivery, and Grace disconnected. The next thing on her list was to call the florist and the caterer. She dutifully checked off each item as she completed the task. Finally, she headed to the gallery. They had painted the walls as pale a gray as they could get without it being white, and installed track lighting that could be moved to spotlight individual pieces of art. Twelve empty easels stood around the periphery of the room waiting for Grace's new collection. As she stood in the middle of the room, her hands on her hips, the doorbell rang. The folding chairs were being delivered. She directed the men where to stack them, pulled the list from her pocket, and ticked that item off. That was the day's final task, and after locking the front door, she checked her studio to ensure each canvas was properly covered. She then retired to the family area and plopped on the sofa, the remote control in her hand.

Grace didn't know what time it was when she woke up, but darkness startled her—both outside and inside the house were dark. When she reached for her phone and realized it wasn't in her pocket, she panicked. She searched the sofa cushions and came up empty.

"What in the world did I do with it?" she asked, speaking out loud to thin air. Just as she was about to head out the door to Evie's house, the faint sound of her phone ringing led her up the stairs to her studio. She grabbed the phone off her desk, but not in time to answer the call.

"Twelve missed calls? Good grief."

She pushed redial beside Taylor's caller ID and prayed everything was okay, and that Taylor wouldn't kill her.

"Where are you?" Taylor's voice was full of worry and tears. "I've been trying to call. Your mother's been trying to call, and you're not answering, and the house is dark, and your mudda said the doors are locked. I was about to call the police and the hospitals and—"

"Taylor, slow down, hon," Grace said. "I'm sorry. I am home. I left my phone upstairs in the studio and fell asleep on the sofa with all the lights off. I didn't hear the phone ring or

Mudda come to the house. I'm sorry. Oh, sweetie. I'm okay. Please don't cry. Where are you?"

"I'm still at the studio. My car broke down. Your mothers are on the way to pick me up, and then we were going to come to the house. I thought you'd given them keys to the house. We've been beside ourselves."

"I'm sorry, sweets. Really. I don't know why I slept so hard. You know I don't usually. Do you want me to wait here or go to Grams'?"

"Either call Pepper and let them know you're okay or go over so they know."

"Does Grams know I'm missing?" Grace was back downstairs and in the family area. She sat on the sofa and pulled her shoes on, ready to run across the yards.

"No. We didn't want her to worry until we knew there was something to worry about." Grace heard voices in the background. "Your mothers are here. I'm handing the phone to your mom."

†

"How many times do I have to say, 'I'm sorry?'" Grace said to Taylor's back. "I didn't leave my phone upstairs on purpose. Or fall asleep on purpose."

Taylor didn't say anything. She shrugged her robe on over her pajamas and left the room, carefully pulling the door closed behind her with a gentle click. Grace would have preferred she had slammed it, but she knew better than to expect that. Taylor had the silent treatment down to an art, including walking across a room and closing doors. Grace wished she could learn to be like that, but her temper was loud and volatile. She had realized over the past few years that the silent treatment was much more effective and hurt worse than she had ever hurt before.

With a deep breath, she opened the bedroom door. She looked down the dark hall and almost cried when she saw the light shining from beneath one of the guest room doors. *I don't want to sleep alone tonight. Or any night.* She walked to the door and leaned her forehead against it. She tapped on it but, as she expected, heard nothing from the other side.

"Please don't do this, Taylor," she begged. "I'm sorry. I love you. Please, let's not sleep alone tonight. Please, honey. Please."

The door opened, and Grace almost fell forward. She started to smile until she saw the look on Taylor's face.

"Begging is not becoming to you, Grace Marie. I am beyond angry with you right now. And I'm tired. And I have a lot to think about. And I think you have a lot to think about. So, please, leave me alone. We'll talk tomorrow."

And with that, the bedroom door closed, once again with a gentle click. Grace leaned on the door until the light beyond it went out. She went to the kitchen and pulled a Dr. Pepper from the refrigerator. For the first time in a long time, she wished it were something stronger. She slid the patio door open and stepped outside. It was oppressively warm for an early-June night. She didn't last long as the mosquitoes wasted no time in discovering she was without repellent.

With a deep sigh, Grace plopped into the easy chair and propped her legs on the ottoman.

"What do I do now?" she asked the darkness. "Have I screwed up beyond repair this time?"

There were no answers coming to her. The tears that had threatened ever since she'd talked to her mother earlier in the evening began to flow. With her elbows on her knees and her face in her hands, she sat forward, sobbing. She sobbed out of fear, grief, exhaustion, and more fear. She sobbed until she had no tears left, and then she hiccupped. But she still had no relief. She curled into a ball in the chair and finally fell asleep, a restless sleep that left her more exhausted than when she fell asleep. The morning sun peeking over the neighborhood's mature trees and into her back window woke her. Her restricted muscles sprang back to life as she stretched.

She limped into the kitchen, put water in the Keurig, and chose a coffee pod from the rack. She reached into the cabinet for a mug and almost dropped it as arms snaked around her from behind. Taylor kissed her earlobe.

"I'm sorry," Taylor said. "I shouldn't have been so horrible last night."

Grace wanted to agree but knew from hard experience that it wasn't prudent. Instead, she turned and wrapped her arms around Taylor and kissed her.

"I'm sorry too," she said. "I really didn't mean to leave you stranded and worried."

"I know." Taylor hung her head. "I—well, I did something stupid that just made how I felt all that much worse."

Grace used a finger under Taylor's chin to lift her head so she could see her eyes. "What, sweets? What did you do?"

Taylor shook her head as tears flowed down her face. "I called my dad and asked him to come help me. He's a mechanic, for God's sake, but he said no. Actually, he said, only if I came home with him and promised never to see you again."

Grace pulled Taylor close. "I'm sorry he said that. But I'm so glad you chose to come home to me. I'm sorry I wasn't available when you needed me."

"We've got a lot to do today," Taylor said. She stepped out of Grace's arms. "I'll scramble us some eggs if you'll make me a cup of coffee. You can tell me what you got accomplished yesterday so we can coordinate our efforts today."

Grace's arms felt empty as she watched Taylor pull the bowl of eggs from the refrigerator. She turned back to the Keurig and hoped Taylor wouldn't hear the tears in her voice as she told her everything she had done the day before. They ate breakfast and planned their day, but Grace still had a sense of emptiness, of something still unresolved, as she put her dishes in the dishwasher and headed for the shower.

†

"I cannot believe you," Cecelia said when Grace called her after Taylor took Grace's car to run some last-minute errands. "What if we hadn't been available to help Taylor? What if you hadn't woken up when you did? Have you thought about any of that? I thought you were more responsible than that."

"Good-bye, Mother," Grace said through gritted teeth. "I'll call back later, maybe."

She could hear Cecelia yelling, "Don't you hang up on me," as she disconnected the call. The thought of silencing her phone tempted her, but she had learned her lesson about that. Instead, she chose "Ignore" instead of "Accept" when Cecelia called her back. She did the same when Marie called.

The pounding on the patio door a few minutes later didn't surprise her. She fought the urge to ignore them but went downstairs as slowly as possible. Turning the corner, she was surprised to see Evie and Freddy instead of Cecelia or Marie. Evie was in her wheelchair, pounding on the door with the head of her cane as Freddy clung to the wheelchair's handles. Grace rushed over and slid the door open.

"What the hell are you up to, young lady?" Evie said, swinging the cane at Grace. Grace jumped back but still felt the sting of the cane on her shin.

"Damn it, Grams. That hurt. Good grief. I've already been through the mill with Taylor and Mom. I don't need you yelling at me and abusing me with that damn cane. Freddy, come in and get a drink of water, and then wheel this old woman back to her house."

"Don't you talk to me like that," Evie warned, her voice low.

"Grams, for once you're in the wrong," Grace said, her hands on her hips. "I messed up last night. I know that. Taylor and I talked about things. I've made my apologies, groveled to her, and slept alone last night. Now, at least as far as I know, we're okay. I'm sorry I worried Mom and Mudda, and if they'd give me a chance without chewing me up and spitting me out, I'd tell them so. I'm not even sure what your problem is since Taylor told me they hadn't told you what was going on. So, unless you have a valid reason for treating me like this, I suggest you go back and start over again."

"You are standing in the house I bought for you—"

Grace put a hand up to stop her. "If you're going to use this house for ammunition whenever you're mad at me, then I'll be moved out by this evening and have the deed back in your name as soon as the courthouse opens Monday. You go ahead and have your birthday party and wedding here, but I won't be in attendance. Now, if you'll excuse me, it seems I have some packing to do."

She turned to walk away, pulling her phone from her pocket and trying not to let Evie see the tears that threatened.

"Wait, Grace." Grace stopped when she felt Freddy's hand on her arm. "I don't think I understand what's going on here, but everyone being so upset is scaring me."

"I'm sorry, Freddy." Grace put her arm across the smaller woman's shoulders. "I don't mean to scare you. I don't know what Grams' temper was like when y'all were young, but right now it's out of order, and it scares me too. I love you, Freddy. I wish I'd known you when y'all were younger."

"You are so like she is," Freddy said. She grinned. "I was on the receiving end of her anger more times than I can count, starting as soon as we could walk and talk."

"I don't like that y'all are talking about me, and I can't hear what you're saying," Evie said.

"We're talking about your temper, my dear," Freddy said as she walked back to Evie's wheelchair. "Neither of us is sure why you're so angry. I told Grace that it's scaring me."

Evie pulled Freddy down and kissed her on the cheek. "I'm sorry I scared you, Freddy. I love you and never meant to do that. But I'm mad at her, not at you, so there's no need to be afraid."

"But, Grams, I don't even know why you're mad at me," Grace said. She pulled a dining chair close to Evie for Freddy, and then one for herself. "You know I'll own up when I've done something wrong, and that I'll do everything in my being to make things right. But I don't deserve double jeopardy, or triple, or more. Taylor had a right to be pissed at me. Mom and Mudda have a right to be pissed at me, but they should at least give me a chance to apologize. But why are you so upset?"

Evie shook her head. She took Freddy's hand. Seeing how much her great-grandmother trembled alarmed Grace. She reached over and covered their clasped hands with one of her own.

"What's up, Grams?" she asked.

"Cee said you hung up on her and then wouldn't answer your phone when she or Marie called. She didn't tell me why, and I'm not even sure what all happened last night that got everyone so riled up. I could just see how hurt and upset it made her when you wouldn't talk to her, so I asked—"

"Told," Freddy said.

"Told," Evie corrected herself. "Told Freddy to wheel me over here so I could knock some sense into your head. I guess I should have found out more before I did that. I'm sorry."

"Thank you, Grams. I love how much you care for all of us. But why do I have a feeling there's more to this than that? Why are you shaking so much?"

"I was wondering that myself," Freddy said. Grace felt her squeeze Evie's hand. "Are you sick, my dear?"

Evie shook her head. "No, I'm not sick. I think I'm more nervous about tomorrow than I thought."

"About getting married or turning ninety-five?" Freddy asked. "I can stop one but not the other."

Evie chuckled, but the laugh didn't reach her eyes. "Neither. I'm nervous about Taylor's documentary. I know they're going to film tomorrow and that has me on edge."

"Do you want me to call Taylor so she can come talk to you about it?" Grace asked.

Evie and Freddy shared a look, then looked at Grace, and nodded in unison.

"I think that would be a good idea," Evie said.

Thirty minutes later, Lois and a man Grace hadn't met yet arrived, and Taylor returned a short time later. The six of them gathered in the gallery. Grace checked her watch.

"We have about forty minutes before some more stuff for tomorrow is being delivered," she said.

"In that case, let's figure out what the problem is," Lois said. "Evie, can you tell us what makes you so much more nervous about this than the other times we've taped you?"

"I honestly am not sure," Evie admitted. "To tell the truth, I'm not so sure it's about this taping as it is knowing y'all are going to put it on TV for the whole world to see."

"That's not going to happen right away," Taylor said. "Right, Jeb?"

The man turned out to be one of the financial backers of the documentary, and also one of the producers. "That's right. Once we finish taping and editing, we have to find a channel to air the documentary. The other backer and I feel one of the public networks will be most interested. It could feasibly be early next year before it airs."

"And you and Freddy will see the film before any other decisions are made," Taylor said.

They talked for another fifteen or twenty minutes before Evie felt more comfortable about the process. Lois and Jeb left out the front door, while Freddy pushed Evie's chair out the back door and headed across the yard. Grace hugged Taylor.

"Thank you," she said. "Everyone's in the worst moods I've seen in a while. After the delivery, I'm going to go talk to Mom and Mudda. I love you."

"Do you mind if I go to the studio and go over things with Lois?" Taylor asked. "I want to be sure there won't be any snafus to make Evie nervous tomorrow."

"I think that's a good idea." Grace gave Taylor a quick kiss. "I'll see you later. I love you."

CHAPTER THIRTY-FIVE

Saturday, June seventeenth, dawned clear and warm. The high for the day was in the mid-nineties, and Grace was glad the party and wedding were going to be indoors rather than outside. Taylor lay on her stomach, her arms crossed under her head, the sheet barely covering her butt. The urge to trace her partner's spine from neck to tailbone tempted Grace, but she knew starting that would make them late, and they had a lot left to do before their guests arrived. Instead, she kissed one of Taylor's shoulders and headed for the en suite bathroom.

Even though it was already hot outside, Grace ran her shower as hot as she could endure. As she rinsed the soap from her body, she heard Taylor moving around the bathroom. She turned the water off, but before she could get out of the shower, Taylor stepped in and wrapped her arms around her. Grace loved the feel of her partner's bare body against her own, but she knew they didn't have time.

"Mmm, I love you," she said as Taylor kissed along her collarbone and squeezed her butt cheeks. "I love you, but we don't have time. Oh, gawd, I want to tell you not to stop."

"Then tell me not to stop," Taylor mouthed into Grace's chest as her mouth moved to the hardened nipple of one of Grace's breasts. One of Taylor's hands slid to Grace's front and between her legs. Grace leaned against the shower wall, bent her knees, and spread her legs even while her brain told her to tell Taylor to stop.

"Oh, gawd," she groaned as she felt her body respond to Taylor's ministrations. She pumped against Taylor's hand as an orgasm grew and erupted from her groin.

She fell limp against Taylor, who held her up while she kissed her. Taylor guided her to the built-in bench and turned the shower back on. Grace leaned against the wall and watched as Taylor soaped up the scrubby. She washed the sex perspiration off Grace before bathing herself. Taylor made taking a shower into a sexually provocative dance. Grace felt the heat growing once more and knew if she gave in, their entire day would be behind. She stood up, gave Taylor a quick kiss, and escaped from the shower stall.

After getting dressed, she went to the kitchen, turned on the Keurig, and poured herself a bowl of cereal. It wasn't long before Taylor joined her with a slightly evil grin on her face.

"Good morning, dear," she said as she trailed a finger under Grace's nose. "I love you."

Grace grabbed her hand and sucked the finger into her mouth. She watched as Taylor's eyes glazed over for a moment before pulling her finger from Grace's mouth with a pop.

"Tomorrow, we don't get out of bed unless we absolutely have to," Taylor said. "It's been too long since we had a truly decadent day in bed."

"Now that sounds like a plan I can live with," Grace said. "Especially since we get to do the same thing again next Sunday."

"Wow. Twice in a week." Taylor laughed as she waited for the Keurig to dispense her cup of coffee. She took it and sat across the table from Grace. "Okay. What is first on our list to do?"

"We need to set up the chairs, and I need to bring my collection downstairs."

"That doesn't sound like that much," Taylor said.

"That's because I paused to take a breath." Grace laughed and continued to enumerate things that needed to be done before one-thirty that afternoon when they expected guests to show up.

Taylor held both hands up. "Damn, girl. What have you done all week? I thought you were getting things ticked off that list."

"I'll have you know I have ticked a great number of things off the list. These are the things that couldn't be done before today, such as taking delivery of the refreshments and flowers."

As she finished speaking, the front doorbell rang. She grinned at Taylor and mouthed, *And off we go.*

Over the next few hours, the two of them, joined by Marie and Sonya, scurried around the house to complete the arrangements for the afternoon's festivities. About noon, they stopped and looked around at their accomplishments.

"Wow. I don't think we could have gotten all this done without y'all's help," Taylor said. "The place looks wonderful."

They had tied white and silver ribbons to each chair, and fresh white roses stood in vases around the room. An arch stood at the front of the room, also draped with white and silver ribbon and garlands of roses. The room was brightly lit now, but Grace had the timer set for the lights to dim at about the time the wedding was to start, with spotlights aimed at where the officiant would stand and the brides would exchange their vows.

Easels evenly spaced along each side of the room had a canvas draped in white or silver linen. Two easels sat up front, holding the two largest paintings.

In the family room, tables were ready for a small buffet to be laid out. Three attendants from the catering company milled around, making sure everything was in order, while a bartender continued to set up the open bar. The cake from the Dairy Queen manager waited in the freezer to be presented to the newlyweds, as well as individual sundaes for each of the guests.

"I need to get back to the house to get ready. Dauda and future dauda-in-law, I do believe you've outdone yourselves. See you soon." Marie gave the younger women a hug. Sonya followed suit.

Grace closed and locked the sliding door behind them and turned to Taylor. "Let's go take a shower. We have a little bit of time for me to repay you for this morning."

Taylor squealed and ran for their bedroom, unbuttoning her blouse as she went.

†

About an hour later, they stood at the front door, greeting their guests. Cecelia and Marie had wheeled Evie through the two backyards a little bit earlier and had her sequestered in the master bedroom. Pepper and Sonya showed up just a few minutes later with Freddy. Grace escorted them to one of the guest bedrooms.

"I don't understand why we have to hide," Freddy complained. "I want to be out there with everyone else."

Grace led Freddy to the bed and sat down with her. "You'll get to be out there with everyone in just a little while. Remember, this was supposed to be a surprise, but Grams figured it out. So let a little bit of it be a surprise. Okay?"

Freddy nodded but still looked unhappy.

"Would it be easier to wait if you had a puzzle to work on?" Grace asked.

Freddy looked up and grinned as Grace walked to the dresser and pulled a puzzle depicting puppies in a basket from a drawer in the bedside table.

"You can work it here on the bed. I'll be back to get you in a few minutes."

Pepper put a hand on Grace's arm as Grace was leaving the room.

"Thank you, Grace. Remembering to get her a new puzzle was so thoughtful of you."

Grace hugged her. "It wasn't anything. I'll be back in a little bit."

Just as Grace got back to the living room, the wedding officiant arrived.

"Reverend Holt, thank you so much for coming today," she said. "Would you like to say hello to the brides before we get started?"

"Please, call me Sharon," the reverend said. "And yes, I would like to say hello to the girls. I have so enjoyed getting to know them over the past few weeks."

"They are definitely one-of-a-kind times two," Grace said. She motioned to Taylor to join them. "Sweetie, will you take Rev—, I mean Sharon, to see Grams and Freddy?"

"Certainly." Taylor offered the reverend an elbow and led her down the hall.

Grace looked around and was gratified to see that almost all the chairs were full. It looked like everyone who had sent a positive RSVP had actually shown up. She walked around the room and greeted some guests who had arrived while she was with Freddy.

It wasn't long before the reverend returned to the gallery. She picked up her bag and went to the small table behind the arch. She unpacked a small silver cloth and draped it over the table. On the table, she placed a small book, a folder Grace knew held the marriage license, and the white and silver ropes for the handfasting, an element that had surprised Grace when Evie and Freddy had insisted on it. The reverend turned and gave Grace a slight nod. Grace went to the front of the room and cleared her throat to get the attention of the guests.

"Thank you all so much for coming today," she said. "When we first started planning this, it was supposed to be a surprise ninety-fifth birthday party for Grams. But then, we were blessed to have Freddy enter our lives, re-enter Grams' life, and the party became a party for the two of them. Then, Grams figured out we were planning the party and threw a fit—"

She stopped long enough to let the laughter die down.

"And so, we planned the party to her specifications, and everyone was happy. But then, the ultimate twist—"

Again, laughter stopped her.

"The final twist was Freddy proposing to Grams, and then they made the decision that today would also be their wedding date. I want to thank everyone who has helped put this day together. In just a moment, the happy brides will join us, and Reverend Sharon Holt will do them the honor of overseeing their marriage vows."

She gave a slight nod to the tall, skinny man standing next to the Chinese screens. He picked up a violin and started playing "Evie's Opus" while Grace and Taylor went to give the brides and their escorts the signal that it was time to join the celebration.

Pepper, Sonya, and Freddy were the first to enter the room. Freddy's face lit up when she heard the violin playing. She detoured to the young man, who bent so she could kiss him on the cheek. He motioned to the stool beside him, where Freddy's violin waited. She picked it up and seamlessly joined him.

Cecelia and Marie escorted Evie into the room, one on each side of her, her hands in the crook of their elbows. The smile that lit her face was one Grace had never seen on her before. It was tender, excited, and full of love. The sight brought tears to Grace's eyes. Taylor took her hand and squeezed it. Grace looked at her and saw that she, too, had tears in her eyes.

Two chairs stood in front of the arch. Cecelia helped Evie into one of them and stood behind it. Pepper waited for Freddy to complete the song, but Freddy had her own ideas. Continuing to play, she meandered around the room, ending in front of Evie. She finished the opus with a flourish, handed the violin to Pepper, and sat down in her chair with a thud. The guests burst into applause and laughter. After Pepper took her place behind Freddy's chair, the reverend stood in front of them, waiting for everyone to quiet down.

"Today, I am honored to stand in front of you and these two beautiful women who are joining their lives in matrimony. It's not every day I get to officiate at a wedding for two ninety-five-year-olds."

Laughter again filled the room. Evie smiled at Freddy and took her hand.

The reverend opened her book and, within a short time, had led the two women through their vows. She picked up the cords and wrapped them around their wrists in the infinity sign. After a few more words, she declared them married. Freddy and Evie leaned over and shared a sweet kiss. Pepper and Cecelia unwrapped their hands, helped them to their feet, and turned them to face the crowd. The guests rose to their feet, applauding and cheering. Grace realized her face was wet with tears. Marie pressed some tissues into her hands.

"Sweetie, it's your turn," Taylor said. Grace gave her a quick peck on the lips and dried her face with the tissue before moving to join the newlyweds. Pepper and Cecelia helped the ladies back into their chairs after turning the chairs to face the guests.

"Grams, Freddy, I'm so proud of y'all, and I love you so much," she said. "Your history is mind-boggling, sad, and uplifting, and so many other adjectives I can't think of. I racked my brain for what to give you for your wedding gift."

She nodded at Taylor, who moved to stand between the easels. Marie, Sonya, Cecelia, Pepper, and the reverend did the same thing.

"So, I did the only thing I know I'm good at."

She stepped to the two easels next to the arch.

"These are yours to hang in your room," she said. She pulled the cloth off the easels, and the guests gasped in unison.

One painting was the portrait of Evie, which had started the collection to begin with. Above and to the right of Evie's head, which she painted as if she were looking up at it, Grace had painted Freddy as a young girl, holding her violin to her shoulder, her eyes looking down at Evie. The effect was breathtaking.

The second painting was of Freddy as she was at ninety-five, her eyes bright and her smile impish. Her portrait faced left, and just above her, in the left corner, was a portrait of Evie as a young woman, her hands clasped below her chin, her eyes beaming.

"Oh, my goodness," Evie said.

She held her hand out to Grace, who took it and helped her to her feet. Freddy joined them, and the two stood in front of the paintings, holding hands. Grace couldn't wait to see the photographs the photographer was getting of their first reactions. Evie turned to Grace and held her arms open. Grace stepped into her embrace, and Freddy joined them in a group hug. Grace dried her tears as the two older women returned to their chairs.

"But this isn't all," she said. "My new collection is also because of you and your story and how much you mean to all of us."

She nodded, and the women standing between the easels simultaneously pulled the linens from the paintings. Evie and Freddy were the subjects of all the paintings, some as they were in the present, some copied from photographs from their youth. Grace's favorites, however, were those of the two women's hands entwined. She'd painted youthful hands as she pictured how they looked as a young couple, as well as hands replete with age spots and a map of veins.

"Thank you," Grace said as everyone stood and applauded. She kneeled on the floor in front of the newlyweds and gathered them into another hug.

Chapter Thirty-six

Grace fell backwards in bed, and Taylor fell on top of her.

"You're not too tired for a little fun, are you?" Taylor asked as her hand found its way inside Grace's blouse.

Grace wrapped her arms around Taylor and flipped them so that she was on top. She grinned when Taylor squealed. She bent down and stopped the squeal with a deep, sensual kiss. When they came up for air, neither of them wasted any time in helping the other out of her clothes.

A while later, they lay in each other's arms. Grace knew Taylor's tuneless humming meant she was thoroughly satisfied.

"Think Evie and Freddy are having as much fun as we just had?" Taylor asked.

Grace laughed. "If they are, I hope Mom has the defibrillator charged and ready."

"Today was magical, hon." Taylor turned over so that they were face-to-face. "Your paintings are the best I've ever seen."

Grace kissed Taylor on the forehead. “Thank you. I have to admit I’m happy with how they all turned out. And I’m really glad Grams and Freddy liked them. I was afraid they’d be hurt or feel as though I’d invaded their privacy.”

Taylor shook her head. “I don’t think you can do any wrong when it comes to what your grandmother thinks.”

“Great-grandmother,” they said in unison and then laughed together.

Grace covered her mouth and yawned so big her jaw cracked. She rubbed it. “Ouch. I’m so tired, I feel like I could sleep for a week.”

“Don’t do that.” Taylor kissed her cheek. “You’ve got another wedding to prepare for.”

Grace leaned over and kissed Taylor on the lips. “And if it goes even half as well as today did, we’ll have a wedding day we’ll never forget.”

“And if our honeymoon is half as good as tonight, neither of us will be able to walk the next day.”

†

The next morning, Grace slid out of bed while Taylor was still sleeping. She took a quick shower and dressed in shorts and a soft T-shirt. When she came out of the bathroom, Taylor was still snoring softly, so Grace tiptoed out, pulling the door closed with a gentle click. In the gallery, she stood much as she had the day before, hands on hips, doing a slow three-sixty, but this time it was with a groan. She realized how much work she had to do to get the gallery back to the immaculate space it needed to be so she could start getting ready for her own wedding, and then for the gallery opening the following week.

After she removed the ribbons and flowers from each chair, she folded and stacked them next to the door for pickup early the following day. She rewrapped the paintings for their return to the studio. She was finishing up the last few details when Taylor came into the room, wrapped in her robe and rubbing her eyes.

"You should have woken me up," she said. "I could have helped."

Grace hugged her and kissed her cheek. "You could have, but I'm already done in here. The kitchen's next on my list. I'm almost scared to look at it."

Before Taylor could respond, there was a knock on the back sliding door. Taylor slid the Chinese screen out of the way. It didn't surprise Grace to see Cecelia and Marie at the door, but what they were carrying did surprise her. She went and opened the door.

"What's all this?" she asked as she took the linen-covered tray from Cecelia.

"I figured y'all would probably sleep in and then not want to fix breakfast, so we made you some French toast and scrambled eggs," she said.

"Mudda's special French toast?" Grace asked, her eyes wide.

"Of course, my special French toast," Marie answered with a laugh. "You did such an awesome job planning and putting together the party and wedding yesterday that this was the least I could do for you."

Grace set the tray on the counter and turned to hug Marie. She surprised herself by bursting into tears. Marie rubbed her back and guided her to a chair. Cecelia handed her a couple of napkins while Marie kneeled in front of her.

"What's up, Dauda?" she asked. "Why the tears?"

Taylor stood behind Grace with her hands on Grace's shoulders. "Yeah, babe. Are you okay?"

Grace shrugged. "I honestly don't know why I started crying. It's just, well, oh, good grief—I don't know." Grace wiped her face and nose with a napkin.

Cecelia sat in the chair next to Grace's and took one of her hands. "I think I know at least part of it. You've been burning three candles at both ends and a couple of them in the middle. I think that's why you left your phone upstairs the other day. You subconsciously knew you needed some rest, so you left it where you wouldn't hear it—"

"But you better never do that again," Taylor said, interrupting Cecelia.

Everyone laughed.

"You can count on that," Grace said. "I can't remember the last time everyone was that mad at me, including Grams, and I don't think she even knew why anyone else was mad. Speaking of Grams, have y'all seen her and Freddy this morning?"

"I peeked in on them when I got up this morning," Marie said. "I'm so glad that the larger bed was delivered on Friday. Those two old women were snuggled up together, still asleep but with smiles on their faces. I heard them giggling just before we came over here."

"Giggling?" Grace and Taylor said in unison.

"Yes, giggling. I'm not sure which is cuter, a baby giggling or two ninety-five-year-olds giggling," Marie said, a grin on her face. "It's obvious, so obvious, how much they love each other."

Marie got up off her knees and groaned when one of them audibly popped. "I'm too old to be on my knees," she said as she perched on Cecelia's lap. "Thank goodness we're already married because I wouldn't be able to get up off the one knee from proposing to you."

Cecelia kissed her on the cheek and looked at the two younger women. Taylor had pulled a chair around and was sitting beside Grace.

"I wonder if you two know how blessed you are to grow up in a time that is more accepting than it was when we were your age, and far more accepting than in your great-grandmother's time." Cecelia's eyes shone with unshed tears. "I can't imagine my life without Marie. She's been my rock for almost thirty-five years, and with any luck, will be for another thirty-five or more. My heart breaks when I think of Grams and Freddy missing out on almost eighty years of this kind of love."

The four of them were quiet for a long moment. Marie stood up and carried the tray into the kitchen.

"Where can I find a cookie sheet to put these on so I can stick them in the oven to warm up?" she asked.

Taylor stood up and went to join her. "Wouldn't it be faster in the microwave?"

Cecelia and Grace cracked up laughing at the look of mock horror on Marie's face.

"What? What did I say?" Taylor asked, looking between Marie and the mother and daughter laughing at her.

"You never put Mudda's special French toast in the microwave," Grace said. "They get too soggy and don't taste nearly as good."

†

The week that followed was busy, busier, in fact, than the week leading up to Evie and Freddy's wedding.

Taylor spent a great deal of time with Lois at the studio, viewing the interviews and tapes made at the wedding. Grace spent so much time checking off everything on their wedding list that she didn't have time to miss Taylor until she got home each evening. Then Grace would remember how much she loved her and wished they could spend more time together during the day. One evening, as they sat down to dinner, she decided to broach the subject.

"I miss you when you're at work during the day," she said. She used a piece of garlic bread to soak up some of the marinara sauce left in her bowl. "But I have an idea that may allow us to spend more time together."

Taylor tilted her head. "Oh? What, pray tell, would that be?"

"What if we finish the attic over the garage and make that your studio? We could use the money left in Grams' contingency fund. Let's see how much the equipment you need to do whatever you do with film and stuff is, and maybe you could work from home too."

Grace reached across the table, and with one of her forefingers, gently pushed Taylor's chin up to close her mouth. Taylor was, for a moment, seemingly speechless as her mouth opened and closed several times without making a sound.

"Are you serious?" she finally asked.

"Uh, yes. Don't you think it's feasible?"

Almost before she finished speaking, Taylor was around the table and straddling her lap. She took Grace's face in both hands and laid a kiss on her that sizzled all the way to her toes.

"Yes. Yes, I do think it's feasible," Taylor said when they came up for air. "I love you so much."

"It's a good thing since you're going to marry her."

Taylor would have fallen if Grace hadn't caught her. They both turned to Cecelia, who leaned on the open sliding door.

"Mom! What are you doing sneaking up on us?" Grace asked. "What's up?"

"Where are y'all's phones?" Cecelia asked. "I've called both of you twice before I decided to walk over and see if you're still alive."

Grace pointed to the table by the door. "Mine is right there," she said.

Cecelia looked and shook her head. "Wrong. There is nothing on this table."

Grace stood up and went to see for herself. Sure enough, the table was bare.

"Well, I'll be damned. Where did I put that stupid thing?"

Taylor came from the bedroom with her purse in her hands. She sat down and dug through it. "I thought my phone was in my purse, but it's not here. Cee, can you call it and see if we hear it?"

Cecelia laughed. "I just told you I'd already done that. Grace, where were you last? Did you leave it upstairs again?"

Grace bounded up the stairs only to find that she had, indeed, once again left her phone on her workbench. She picked it up and checked for missed calls. Thankfully, the only two were the ones from Cecelia. She descended the stairs slower than she had gone up them. Taylor wasn't with Cecelia, who was sitting at the table, eating a piece of their garlic bread.

"Where's Taylor?" Grace asked as she sat down.

"She went to see if she left her phone in the car. I see you found yours."

Grace nodded. "Yup. I can't believe I did that again. Why were you calling? You didn't leave a voicemail."

"You know I hate voicemail." Cecelia took another bite of bread.

"Well?" Grace asked again.

"I don't talk with food in my mouth," Cecelia said around the mouthful of bread.

Grace shook her head and went to find Taylor.

"You okay, hon?" she asked as she entered the garage.

Taylor was sitting with her forehead against the steering wheel of her car. She shook her head without looking up. Grace knelt by the open driver's side door.

"Why are you crying?"

"I can't find my phone. I don't know where I left it."

"Come inside and let's call Lois and see if you left it at the studio," Grace said, drying Taylor's cheeks with her thumbs. "You didn't go anywhere else today, did you?"

Taylor nodded.

"You did go someplace else?" Grace asked, trying to verify what the nod meant.

Taylor nodded again. "I met my brother for lunch," she whispered.

Grace helped Taylor climb out of the car, and they went back inside.

"I thought y'all had left me here," Cecelia said. She stood up and met them halfway across the room. She slid an arm around Taylor's waist. "What did my dauda do to make you so sad?"

Taylor shook her head but didn't look up or say anything. Grace led her to one of the overstuffed chairs. Taylor slid into the chair and buried her face in her hands. Grace sat on the arm of the chair and rubbed her back while Cecelia sat on the ottoman and put her hands on Taylor's knees.

"I'm sorry if I did or said something that brought this on," Cecelia said. "I was just giving y'all a hard time. I didn't mean to hurt your feelings."

"You didn't." Taylor's voice was muffled by her hands.

Cecelia looked up at Grace, her eyebrows almost disappearing into her hairline. Grace mouthed, *I'll tell you later.*_Cecelia stood up and kissed Taylor on the top of her head and Grace on the cheek.

"I'll bring y'all some dessert in a little while," she said. She bent over and put her mouth near Taylor's ear. "I'm sorry, sweetie. I didn't mean any harm."

Taylor nodded but still didn't look up or say anything. Grace stood and hugged Cecelia, who left without a word. Grace sat on the ottoman.

"Honey, you want to tell me what happened today?" she asked, rubbing Taylor's legs.

Taylor took a long, deep breath and rubbed her face. "I should have told Cecelia not to worry about it, but I just couldn't find any words. I'm sorry I was rude to her."

"Don't worry about that," Grace said. "How did you end up having lunch with your brother? I didn't know y'all were on speaking terms."

Taylor leaned back and rubbed her face again. "Lenny and I were never not on speaking terms," she said. "We didn't speak because of Mom and Dad. They forbid me from calling him and told him he'd go to hell if he did."

She took another deep breath.

"It was my turn to do the coffee run today. Lois always orders everything on her app, and I just have to go through the drive-thru to pick everything up. But the app didn't work today, and neither did the speaker at the drive-thru, so I had to go inside to order. Lenny was leaning against the counter, flirting with the barista. I turned around to leave, but he saw me and caught me before I got out the door. Turns out he's engaged to her."

"Engaged? I thought he was just a kid," Grace said.

Taylor's laugh was bitter. "The last time I saw him, he was. But since then, he's graduated from high school and is a junior out at UTA. You'll never guess what he's majoring in."

"Don't tell me he's majoring in social anthropology."

"No. He's majoring in film. So I guess I won't be, at least for the next couple of years."

Grace held up one hand. "Wait a minute. Just 'cause he's majoring in it doesn't mean you can't."

"I don't want to put him in an awkward position where he might have to explain to Mom and Dad. Especially Dad." Taylor shook her head. "Anyway, I had to get back to the studio. When he walked me to the car and hugged me, I nearly fainted. I can't remember the last time he hugged me. I think I was in middle school. But then he asked me to go to lunch with him. I was glad I'd already set the coffee down, or I would have dropped it."

"Wow. Just wow." Grace leaned back and stretched. "It sounds like he doesn't have the same mindset as your parents do."

"He doesn't. He told me his best friend is gay. I've known that kid since the boys were in kindergarten and pegged him as gay when they were in second or third grade. I never said anything, of course, but I wasn't surprised when Lenny told me about Clarence. Lenny said Clarence is engaged to a football player who plays for UTA."

"Wow—"

"Do not say 'Just wow,'" Taylor said with a hint of a grin.

Grace chuckled. "Okay. But none of this tells me why you were so upset out in the car. Or why you didn't tell me at dinner."

Taylor leaned forward again and put her face in her hands. Even though she made no sound, Grace knew she was crying again. She didn't know what to do, so she leaned her head against Taylor's and rubbed her shoulders. After a moment, Taylor wrapped her arms around Grace and wept on her shoulder. When her sobs turned to hiccups, Grace went to the guest bathroom and came back with a box of tissues.

"Are you going to be okay?" she asked as she pulled a fistful of tissue from the box and shoved it in Taylor's hand.

Taylor nodded as she wiped her face and blew her nose.

"Do you think you can tell me what's going on now?" Grace brought Taylor a glass of water from the kitchen.

Taylor took a deep breath. "Lenny's wedding is Saturday at two."

Grace stopped and stared at Taylor. She had to play her words over and over in her mind before she made the connection.

"Oh, shit. Oh, Taylor. It's not too late for us to reschedule if you want to go to his wedding."

Taylor shook her head again. "I wouldn't be welcome, and I'd just make things uncomfortable for him and his fiancé. Besides, it would cost us a fortune to change things at this late date."

Grace squeezed her way into the chair beside Taylor. "No wonder you're so upset. I can't imagine how you're feeling. I wish I had all kinds of magic words to make things different."

Taylor laid her head on Grace's shoulder. "You do have the magic words," she said. "And you say them all the time. And I'm so blessed I'm the one you say them to."

"I love you, Taylor. With all my heart and all my soul. I'm the one who is blessed."

†

Grace took Taylor to retrieve her phone from the restaurant the next day. From there, they went to Best Buy and bought a gift card to send, anonymously, to Lenny and his bride. When they arrived at the studio, Taylor encouraged Grace to come in with her.

"We're so close to being ready to market the documentary," she said. "I want you to see it first. You might catch some things we need to change, leave out, or add that we're not seeing. Please?"

"I'd love to, hon, but I have an appointment with an art broker who might be interested in backing the studio and my work. I told you about him a couple of days ago."

Taylor's face fell. "You did. I forgot. But I really do want you to see this before we get much further. When do you think you can come see it?"

"Aren't you planning on screening it for Grams and Freddy?"

"Yes. But I want you to see it before that. I'm nervous about them seeing it, and I want you to troubleshoot for me."

Grace watched Taylor fight back more tears. She hated seeing her partner in so much pain. Normally strong, Taylor was struggling with her self-confidence and self-esteem, and Grace wanted nothing more than to have a face-to-face with Taylor's family. But she knew that wasn't possible and would only do more harm than good.

"Here's what I'll do," she said. "Let me get through this meeting with Mr. Anderson. If we're done fairly fast, I'll come back and see the film this afternoon. Otherwise, is there any way I can see it when I come to pick you up?"

Taylor smiled. "Let me check with Lois. I'll text you what she says, but I think when you pick me up will work."

Grace checked the clock. "I've gotta go, sweets. I love you."

†

That evening, Grace sat stunned as the lights came up in the screening room. Taylor squeezed her hand.

"Are you okay?" Taylor asked. "What do you think?"

"Wow. Just wow." Grace couldn't find any other words. "Wow."

"Just wow," Taylor said with her. "Is that all you can say?"

Grace nodded. She kept replaying scenes from the film in her head. She'd never thought of her great-grandmother in quite the same terms as the film crew saw her. Yes, she knew her great-grandmother was intelligent and could draw, but she never realized how much she knew about art. The things she said and how she said them made Grace realize Evie had lost more than time with Freddy by marrying her great-grandfather.

"And Freddy. Why wasn't she more famous than she was? She's so frickin' talented."

Taylor waved a hand in front of Grace's face. Grace blinked. "Lois asked you a question," Taylor said.

"I'm sorry," Grace said. She turned to Lois. "This is beautiful. I see so much about my great-grandmother and her wife that I'd never have known otherwise. Thank you so much."

"Thank you," Lois said. "That means a lot to me and the crew. Is there anything in it that you saw or heard that needs to be changed?"

Grace grinned. "Just one thing. There's a couple of places you refer to Grams as my grandmother. She'll have a fit if she hears that. She's my great-grandmother, and she'll let you know in no uncertain terms if that's not fixed."

"I can't believe I didn't catch that," Taylor said. "We can fix the soundtrack tomorrow. I'm glad you caught it."

Grace yawned. "Oh, I'm sorry."

Lois patted her arm. "That's okay. I know there's a lot going on in your life right now. Are y'all ready for Saturday?"

Grace and Taylor nodded in unison. "I hope so," Grace said. "Tomorrow the chairs are delivered, again, and the wedding cake and flowers will be delivered tomorrow afternoon."

"At least Taylor will be there to help you this time," Lois said. "If y'all need any more help, give me a holler. I'm taking some time off from this place until next week."

"Thanks." Grace stood, yawned, and stretched. "Taylor, do you mind driving?"

Chapter Thirty-seven

The next day was a flurry of activity from the time the girls woke until Cecelia and Marie came to whisk Grace away to spend the night at a nearby hotel. The mothers waited in the car while Grace and Taylor said their goodbyes.

"Are you sure you're going to be okay here alone?" Grace asked for the twentieth time. "Maybe Pepper or Sonya will stay with you."

"I'll be fine," Taylor said. "Sonya is coming over early in the morning to help with last-minute stuff. I'll miss you. I'm not going to sleep in our bed. That would just be too lonely."

Grace pulled Taylor to her and kissed her long and deep. Just as they were pulling apart, a car horn sounded out front and Grace's phone rang. The girls laughed.

"You better go before they come in here and drag you out," Taylor said. "I love you. I'll see you tomorrow at two."

"You better believe it," Grace said. She leaned in for another kiss, but Taylor leaned back.

"Go. Now," Taylor said. "If I let you kiss me again, I won't let you go."

Grace sighed and headed out the door. She turned for one more look at Taylor. "Don't forget to set the security system," she said.

"Yes, Mother," Taylor said with a laugh. She started closing the front door. "Go."

"Come on, Grace," Marie called from the car. "We're hungry. And the buffet at the restaurant ends in an hour and a half."

"Isn't an hour and a half plenty of time?" Grace asked as she got in the car.

"Not for her," Cecelia said. "You should know that."

†

The next day, Grace stood in front of the full-length mirror that hung on the back of the hotel room door. She pulled the sleeves of her white shirt down so that the cuffs were lower than the sleeves of the ivory dress coat. Cecelia stood behind her, a huge smile on her face.

"You look suave," she said. "I don't think I've ever seen you look so good."

"I don't marry the love of my life every day," Grace said.

Her heart skipped a beat as she thought about Taylor. She'd hated sleeping alone the night before, and it was worse that her mothers had not only confiscated her phone, but they had also taken the house phone from her hotel room. Her plan had been to call Taylor and fall asleep with her.

"You are beautiful," Cecelia said as she pulled Grace into a tight hug. "And I'm so proud of you. Everything that you've accomplished over the last few years boggles my mind. And now you're not only getting married, but you also own your own art studio."

"I can't take credit for that last part," Grace said with what breath she had left. "That was Grams' doing."

"That she wouldn't have bothered with if she didn't think you were worthy."

The door between Grace's room and her mothers' room opened, and Marie joined them. The two mothers wore almost identical outfits, but in reversed colors. Cecelia wore blue linen slacks and a jacket with a rose-colored blouse, and Marie wore burgundy linen slacks and a jacket with a pale blue blouse.

"Y'all look like recently reconnected twins," Grace said with a laugh.

Marie slid an arm around Cecelia's waist. "I think we look a lot better than any set of twins ever has or ever will. The desk just called up. Our car is waiting downstairs."

"Our car?" Grace frowned. "What do you mean 'our car?'"

The mothers looked at each other and grinned. "One of our wedding gifts to you is a limo ride from here to the house and then, after the reception, for a ride back here."

"Back here?"

"Is there an echo in here?" Marie asked with a laugh.

"Yes, my dear, back here," Cecelia said. "We've booked the honeymoon suite for y'all for tonight and tomorrow night."

Grace was glad she didn't wear makeup because her tears flowed. Her mothers gathered her in a hug and laughed.

"Dry your tears," Marie said. She stepped into the bathroom, grabbed a handful of tissues, and handed them to Grace. "We got a wedding to get to."

Once at the house, Marie wouldn't let Grace get out of the car until she made sure the coast was clear. She motioned from the door for Grace and Cecelia to come inside.

"Sonya has Taylor sequestered in one of the guest rooms," she said. "Some guests have already arrived, so we're going to go to the other guest room."

"Why not the master?" Grace asked.

Marie shrugged. "I don't know, but I was asked to keep you out of there for now."

"Oooo-kay," Grace said. She wondered what Taylor was up to, but she didn't argue. "What are we going to do in the guest room until two?"

Cecelia rolled her eyes. "Play cards. What else?" She brandished an unopened deck of cards.

Grace shook her head. "No way. I always lose and end up owing y'all something I can't pay back."

"No wagering this time, I promise." Cecelia took Grace's arm and rather forcefully led her to the guest room.

After losing several hands of Hearts, the knock on the door came that Grace had been waiting for. She stood and checked her appearance in the mirror before pulling the jacket back on. Cecelia opened the door, and the beautiful sound of Freddy's violin floated into the room. Cecelia and Marie smiled at Grace.

"Freddy wrote this just for you and Taylor," Cecelia said.

The mothers flanked her as Grace went into the gallery. Evie sat in a chair next to where Grace would stand, and Pepper stood as Taylor's witness. Freddy stood to one side of the flowered arch, playing her violin. Her eyes were closed, and she swayed to the movement of the bow over the strings. Evie reached out and tugged on her shirt. When Freddy opened her eyes and saw Grace, a grin spread across her face, and she began playing the wedding march.

Grace turned toward the hallway, ready to greet her bride. When Taylor appeared, escorted by Marie, Grace almost fainted at the sight of how beautiful Taylor looked. She wore a simple white gown that accentuated her curves and made her already tan complexion seem even darker. She carried a small bouquet of lilies and wore a tiny pill-box hat, her beautiful hair pulled up into a French twist.

Marie led Taylor to Grace and put Taylor's hand in Grace's outstretched one.

"Hi," Grace said in an awe-struck whisper. "You're beautiful."

Taylor smiled at her, and the two turned to Reverend Holt, who wasted no time in leading the girls through their vows.

"I pronounce you married," she said with a smile. "You're welcome to seal these promises with a kiss."

Taylor handed her bouquet to Pepper before turning and wrapping her arms around Grace. Although Grace planned to dip Taylor, Taylor surprised her by beating her to the punch. Everyone laughed as Taylor bent Grace over backwards and laid a sensual kiss on her lips. Once back on her feet, Grace pulled Taylor into a tight embrace.

"I love you," she said in her ear.

†

Two nights in a luxury honeymoon suite with all the amenities anyone could ask for was more of a honeymoon than the girls had expected to have. However, they didn't take advantage of many of the amenities, as they only left the bed for the bare necessities.

Grace stretched as she climbed out of the back of the limousine in front of their house and grinned when she saw the "Welcome Home" banner strung across the front porch. Taylor slid an arm around her waist.

"It is home, isn't it?" she said. "I still have a hard time believing this house is ours."

The girls walked to the front door and, after Grace unlocked it and pushed it open, Taylor swept her off her feet and carried her across the threshold. She kicked the front door closed as she set Grace on her feet and backed her up until Grace's back was against the door. The kiss they shared was long and sensual.

"I think we'd be more comfortable in the bedroom," Grace said when Taylor finally stepped back.

Taylor grinned at her, took her by the hand, and the two headed down the hallway. Taylor stopped at the bedroom door and kissed Grace again before stepping back.

"You first," she said with a slight bow.

Grace raised her eyebrows, cautiously turned the doorknob, and peeked into the bedroom. Her mouth dropped open when she saw their bed strewn with rose petals and a gift box sitting in the center of the bed. Vases of roses adorned the dresser and each side table. She turned to Taylor, who was grinning like a madwoman.

"I thought we were staying here the other night," Taylor explained. "And I wanted to make things as romantic as possible. Cecelia made sure the roses stayed watered while we were gone."

Grace stepped into Taylor's arms and hugged her as she fought back tears of true happiness.

"Don't start crying," Taylor said as she sniffled. "If I start, I may not be able to stop. Open your gift."

"Let me go and get yours first," Grace said. "We can open them together."

After a quick kiss on Taylor's cheek, Grace ran up to the studio and retrieved the painting she had done for Taylor. She carried it back to the bedroom, where Taylor stood holding the box that Grace's gift was in. The two sat on the edge of the bed and exchanged packages.

"You first," Taylor said, smiling that smile that melted into Grace's soul.

Grace carefully untied the bow and, with a quick glance at Taylor, lifted the lid off the box. She gasped when she saw the sign nestled in tissue paper. It simply said "The Art Gallery and Studio of Grace Jenkins" in ivory-colored lettering on a hunter-green background. Grace lifted it out of the box and hugged it to her before turning to Taylor.

"This is beautiful," she said. "Thank you so much. I can't wait to hang it out front."

They shared a soft kiss before Taylor laid her package across her lap.

"I can already tell this is a painting," she said. "But what did you paint?"

She tore the white covering from the canvas. Grace watched as tears flooded her eyes, and she held the painting out in front of her. The painting was of the first picture Cecelia had taken of them together. Surrounding them were smaller portraits of Freddy and Evie, Cecelia and Marie, and Pepper and Sonya. Across the top was the word "Family," and at the bottom was their wedding date.

Taylor leaned the painting against the dresser mirror, stood back, and stared at it. Grace watched Taylor's reflection in the mirror for a moment before standing up and wrapping her arms around her waist.

"Our family," she said.

Taylor turned and kissed her as she backed her up to the bed.

CHAPTER THIRTY-EIGHT

Six months later, Grace watched Evie and Freddy as the lights went back up in the theater and the crowd in attendance rose to their feet as one, applauding. The two nonagenarians looked like they were slightly in shock. Both Grace and Taylor kneeled in front of them.

"Are you okay?" Grace asked as she took Evie's hands.

Evie nodded and smiled through her tears. Freddy leaned her head on Evie's shoulder and sniffled.

"It's beautiful," Evie said. "Even though I've seen it before, this is so much more special. I can't believe all these people really care about two old women and their lives."

Lois tapped Taylor on the shoulder.

"Do you think they can stand up with us?" she asked. "I'd like to introduce them to everyone."

The younger women offered the older women their hands and helped them to their feet. All of them turned to face the audience.

"I'd like to introduce you all to the stars of this wonderful documentary. Ladies and gentlemen, this is Evie and Frieda. These ladies have seen and endured more in one lifetime than the whole of us put together ever will."

The audience once again was on its feet. Evie blushed so red that Grace worried about her blood pressure. She tightened her hold on Evie's elbow as the older woman swayed a bit. Evie smiled at her and patted her hand.

"Would either of y'all like to say anything?" Lois asked. Evie shook her head, but Freddy nodded and grinned. Lois held the microphone out to her.

"Thank you all for coming today," Freddy said. "I want you to know I never stopped loving this woman in all the years we were apart. You heard some of the song I wrote for her in the film, but with your permission, I'd like to play the full 'Opus.' I brought my violin if that's okay."

A young man came from the side of the theater with Freddy's violin. She took it and plucked one or two of the strings before tucking it under her chin. Grace helped Evie to her seat as Freddy drew her bow over the strings. Within moments, the theater filled with the dulcet tones of the 'Opus,' sometimes upbeat, sometimes melancholy, but every note full of love. Freddy closed her eyes and swayed as she played. Evie clasped her hands to her heart throughout the performance. When Freddy slid the bow over the string with the last note, there was a moment of pure silence before the audience erupted in cheers.

Freddy smiled at Evie, bent over, and kissed her. Grace couldn't hear her over the ovation, but she saw Freddy say *I love you* and Evie nodding.

†

That night, Taylor and Grace lay in each other's arms, quiet, each with her own thoughts. Taylor turned onto her side, and to Grace's surprise, Taylor's eyes were wet with tears. She put her palm on Taylor's cheek.

"What's wrong, babe?" she asked. "Tonight was a resounding success. You should be so proud of yourself. I know I'm proud of you."

"Thank you. I was so overwhelmed at the love in that theater tonight, and now I'm lying here wondering what's next. This project has been my whole life, well, except for loving you, for the past year."

"You have a list of projects, don't you?" Grace asked. "And school. Are you still planning on going to school?"

Taylor turned onto her back and put an arm over her eyes. Grace sat up and stroked Taylor's hair.

"What's going on up here?" she asked, tapping the top of Taylor's head. "I thought school was what you wanted to do, and major in film and cinematography. Have you changed your mind?"

"No," Taylor said. "I still want to do that, but, oh, I don't know how to explain how I feel. How do you feel after you've had an opening and suddenly everything you've worked for is out there for the world to see? Isn't there a bit of an empty feeling?"

Grace thought about it for a minute. She slid down so that her face and Taylor's face were next to each other.

"Sometimes. It was sort of like that after I unveiled the paintings I did for Evie and Freddy's wedding. For some reason, it was so hard to figure out what to do next. If Reverend Holt hadn't commissioned me to do those paintings for the church, I probably would have been lost."

She kissed Taylor on the cheek.

"Why don't we get some rest tonight, and tomorrow we can look over your list, and you can decide what's next? I have a feeling it won't take long to figure something else out."

Taylor rose on one arm and smiled down at Grace.

"I have a better idea," she said as her hands started caressing Grace's body. "Why don't we do something else to get my mind off things?"

Chapter Thirty-nine

Five years later

"I can't believe we're celebrating their one-hundredth birthday," Cecelia said as she watched Evie and Freddy being feted by the mayor of Fort Worth, as well as a large crowd of people who knew them through Taylor's documentary.

"I can't believe the entire city of Fort Worth turned out like this," Grace said. She looked around the banquet hall and then smiled at Taylor. "This is all your fault, you know."

Taylor grinned back as she hugged her wife. "Look at them, though," she said. "They're eating this up."

Evie and Freddy looked like they were having the time of their lives. Evie looked over and gestured for them to join them. The four women made their way through the crowd and bent over for hugs from the centenarians.

"This is some party y'all set up," Freddy said. "I never thought that little film would make us so famous."

"You would have deserved this even if I hadn't made the film," Taylor said. "There aren't many couples who turn one hundred together."

"Well, I'm tired," Evie said. "I think we should say our good-byes, and you all take us home."

†

Later, after making sure the two old women were safely tucked in bed, the other women lounged in the living room.

"The past five years have been something else, haven't they?" Cecelia said.

"That they have." Grace reached over and squeezed her mother's hand. "But I wouldn't change a thing, except for missing y'all when you're out gallivanting around the country. Where, and when, are you off to next?"

Cecelia glanced at Marie, who lay stretched out in the recliner with an arm over her eyes.

"I'd ask her, but I think she's fallen asleep," she said with a grin. "We talked about exploring up the Mississippi, starting at New Orleans."

"That sounds like fun." Grace yawned. "You'll have to tell us more about it another time. I'm like Marie, plain exhausted."

She stood up and offered her hand to Taylor, who allowed herself to be pulled to her feet. Cecelia stood and walked them to the back door, where they traded hugs and promises to see each other the next day. Taylor and Grace linked arms and made their way through the dark backyards to their own home. Once on the back porch, Taylor stopped and pulled Grace into a hug.

"I love you," she said into her hair. "And I love your family."

"Your family too," Grace reminded her.

†

"Both of them?" Grace choked on her words and her tears as she stared at her mother's grief-stricken face. "But they were okay last night when we came home. What happened?"

"I don't know," Cecelia said, her voice cracking. "When I hadn't heard anything out of them by the time Sonya was leaving for work, I decided to check on them. They didn't answer when I knocked, and I got a sick feeling in my gut. Sonya came back in when she heard me knock louder and went in. And oh, God, baby, they were holding each other and looked like they were asleep, but…"

Taylor kneeled in front of Grace's chair and gathered her in her arms, and the two sobbed together. It took a long time before either could say anything. Taylor's phone rang, startling them. She pulled it out of her pocket and looked at it without answering.

"How can the world go on?" she asked. "I can't imagine facing each day without them."

Grace took the phone from her and saw that the missed call was from Lois.

"Babe, you need to call her back and let her know what happened," she said. "She should know. She loves them, too."

By that afternoon, the media knew of Evie and Freddy's passing, and it was the opening story on almost every local news broadcast. Grace threw the remote across the room, barely missing the TV.

"This should be just our business," she railed as she stormed around the room. Taylor stepped into her path and tried to hug her, but Grace couldn't accept the embrace. She stepped back and glared at Taylor. "It's because of that stupid film that we can't just grieve them."

Taylor's mouth fell open, and tears spilled from her eyes. She turned and walked away, out the back door. Grace didn't follow her.

An hour later, Taylor came back in, her face puffy and red. She pulled one of the dining chairs over beside where Grace was curled in the overstuffed chair.

"I'm sorry," she said. "I thought their story was important. If I had known it would cause you this much pain, I would never have made it. But I can't undo things. Evie and Freddy have been adopted by the city, and now everyone loves them, and they have a right to know they're no longer with us. I'm just glad they went together. I hope, if you let me stay in your life that long, that we go together also. Life without you is unimaginable to me."

Grace uncurled herself and looked at Taylor. She was out of words, out of tears, out of everything. She felt as if she'd lost her guideline, her muse, a huge part of her heart.

"I know you had no idea something like this would happen," she said, reaching out and taking Taylor's hand. "I'm sorry about what I said. I'm just so angry, so confused. Mom needs us, and I need you, but I really just want to curl up and stay that way until the end of time."

Taylor nodded. She leaned over and kissed Grace on the cheek.

"Curl up, babe. I'm here for you. I promise."

†

After a memorial service in the same ballroom as their birthday party, they interred Evie and Freddy's ashes at the family cemetery in Gilead, next to baby Christina, who finally had a headstone. The family had a private gathering at the cemetery and later at their house.

"What's going on with you and Taylor?" Marie asked Grace when she caught her alone in the kitchen. "Y'all barely look at each other, and I haven't seen you touch all day."

Grace shook her head. "We're both trying to come to terms with the fact that the glue that held the world together is gone. It's been such a circus that we haven't really had a chance to just grieve. If Taylor hadn't insisted on making that documentary, it wouldn't be like this."

"Whoa, Nelly," Marie said. She pointed at a kitchen chair. "Sit down right there."

Grace balked, and Marie grabbed her arm. "Now," she ordered.

It had been a long time since Marie had asserted her authority, and Grace did as she was told. Marie pulled another chair close and took both of her hands.

"What you just said is mean, and it's ludicrous," she said. "Making that documentary made Evie and Freddy happy, and it gave Freddy a chance to show the world she's still an amazing violin player. How many other ninety-seven-year-olds get to be the guest violinist with the Dallas Philharmonic? It helped a lot of other people come together in ways that may not have happened otherwise."

"But if she hadn't made it, there wouldn't have been reporters on our doorstep or at the memorial service. It would have been us, their family, and maybe I'd be able to figure out what to do next." Grace shook her head. "It's so fucking hard to be in this house and know they aren't in the other room. I can't even paint. I can barely breathe."

"Stop it."

Grace whirled around to see Taylor and Cecelia standing behind her.

"None of this is Taylor's fault. They were old, one-hundred-years old. We knew they wouldn't live forever." Cecelia's hands were on her hips, and her lips were thin lines across her face. "This is hard on all of us, God damn it, not just you."

She turned and ran into Taylor, who wrapped her arms around the older woman. Taylor wouldn't look at Grace as she led Cecelia from the kitchen. Marie stood up and followed them, leaving Grace alone, in shock and in pain. Grace slipped out the kitchen door to the side porch and almost tripped over JB, Evie's cat. He looked up at her and gave a plaintive meow.

"Oh, JB," she said as she scooped him up. In the time he had been Evie's pet, he had never allowed Grace to touch him, but now he cuddled up to her. She took him back inside, sat back down, and rocked him. "You must be so confused. Your mommas are in heaven now. Oh, my God,"

Grace buried her face in the cat's thick black coat and sobbed. He lay there without complaint while her tears soaked his fur. At one point, Grace felt a hand on her cheek, but she didn't look up. She couldn't. Everyone was angry with her, and she didn't blame them. Once her sobs subsided, she put the cat on the chair while she went to the sink and washed her face. She looked at her reflection in the window.

"You're a stupid idiot," she said to it. "How are you going to fix this?"

"There's nothing to fix." Taylor had come into the kitchen without Grace hearing her. "We're all hurting, and it's not going to go away anytime soon. Our new normal is unfathomable right now. But we have each other if we're willing. And right now, you don't seem to be willing. Pepper and Sonya are going back to Weatherford, and they've invited me to go with them if you're not ready for us to be together."

"You're leaving me?" Grace whispered.

Taylor shook her head and leaned on the counter next to the sink.

"I don't want to, Grace. I love you so much, and I don't want us to be apart. But you're pushing me away. You're blaming me for your pain. I didn't do anything wrong. I didn't make Grams and Freddy die. Didn't you see how happy they were at their birthday party? Can't we try to focus on that instead of the fact that there were reporters at their memorial service? Can't you try to understand that the reporters were there because so many people love them? Cecelia was spot on when she said you're not the only one hurting. My heart is broken, and you're making it harder…"

Taylor crossed her arms and turned her back to Grace. Grace leaned her head against Taylor's back.

"I'm sorry won't suffice, will it?" she said. "I don't know why I've been so ugly. It's not your fault. I know you made the film to tell their story, not to make it harder when they died. Oh, God."

She caught her breath as the reality of it all hit her once again. JB stood on the kitchen chair and meowed at her. She went to him and picked him up again.

"I bet you're hungry, huh?" she said. "Let's get your food together."

She set him back down and went to the cabinet for his food. The small actions of taking care of the cat calmed her. She felt Taylor's eyes on her and turned to look at her.

"JB is hurting too," she said. "He doesn't understand."

"Do you want to take him home and help him try to understand?" Taylor asked. "Maybe he'll help you too."

"I'd rather have you help me. I'm truly sorry, Taylor. To me, you are more precious than life. Please don't leave me."

Taylor enveloped her in her arms and kissed the side of her head.

"Let's let your mom know we're going to be okay," she said. "And let her know we're adopting JB, so she doesn't have to worry about him."

EPILOGUE

One year later

"Hi, Grams. Hi, Freddy." Grace sat cross-legged in front of their gravestone, tracing the engraved names with her fingers before laying her palms against their pictures. "I miss you. Everyone misses you. We're figuring out how to live without you, but it's hard. Pepper and Sonya moved back to Weatherford, and your house feels so empty. And it is empty when Mom and Mudda are traveling. They're thinking of selling it and living full-time in the RV. They might change their minds after Taylor and I tell them our news tonight."

Grace could almost picture Evie holding her clasped hands beneath her chin with a huge smile on her face while Freddy bounced in her chair, clapping her hands. She wished they could be with them that night at the restaurant—she knew their spirits would be there, but it just wasn't the same. She looked up when she felt hands on her shoulders.

"You 'bout ready?" Taylor asked. "If we don't leave now, we'll be late, and you know how much Mom would like that."

Grace laughed as Taylor hauled her to her feet and then into a hug.

"How are you doing?" she asked as she nuzzled into Grace's neck.

"I'm sad," Grace admitted, trying to hold back the tears. She didn't cry every day anymore, but it was hard not to on this day, the anniversary of their death. "But I know they're with us and are proud and happy for us. And that helps."

The two young women walked to the car arm in arm. Taylor pulled the passenger door of her new VW Tiguan open. After Grace buckled in, Taylor leaned over and kissed Grace on the cheek. Grace smiled at how it seemed, more than ever, that Taylor couldn't stop touching her as though she had to remind herself that Grace was truly there. After Grace had spent three long weeks in Omaha painting a new mural at the children's hospital, and then came home to much-anticipated news, it was almost like they were on their long-overdue honeymoon.

When they arrived at the steakhouse, they found Cecelia and Marie waiting for them in the lobby. After hugs and kisses all around, Marie let the hostess know they were there for their reservation. The hostess quickly seated them in a comfortable booth near the back of the dining room.

"May I take your drink order?" the server asked.

"I'll have a glass of water with lemon," Grace said with a small smile. Taylor covered her hand with her own as she ordered her iced tea. Grace noticed Cecelia giving her a weird look.

"You usually order a margarita," Cecelia said. She looked at Taylor. "Or a beer."

"I'm just not in the mood for alcohol tonight," Grace said. "I'm still tired from my trip, and alcohol makes it worse."

"You've been back for almost two weeks," Marie said, a worried look marring her face. "You're not sick, are you?"

Grace and Taylor glanced at each other.

"I'm not sick," Grace assured her.

"Well, something's going on." Cecelia's mouth was a straight line across her face, a look Grace recognized from when she was a teenager and not telling her mother the whole truth about something. But before the conversation could go further, the server was back with their drinks and to take their orders.

Once the server had left the table, Cecelia opened her mouth to say something, but Grace put her hand up to stop her.

"I'm going to stop painting murals for a while," she said. Taylor took her hand and squeezed it. "I don't want to travel anymore."

"Can y'all afford for you not to take those commissions?" Marie asked.

"We can," Taylor said, speaking for Grace. "The money I made on Evie and Freddy's documentary, and the royalties still coming in, is enough to tide us over. Plus, the film I helped make about LGBTQIA homeless youth has been bought. That's a pretty good chunk of change right there. We can afford for Grace to stay home and do her own art for the gallery."

"And I'm getting good commissions off Audrey's sculptures," Grace added. "Her stuff is flying out of the gallery so fast, I might have to hang some of my pieces to fill the empty spaces."

"That's all well and good," Cecelia said with an edge to her voice. "But I have a feeling there's something you're not telling us."

Grace and Taylor looked at each other and grinned.

"Spill it, girls," Marie said.

"How would y'all feel about being grandmas?" Grace said. "In about seven months?"

Cecelia and Marie sat in stunned silence, their mouths hanging open. Grace and Taylor laughed.

"I think we've found a way to make them speechless," Taylor said.

"Are you kidding me?" Cecelia said as she reached across the table for Grace's hand, a single tear slipping down her face. "You're pregnant? Y'all didn't tell us you were trying."

Grace found she couldn't say anything as she nodded. Taylor rubbed circles on her back.

"I'm sorry I didn't tell you we were trying, but I didn't want you to be sad or disappointed if the insemination didn't work. We're all still trying to figure things out without Grams and Freddy, and you didn't need another thing to worry about. Please, don't feel you're the 'Oh, yeah' mom. The only people who know besides me and Taylor are Grams and Freddy. I went to the cemetery today and told them."

Cecelia slid out of the booth and kneeled in front of Grace, taking her in her arms as they both cried.

"Oh, baby," she said. "My baby is having a baby. Grams would be over the moon. I'm glad you told her and Freddy first."

Once they could catch their breath and Cecelia was back in her seat, the conversation turned to due dates and which room would become the nursery—both at Grace and Taylor's house, and at Cecelia and Marie's house.

"So, I guess this means you aren't going to sell?" Taylor asked, a grin on her face.

"Hell, no," Marie said. "We'll still travel, but there's no way we could babysit in the RV. We have to keep the house."

Grace laughed and held out her hand. "We're starting a cursing jar," she said. "Anyone who says a curse word near this baby has to put a five in it."

"A five? Isn't that kind of steep?" Cecelia laughed as Marie pulled her wallet from her back pocket and passed a five-dollar bill to Grace.

"The money is for diapers and college," Grace said with a grin.

Even after their food was served, the four women talked about the future new addition to the family.

"Have y'all considered names yet?" Cecelia asked.

Grace and Taylor looked at each other, and tears stung Grace's eyes.

"We know we want to honor Grams and Freddy," she said. "If this little bean is a girl, we're going to name her Evelyn Frieda Grace; and if it's a boy, his name will be Frederick something—we haven't decided on a middle name yet."

There wasn't a dry eye at the table. The server tiptoed up and put a stack of fresh napkins on the edge of the table, causing the family to giggle.

"How about Evan?" Marie suggested, once they could talk again. "It's close to Evelyn."

"Ohhh, I like that," Taylor said. She turned and looked at Grace. "Frederick Evan. What do you think?"

"I think Grams and Freddy would like these names," Grace said. She put a hand on her tummy. "In fact, I know they like these names and will watch over this baby for the rest of eternity."

About the Author

Glenda Poulter has been writing poetry, short stories, and novels since she was ten years old, well over a half century. Slice-of-life novels with women who love women as her main characters are her specialty. Strong women with human weaknesses and foibles populate her stories along with their sometimes-quirky friends. Her past published work includes *Welcome Home* and *Out of the Past.*

Glenda lives in central North Carolina with her long-time partner, Lisa, and the felines that rule their lives. She is the proud mother of a daughter and son and doting grandmother of two. Other interests include collecting seashells, the fiber arts (crochet, knitting, quilting), reading, and photography. Glenda seldom meets a stranger, and she strives to leave everyone she encounters with a smile. Glenda has an affinity with the ocean, and she is sure she was a mermaid in a previous life. The gift of seashells calls her name on a regular basis.

OTHER AFFINITY BOOKS

A Moment in Time by Annette Mori

With the future of civilization hanging in the balance, elite Time Enforcer Saron Bahl is sent back to the twenty-first century to protect the one woman whose survival will ignite a new Age of Enlightenment. But when the mission collides with secrets from Saron's past, the timeline—and her heart—begin to fracture.

Avery Simpson, a pacifist and the reluctant leader of the Sapphites, is skeptical of the tall, imposing stranger who claims to be from the future. Yet despite her doubts—and her disapproval of Saron's ruthless methods—Avery can't deny the magnetic pull between them.

As the relentless Traditionalists close in, survival may depend on more than strategy and strength, but the Sapphites prove far more formidable than anyone ever imagined.

Caught between duty and desire, Saron and Avery must decide what they're willing to sacrifice—for the world, for their cause… and for each other.

Noble Intentions by LJ Reynolds

Agent Charlie Matthews returns to her hometown to piece together the remnants of her once-perfect life, only to hit the ground running on what may be the most significant case of her career.

Detective Noble Gentry's sole focus is ending the hunt for the killer before additional lives are lost.

Two strong women, both dedicated to their jobs. Thrown together, they unite on a mission to stop a killer with nothing to lose.

Will they catch the killer?

Will their growing attraction get in the way? Sometimes love is closest when it seems gone forever.

The Princess Needs a Wife by JM Dragon

Since birth, Princess Sophia Osric has led a charmed life. When a family tragedy forces her to shift from casual obligations to specific royal duties, it results in a decree from her father to find a wife or risk losing her special privileges. But there's always a catch—it must be a commoner. How on earth can she do that? Where will she find a commoner other than someone to wave or smile at?

Perhaps fairytale romances happen for princesses, too.

Without Borders by Stacy Reynolds

When the opportunity to become a war correspondent opens at her news agency, journalist Nicole Sheppard jumps at the chance to go to Ukraine. Her lifelong goal to gather news firsthand in the heat of battle and to test her mettle against the turbulence of war will finally be realized.

What she doesn't anticipate is having her heart and emotions tested as well when she meets the beautiful French doctor, Marie Dubois. As Nicole dodges bullets and Marie extracts them from the wounded, the two women struggle against a growing attraction to one another.

But when Nicole and Marie are kidnapped by a ruthless Russian mercenary, they must work together to find a way to escape.

The only thing they can't escape is falling in love.

The Invisible Woman by Annette Mori

In a world where logic meets the extraordinary, Tamara, a brilliant forensic scientist, discovers a mysterious purple plant that blesses her with superhuman abilities, including invisibility. Teaming up with her best friend, Annalise, a passionate FBI agent haunted by scars from her past, the two friends embark on a quest to bring down a brutal serial killer known only as The Hunter. As the danger intensifies, their bond deepens, and secrets are revealed. Will Tamara and Annalise finally admit to their feelings despite being polar opposites? Join these extraordinary women in this gripping tale of love, friendship, and the fight for justice, where heroes are born from pain.

Never Too Late by Glenda Poulter

After the death of her long-time partner, and a scandal at the school where she taught music and art, Janice Halston emerged as a shadow of herself. Feeling shaken, cautious and artistically blocked.

Tam Murphy lost her wife and son within a short time of each other. She tries to fill her emptiness with her daughter Mae, and granddaughter, Ocee.

Janice and Tam are brought together by the precocious Ocee. As their friendship deepens, so do their feelings for each other. Their deepening feelings send both women spiraling…in different directions. One toward what could be, the other away from fear of another loss. Will their spirals lead them back to each other, or further apart?

Nothing But Net by Ali Spooner

Hunter James, a rising star in college basketball, has her career and life sidelined after experiencing a family tragedy.

An opportunity for a fresh start opens the door to return to what she loves most: playing basketball. Hunter rushes through that door to make the most of her second chance.

Back in the basketball arena, doing what she loves, will she open herself and her heart to another chance to forgive herself and fall in love?

The Kitten Trap by Annette Mori

Inspired by the classic movie, *The Parent Trap*, two adorable black kittens, Midnight and Onyx, play matchmakers for their human mothers, Mac and Carmen. Struggling with the complexities of farm life, Mac can barely believe her beautiful girlfriend, Carmen, has agreed to move to the drafty old farmhouse to live with her and her beloved Pops. When Carmen is forced to leave the farm to care for her ailing mother, Midnight and Onyx as well as Mac and Carmen must struggle with the difficult separation. Just when it appears Carmen and Onyx may come back home to the farm, cruel fate raises a further challenge, one that will need the help of two mischievous kittens to overcome.

To Autumn by Katie M Hall

Sixteen-year-old Robyn Gale, along with her younger sister Anne, is sent away for the summer holidays of 1997 to stay with her grandmother at a caravan park in Devon. Robyn's had a tough few months: trying to cope with the fallout of their mother's attempted suicide, messing up her GCSEs, and finding herself attracted to girls. Perhaps getting away from her real life is just what she needs…she can focus on finding a boyfriend, watching *Neighbours,* and swimming. A solid plan, until she meets charismatic Australian lifeguard, Autumn, and her life is turned even more down under.

Fairytail Farm by Ali Spooner

Dr. Hill McCall and her wife Alice dreamed of developing a sanctuary for unwanted cats and dogs to live out their lives as a retirement project. Hill has secretly worked on the project for months when a wealthy benefactor surprises her with a large donation, allowing Hill to be more aggressive with the project's opening. A group home operator approaches Hill about summer volunteer positions for four girls as Fairytail Farm becomes more than just a sanctuary for the animals. It creates an environment of love and kindness for the animals and all that support the project. Several love stories develop from first love to mature couples who have found their forever person. Fairytail Farm is more than a dream come true. It is a home for happily ever afters.

Affinity
Rainbow Publications

eBooks, Print, Free eBooks

Visit our website for more publications available online.

https://affinityebooks.com/

Published by Affinity Rainbow Publications
A Division of Affinity eBook Press NZ LTD
Canterbury, New Zealand

Registered Company 2517228

www.ingramcontent.com/pod-product-compliance
Lightning Source LLC
LaVergne TN
LVHW020702110826
845149LV00012B/2077

* 9 7 8 1 9 9 1 3 5 7 4 0 3 *